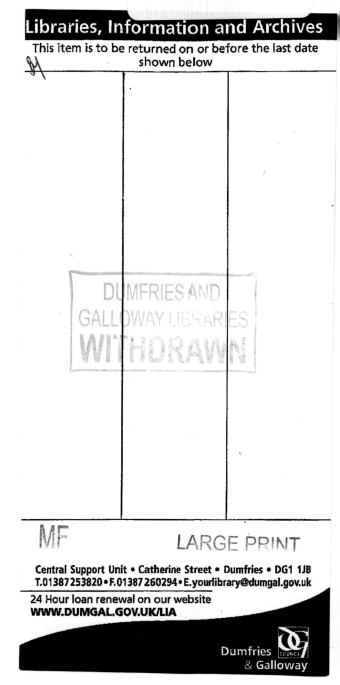

Ali Carter was born in Scotland and read art history at St Andrews. There followed an eclectic career in investment management, retail and technology; then in 2011 she had a catastrophic bicycling accident. After major brain surgery and a long recovery, Ali set herself a challenge to walk alone from Canterbury to Rome, a three-month pilgrimage. From then she decided to follow her passion and become a fine artist, specialising in oil paintings from life with an emphasis on colour. Ali lives in East Sussex with her husband.

THE COLOURS OF MURDER

Flirtatious American blonde Miss Hailey Dune should never have accepted a summer weekend invitation to Fontaburn Hall. But when the Honourable Archibald Wellingham's gentrified house party are woken in the early hours of Sunday morning, it's too late: Miss Dune's blood is on their hands. With the aid of well-mannered Detective Chief Inspector Reynolds, intelligent Sergeant Ayari and loyal friend Dr Toby Cropper, Susie Mahl, on a timely commission drawing six racehorses nearby, seizes the opportunity to play detective for a second time. Her inquisitive nature, tenacity for truth and artist's eye for detail make her ideally suited to the task in hand. But is she getting carried away by her previous triumph — even to the extent of endangering her reputation and her burgeoning relationship with Toby?

Books by Ali Carter
Published by Ulverscroft:

A BRUSH WITH DEATH

ALI CARTER

THE COLOURS OF MURDER

Complete and Unabridged

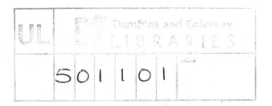

CHARNWOOD
Leicester

First published in Great Britain in 2019 by
Point Blank
an imprint of Oneworld Publications
London

First Charnwood Edition
published 2019
by arrangement with
Oneworld Publications
London

A catalogue record for this book is available from the British Library.

ISBN 978–1–4448–4250–0

Published by
F. A. Thorpe (Publishing)
Anstey, Leicestershire
Set by Words & Graphics Ltd.
Anstey, Leicestershire
Printed and bound in Great Britain by
T. J. International Ltd., Padstow, Cornwall

This book is printed on acid-free paper

For Ma and Emily

A more loyal sales force I couldn't wish for.

Author's Note

'Literature always anticipates life. It does not copy it but moulds it to its purpose.'
Oscar Wilde

This is a work of fiction. Don't be fooled by the first person nor look for direct correspondences. I have created a world for you to live and dream, not dissect. Susie is smarter, funnier, better company and much more talented than me. Her parents, not a patch on mine. Names, characters, places and incidents are used fictitiously. Any resemblance to actual events or locales or persons, living or dead, is entirely coincidental.

Prelude

On the 18th of January this year ten men received the following invitation,

Gentlemen,
Planning ahead to the summer . . . I will be hosting the annual cricket match at Fontaburn on Saturday 18 August and would be delighted if you would like to come and play. You and your respective wives are most welcome to stay both Friday and Saturday night.
I look forward to hearing from you.
Kind regards,
Archibald

The Honourable Archibald Wellingham, son of Lord Norland, was of the following opinion: if you want your A-list friends to come, an invitation must be sent well in advance. He was a conventional man in this respect. He came from good breeding with an estate in Norfolk to boot and, although unmarried and getting on a bit, he was perfectly capable of throwing a party single-handed. His boundless generosity enjoyed nothing more than filling Fontaburn Hall for a raucous weekend.

The hall was a place where people arrived and immediately felt at ease. The old formalities of past generations nestled in those cobwebs high

1

in the ceiling corners, but Archibald's style was more 'pile in and help yourself'. So when invitations to the cricket weekend fluttered through the letterboxes of staple old friends, enthusiastic acceptances returned in no time at all. Four out of the ten men were keen to stay both Friday and Saturday nights and only Stanley Gerald thought he might bring his wife.

Stanley had recently walked up the aisle with Archibald's childhood sweetheart Primrose. He didn't boast any form on the cricketing front, and hadn't been included in the weekend before, but having bought a castle nearby, inviting him seemed to Archibald a friendly thing to do.

The winter whizzed past with back-to-back shooting invitations, spring was spent on the Swiss slopes and as the summer weekend appeared on the horizon Archibald found himself in his study reviewing his guest list.

The Geralds' RSVP had been the first to return, confirming they'd arrive in good time for kitchen supper — they wouldn't want to miss out on fish pie. Yes! thought Archibald, this was immensely reassuring. Primrose had been to stay many times before, she knew the form and would be a great help at keeping the show on the road. Not that Fontaburn house parties had failed in the past, but the next name on the list, Charlie Letterhead, gave him pause. Charlie hadn't been seen on the circuit for months, ever since returning from tour in Afghanistan in fact, and rumour had it he wasn't in a good place. But Archibald, a man of routine and convivial nature, wasn't going to let that get in the way. A friend in need is a friend indeed and a weekend away might be just what Charlie needed.

As for Daniel Furr Egrant and George, Duke of Thelthorp . . . These men rang last week to say they'd be arriving late. Not at the end of a day's work, oh no! — they didn't do nine-to-five jobs. Daniel, the perfect mixer on a country weekend, was coming fresh off a private jet and George, no surprise with the grouse season in full flow, would be taking his usual detour through St James's to pick up more cartridges. This meant supper would be over when these two arrived. So, avoiding any grumbles on their part, Archibald tore a piece of paper off his pad and made a note to stock up on malt whisky. Then returning to his list of guests he put a little tick by each of their names.

It was now time to even out the numbers, and as Archibald gently rocked back on his chair a smile swept across his face. Princess Tatiana Davitoff's name was scribbled down. This minxy Russian had sidled up to him at a recent Sotheby's sale and he'd dined with her twice since in quick succession. As he sat here now, staring out the window, recalling her enthusiasm for his great summer weekend, he saw her green eyes, those thick black lashes, her ruby lips yet to part, that rumple of glistening dark hair pouring over one shoulder leading his eye to her bosom. Then blast! — the moment was dispelled by his mother's words ringing in his ears, 'Darling it's very important you stay focused on producing an heir.' Lady Norland, a dutiful mother, never shied from pushing broody members of the

3

English upper classes her son's way. And as Archibald sat at his desk he took in a deep breath and siphoned through his mother's options for the three remaining female spots. Nope, not one was going to make the cut. So instead he grasped the telephone and dialled Charlotte Mapperton's number.

Charlotte was an old friend. Her husband Hugh, on the other hand, was not, for the simple fact Archibald couldn't stand venture capitalists who were after his money. But it was now August, Hugh would be swanning around Silicon Valley, and Archibald had the phone to his ear ready to convince Charlotte she should come and stay.

'How marvellous,' she exclaimed. 'I'm heavy with child but I'd simply love to.'

'I'm not expecting you to play cricket.'

Charlotte chuckled, 'Arch?'

'Yes?'

'Are you *still* single?'

'Yes.' He veered away from mentioning the Princess. It's not like something was going on . . . yet.

'Excellent! I have an all-singing, all-dancing new American friend. Please, *please* can I bring her?'

'Do,' said Archibald, always being one for the more the merrier.

'What's she called?' he asked, and with Charlotte's reply Hailey Dune's name was added to the list.

★ ★ ★

4

Archibald laid down his pen and reached for his address book. One more girl and the numbers would be even. Then, after a quick flick through the names he snapped it shut, got up from his desk and left his study muttering to himself, 'For heaven's sake there are still two weeks left for a girl to land on my lap.'

His dogs Yin and Yang were ragging around in the hall. 'Do stop it,' Archibald barked as he flung open the front door and out they shot, bounding into the fresh air, full of excitable energy and ready for six o'clock walkies. Letting them be for a sec, Archibald stood on the doorstep of Fontaburn Hall and admired the beauty of his garden stretching out in front of him. His fortunate circumstances were gilded by the early evening summer light. A particularly beautiful time of day he thought, as he pulled the door shut with a bang, marched after the dogs and didn't once turn around to glimpse what lingered in the wings of this fine example of Tudor architecture. No, no he was far too preoccupied dreaming up the ideal final girl for his weekend.

★   ★   ★

The following week — in the most roundabout way — Archibald happened to hear of an attractive artist on commission drawing race-horses nearby. Her name was Susie Mahl . . .

1

The Honourable Archibald Barnabas Cooke Wellingham is my mother's second cousin once removed's goddaughter's husband's cousin. How Norfolk's most eligible bachelor came to hear I was temporarily living nearby should be inexplicable, but the crème de la crème of the British social class can drum up a connection, as tenuous as it may be, in every civilised country, capital, county or state round the world at best, and throughout Europe at least.

Now, please don't mistake my family, the Mahls, for being this high up the social ladder; we're middle class and always have been. But Sarah Smith, the goddaughter of my mother's second cousin once removed, married well and left her modest home in north-west London to land comfortably in a Wiltshire mansion of great proportions, with a bank balance to match and a title in tow. This stratospheric leap of social class sent verbal repercussions travelling at great speed down the maternal line of my family. So, when Mum, who has always been hot on genealogy, heard I had a commission to draw racehorses in north Norfolk, she immediately informed me 'it's no distance at all' from said goddaughter's husband's cousin's country seat. And within seconds she'd stopped talking to me and picked up the telephone to call her second cousin once removed and make the connection.

Within forty-eight hours, much to my mother's triumphant joy, I received a formal invitation to join Archibald Barnabas Cooke Wellingham's house party on the evening of Saturday 18 August at Fontaburn Hall.

My mother having gone to such lengths left me feeling I couldn't possibly refuse and so, despite the fact I'd never met any of the tenuous links, I signed myself up for a dinner party and night with a houseful of grand strangers.

It's not that I'm unfamiliar with this type of company, as several pet portrait commissions have led me to family piles in the past and my years in private education (albeit on a fully funded scholarship) have stood me in good stead, but Fontaburn Hall fell bang in the middle of a week's work. Not something I ever like to break.

I'd been commissioned by the renowned Norfolk trainer Aidan McCann, or 'Canny', as he's better known amongst friends and rivals who envy his ability to pip them to the post. He wanted me to draw six racehorses, his 'yard favourites' as he calls them. *Cha ching*! went my dormant commercial side, waking to the realisation that, if these drawings were a success, I could go on and sell prints to the owners as well as every winning punter from then on in. I had to make these pictures as good as I possibly could, no matter the subject was an animal I knew very little about.

Riding isn't my thing. I didn't grow up with horses so I find it hard to understand what all the fuss is about. It seems to me a black or white matter: you either love them, or you don't. Those who do were weaned off breast and onto saddle — not a moment in between, plonked on Shetlands even before they can walk. Although the selflessness of mothers whose little poppets have been bitten by the bug is remarkable when you come to think about it. Sacrificing lie-ins for mucking out and putting up with that smell both inside and out. Not to mention the expense of it all.

Apart from pony-club camp — and the inevitable snogging — I'm only attracted to one other horse-related activity — a day at the races, rubbing shoulders with champagne socialists and men in top hats.

So, when Canny asked me to draw six of his National Hunt winners, despite the fact I knew I was taking on an enormous challenge (I've only drawn one horse before) I gladly accepted in the hopes an invitation to the Cheltenham Gold Cup or the Grand National might follow.

When we'd struck the deal, he immediately informed me, 'The middle week of August is a good out-of-season time to visit.' The horses would be roughed off still, and with the slight decrease in the amount of work he suggested yard groom Lucy would have me to stay in one of her two spare rooms. Canny would by then have fled Pluton Farm Stables to summer on his yacht in Do We Really Care Where.

It would be the first job I've had when the commissioner is absent, although the names of the horses — Boy Meets Man, On the Pull, Wearing the Trousers for the geldings, and

Mum's the Word, Great Knockers and High Maintenance for the mares — tells you more than enough about Canny's clientele.

2

My head felt heavy as I lifted it off the pillow, waking from a jolly good night's sleep. The air was calm, the curtains weren't even fluttering in front of the open window and I really felt up to the challenge of drawing today. I swung my legs out of bed and gave my whole body a vigorous shake, getting it in the mood for hard work before a late afternoon departure to Fontaburn Hall.

If it wasn't for Lucy Redjacket, chief mucker-out-er and step-in landlady, I would certainly have burst into tears last Tuesday, turned on my heel and gone straight back home to Sussex. Drawing Aidan McCann's horses was proving to be a struggle. Lucy, however, generously welcomed me into her cottage adjoining the stables and despite there being ten years between us we've muddled along together with ease, her never once showing any resentment at giving up precious time each day to help me cordon off whichever horse it is I'm attempting to draw.

Today my sitter was a gelding, Wearing the Trousers, a supreme steeplechaser with thirty-four victories, including a Gold Cup and two King George VI Chases. He may be worth an arm and a leg, so Lucy told me, but his career as a model was quite a different matter. Wearing the Trousers he certainly was. Frisky like you cannot

10

imagine, gallivanting all over the place and absolutely impossible to draw. It really was quite frightening at times, what with a bucking behind and a whiplashing neck.

By the early afternoon the heat had got the better of him and finally he relaxed, although by then time was short and I only just managed to get down a few sketches before the clock struck and maddeningly I had to pack up for the day.

It was all Mum's fault and quite unlike her to have gone to such lengths to get me this evening's invitation. Perhaps she pitied me more than she let on for being unmarried, and hearing that her second cousin once removed's god-daughter achieved it and married above herself, Mum fancied the chances for her own daughter: me.

But, to be fair, as I packed my overnight bag, I thought of Mum, sitting at home in south London bubbling over with excitement anticipating her daughter's time ahead, and I knew deep down inside it was a good thing for me to get out. Weekends away are something the introspections of my art keep me from doing much of the time. And when these rare, out-of-the-ordinary invitations such as Archibald's come along, I'm not one to shy away.

In truth, I am and always have been rather fascinated by privileged people and I confess that I do like to be spoilt once in a while. So, with these happy thoughts in my mind I put on a smile and skipped downstairs.

'Susie!' said Lucy as I approached the yard in my very comfortable new trainers (not the running sort) to say my goodbyes. Her ginger-and-white cat Red-Rum was by her side; a pet I love despite my father's rhetoric, 'Mahls love cooking and hate cats.'

'That's me off, Lucy.'

'Wal, you enjoy yourself,' she said with her recognisable Norfolk intonation. 'You'll be finished and leaving me for good far too soon now we've got the knack of cordoning off these beauts.'

'It's all thanks to you that I've broken the back of them,' I said as I smiled at the horses' heads looming out of the metal-topped stable doors, awaiting their final meal of the day.

Canny has ninety-five National Hunt horses in total, two quads of stables back to back, interconnected by a not-so-pretty red brick arch. And I don't notice it now but the horsy smell of this set-up had initially taken a certain amount of getting used to. It got up my nose like nothing I'd ever come across before, but then I've got a very sensitive nose.

Aside from that pong and the functional aesthetics, Canny's yard is the equivalent of five-star hotel accommodation. High-net-worth animals, kept in cotton wool, fed well and receiving top-class care and attention by some underpaid groom such as Lucy, who is in love with the horses, other members of equally committed staff and the boss, or all three at once.

'Are you sure you don't mind helping me again next week?' I asked, knowing I would struggle without her.

'Would be my pleasure, Susie,' she said, sounding uncharacteristically grown up.

'Thanks so much. I'll be back Sunday night.'

'For dinner?' she asked, and disloyally I wanted to say no. Lucy had many qualities but cooking was not one of them.

'Yes, back for dinner.'

'Great, Sunday's a rest day so I'll have plenty of time to make us something special.'

My tummy churned at the thought as I walked away and waved to her shapely silhouette in the late afternoon sun. Our scruffy work clothes were about all Lucy and I had in common, so when I said my goodbyes wearing a pretty chiffon dress I could tell from her expression it took her by surprise.

Little did she know this summer dress was an excuse for me to wear my new, slinky underwear. I've been longing to put it on since my brief shopping spree in Paris last month. A particularly indulgent trip all thanks to Hillary Trotter, an eccentric spinster from Surrey, who had paid me a lot of money to do a life-sized drawing of her pot-bellied pig, Honk.

'Snort, snort,' I said in my car as I remembered the sound I had to make to get Honk looking alert. The thought cheered me up. A portly pig had been a lot easier to draw than Canny's impetuous horses. Their scooting haphazardly about the paddock as soon as I took out my camera, and then putting their ears back whenever I want to sketch their heads, or eating grass with their backs to me, has made me quite miserable most of the time.

There's something about art, when it becomes a struggle, that strips you bare and makes you feel absolutely dreadful about yourself. It's the lack of aptitude for what you're trying to accomplish that eats away at you and makes you wish you were better at what you do. The only thing that had really picked up my mood this past week was a text on Thursday from my heartthrob Toby Cropper.

Hi Susie, want to join me walking the Peddars Way in Norfolk this weekend? I'm on annual leave. Toby x

Toby and I are in touch but it's sporadic and this last-minute invitation came as a surprise. When I replied saying 'I'm coincidentally also in Norfolk but sadly can't join you,' he'd suggested, 'What about meeting for a crab in Cromer on Sunday?'

As much as I wanted to say yes, I knew it would be rude to shorten my already short visit to Fontaburn Hall. So, I deferred my reply for twenty-four hours in the hopes I could come up with an alternative plan. I discussed it with Lucy whose unconditional enthusiasm at having him to stay clinched the deal and I sent a text.

It's now a day and a half later and I'm still waiting for his reply. But as I beetled along in my car to join the Honourable Archibald Barnabas Cooke Wellingham's house party, I decided that Toby must have intermittent mobile reception on the north Norfolk coast.

3

Fontaburn Hall and its beautiful formal gardens sit well away from prying eyes, concealed in their own quiet calm behind a knapped flint wall. And although the stone is handsome to look at, it is the great height of this uninviting perimeter I should think that wards off the peeping eyes of even a person atop a horse. I have circumnavigated the whole thing and I can assure you there is only one entrance to this historic country seat. As I took in a deep breath and drove through the wrought iron entrance gates, pinned open as if by chance, I did wonder if this family had something to hide?

Topiary pineapples lined the verges, appearing one after the other like welcoming children, and as I travelled up the smoothest metalled road imaginable my car made none of the usual crusty suspension sounds.

The drive took an indulgent bend to the left and funnelled me in between lavender beds without a passing place in sight. After what felt like a quarter of a mile of metaphorical red carpet I was delivered with a reassuring gravelly crunch into a yard full of cars. Or Land Rovers to be more precise. I squeezed my small box into the only available space, disregarding the tin dog bowl that ended up underneath, and as I opened the driver's door a welcome gust of air shot up my dress.

I knew well enough that it's considered unnecessary to lock one's vehicle in places like this, so I turned my back on it and walked through a small, squeaky, decorative gate, up two steps and across an expanse of paving to reach the front door.

Fear God, Honour The King was carved into the lintel above me. This was one hell of a house. *1539* dated it on the stone slab under my feet, although even without this, Fontaburn's architectural provenance marked it as unmistakably Tudor. Not a huge house by any means but its decorative raw sienna brickwork and terracotta tiles exuded wealth. As for the eight extremely tall chimney-stacks clustered into fours, these must be a sight seen for miles in this flat county. And as my neck craned I half expected to come across an 'I'm in residence' flag flying, but no, there was a gentrified modesty to this place.

I dinged the sizeable bell, and as I waited for an answer to the dong I turned to look down an unending avenue of lime trees. The air around me was warm and still and I savoured the moment of calm before who-knows-what lay ahead.

Clitch, went the latch, the door opened, and the wet nose of a hyperactive labrador worked its way between my thighs.

The floppy-haired man beaming at me stood unconcerned.

'Hello lovely, I'm Daniel Furr Egrant,' he said as his long thin neck shot out at alarming speed and his pucker lips pecked me with a, *Mwah, Mwah*, on both cheeks.

'Susie, Susie Mahl,' I said a little flustered, at which point thankfully the labrador, deciding my crotch wasn't what he was after, took off with a surge of energy towards the lime-tree avenue.

'Now, remind me when we last met,' said Daniel.

'We've never met before.'

'Yes, we must have done,' he insisted. 'I know every one of Archie's friends.'

'I'm yet to meet Archie,' I said, incredibly relieved he had a nickname. (As childish as it may seem I knew I'd giggle if I had to say Archibald out loud.)

'Oh, I see.' Daniel flicked back his floppy fringe with one quick swipe of his palm. 'Can I help you? Is it he you've come to see?'

I was puzzled that this man, shoeless and dressed in starched cricket whites, didn't seem to know I was coming for dinner. You'd think it might have been mentioned.

'Archie kindly invited me for the night,' I said.

'Wonderful. That's tremendous.'

Daniel enthusiastically jump-turned into the house and bellowed, 'Archie! Archibald! ABCW!'

A voice called out over the sound of heavy feet on wooden floorboards, 'Oh Dandy do shut up or it will catch on. You know how I hate to be referred to like that.'

'There you go Susie,' said Daniel under his breath. 'Now we all know where we stand.'

'How dare you,' said Archie pulling softly on Daniel's right shoulder.

'This is Susie Mahl,' said Daniel, capitulating behind him.

17

'How d'you do?' Archie's stiff arm protruded and his small right hand gave mine a firm shake, 'I'm so glad you could come. Please excuse my friend.' He turned with a scowl but Daniel had gone. 'This couldn't be better timing; the cricket match is just over.'

'Did you win?'

'No, no, but that's not the aim. We must give them a competitive game but ensure the village wins in the end. It's good for neighbourly relations. Now, do come in Susie.'

'Thank you very much.'

Archie marched me through a gloomy stone hall littered with tweed caps drip dripping off royal antlers. On we went into a vast wood-panelled sitting room at which point I very nearly walked smack bang into the back of him. My eyes had been glued to the splendid staircase in the corner of the room, which rose at a right angle to a minstrel gallery above.

The stairs had the deepest treads I'd ever seen, and from the very top one came an uninhibited American squawk, 'Gin o'clock! That's what you English call it. I just love that saying.'

The blonde Yank trod down to us with saucy rhythm in her slim hips. She clasped both hands onto one of Archie's shoulders and hung off him like a sexy serpent.

'Hailey Dune, this is Susie Mahl,' said Archie.

Hailey's eyelids flicked her long black lashes back as she took a good look at me. 'Susie with an S or Suzie with a Zee?'

'S,' I said with a laugh.

18

'Hailey's obsessed with language today,' said Archie. 'Found the term square leg particularly good at the cricket, didn't you?' He turned his head towards her and she planted a chaste kiss on his cheek.

Then, immediately, releasing his shoulder and motioning her manicured hand towards my slightly fretting, far from manicured hand, she suggested, 'As you have the accent of a gin drinker, why not come play bar lady with me?' Before I had time to consider it our palms clasped together and my rapidly stiffening body was unwillingly pranced towards the door.

'No G&T for me,' called out Archie, having strayed towards the expanse of window, probably in search of the labrador. 'I've still got plenty of Pimm's in my system but you girls help yourself.'

Hailey's blonde curls bounced as I followed them out of the sitting room, down a short dusky corridor and into a walk-in drinks cupboard.

'Fabulous house isn't it?' she said, presuming I'd been here before. 'Us New Yorkers know how to party but I'd rather do it in an English stately home than a loft apartment any day. Much classier.' The 'c-l-a-s-s' of which rung out with her east coast accent.

'This room is incredible.'

It really was.

There were shelves to my right lined with everything from Armagnac to Zaranoff, and shelves to my left with glasses of every shape and size. Straight ahead of us stood two upright see-through fridges, one full of champagne and the other bursting with soft drinks and mixers.

It's no wonder, I thought, the aristocracy can drum up a drunk in their bloodlines so easily, with temptation being the first step in the wrong direction.

'Right, Susie!' squealed Hailey. 'There's ice in that bucket.' She pointed at a mini silver barrel on the solid oak block between us and then excitedly suggested I might like to cut up a lime, there being no shortage of them in the bowl by my side.

I gave her a willing smile, at which point I noticed in return Hailey's cheeks didn't wrinkle when her mouth turned up. They didn't even form the tiniest crease. This, combined with the fact her slim figure had a bounce to it and wasn't yet sagging with the inevitable side effects of age, made me puzzled to think her face needed any work. But then again, ever since I crammed into a small cubicle in my early twenties to feel my friend's enhanced breasts I've understood there can be personal reasons for cosmetic surgery and it doesn't always come down to vanity. Maybe Hailey was a similar case.

She swung around and reached up for one of several brands of gin. 'London Dry, we've got to use this.' She plonked the bottle down between us. 'None of that Indian stuff or Gordon's whoever he is?'

I laughed. Effervescent Hailey was the perfect remedy to put a newcomer at ease.

'Hey Susie, you gotta talk me through it from here, I'm still learning the ropes of you English.'

'Okay, how many glasses?'

'Let's make nine. Lotty might not have one

but in that case I'll drink hers.'

'Right!' I said with a rush of enthusiasm. 'If you put three cubes of ice in each glass, I'll squeeze lime over them and add the gin. Then you top it up with tonic.'

'Tip-top,' came her comically refined reply as our attention turned to the open door. Incoming was the peak of a straw hat under which appeared a woman heavy with child. Her buxom embracement of pregnancy, so far from the fashion of tight clothes over tidy bumps of the younger generation, led me to assume she must be in her late thirties at least.

'Charlotte Mapperton.' Her forthright arm shot out the end of a floaty blouse and before I had time to wipe lime juice off my fingers I shook it.

'Susie Mahl.'

'Daniel told us of your arrival and being the most sober one amongst us I thought it only fair to come and find you. I do hope Hailey's not leading you astray.'

Charlotte put an arm around her friend's waist and gave it a tight squeeze.

'It's all thanks to you,' said Hailey hugging her back, 'that I'm here at all.'

Charlotte gave a wry smile. 'The others are in the pagoda, so you must come and join them.'

Hailey picked up the tray and Charlotte's bottom led the way. Out of the drinks cupboard, down the rest of the corridor and into a drawing room with the most affluent display of porcelain you could possibly imagine. Jugs, cups, saucers, bowls, plates and vases lined

21

the walls and littered the mantelpiece. Being the last in the line I had a brief moment to take it in but there was no time to tarry: I was burdened with the duty of keeping a close eye on Hailey's precarious heels as she tottered out the French window after Charlotte and strutted her stuff across the lawn.

'Susie Mahl everyone!' announced Archie as instantaneously a fiery heat consumed my cheeks.

One by one, with Archie's introduction, bottoms left cushioned bamboo benches and right arms stretched across a glazed ceramic table. 'Stanley Gerald, Primrose Gerald, Charlie Letterhead, Daniel Furr Egrant you've met, George Thelthorp and Tatiana Davitoff.'

Each nodded a 'hallo', as my hand received a firm how-do-you-do shake, not one utterance of a 'pleased to meet you' amongst them.

'Gin for everyone!' said Hailey setting down the tray, and as I dipped my eyes I noticed the table top balanced on the back of a large blue ceramic elephant.

The men moved out on to the vast rolled lawn, which initiated a 'that's right, make way for the girls' from Charlotte, clearly the matron of the bunch.

Everyone other than Archie had swiped a glass and Tatiana, realising there was an uneven number, tried to persuade him to take hers.

'I'm drying out before dinner,' he said.

'In that case, so shall I.' She placed her glass firmly back on the tray.

'Oh Arch, don't be such a party pooper,' said

Charlotte as she motioned him away with a flick of her hand.

'Shoo, shoo,' added Hailey.

Primrose shuffled up the bench to make space for me.

'That's such a wonderful elephant,' I said as I squeezed in beside her.

'Yes,' she claimed, 'I was with Archie when he chose it.'

'Ooooh!' said Hailey, her eyelashes fluttering, 'Maybe I'll bring one back from Wuj-i-ang.'

'Wujiang!' corrected Primrose as Charlotte whispered in Hailey's ear and I thought it a good time to take a swift sip of my gin and tonic.

'Susie,' said Tatiana, 'how do you know Archie?'

'A godchild on my mother's side married his cousin.'

'Marvellous,' said Primrose, 'which one?'

Oh no! Was I really about to spend the night with people more interested in the lineage I come from than who I am? I shouldn't be that surprised as there's nothing that reassures these types more than finding a connection amongst the company they keep. And Primrose is now assuming, if they are Archie's cousins, she'll know them. Charlotte, leaning in to the table as much as her pregnant stomach allowed, clearly thought she might too.

'The Debentures,' I said to two blank faces.

'Nope, I've never met them,' said Primrose.

'Me neither,' said Charlotte.

I looked at Tatiana and Hailey, both of whom shook their heads.

Then not wanting to give up the quest before perusing all avenues, Charlotte asked, 'What was your mother's goddaughter's maiden name?'

'Sarah Smith,' I said, forgiving her mistake in the connection.

'Of course!' exclaimed Primrose, 'Lady Smyth. She's a great friend of *my* mother's. I never knew her daughter was called Sarah, we've always known her as Ra Ra.'

'My Sarah's plain old Smith, no y's and no titles I'm afraid'.

'Oh,' said Charlotte as I caught Primrose's condescending smile.

'Have you met anyone here before Susie?' muttered Tatiana.

'No, Archie included. He heard I was working nearby so invited me for the night.'

'Working?' came Primrose, shocked at the concept.

'Yes, I'm drawing someone's racehorses.'

'You're an artist, how delightful. I dabble a bit when I have time.'

'Someone,' said Charlotte directly to me, 'must have suggested Archie invite you. I'd put a bet on the fact you're single, aren't you?'

Was Archie's situation so desperate that he'd stoop as low as me, a middle-class girl from south London? These cats had nothing to worry about if that was the game we were playing. The Honourable Archibald Barnabas Cooke Wellingham will, when on death doth his father part with the title, become Lord Norland, and as coincidental as it would be for me to end up Lady Norland, the name of the very lane I live on in Sussex, it is a highly unlikely outcome. Not to mention the fact that if I did bag this man with title, enormous wealth and gigantic windswept castle on the northern bank of the Wash estuary (yes, I did do a spot of Googling before the weekend), my mother, I'm certain, would keel over on the spot.

Tatiana looked straight at me, wanting an answer, and no matter what I wasn't going to lose a pawn with my first move. 'Yes, I'm single.' I gave a girly giggle that Hailey carried as she flicked her blonde curls over her shoulder and wafted out the pagoda. Waft, waft, waft, she headed towards a bench in the distance where Archie and Charlie sat, far enough apart for her to place her pert bottom between them. Tatiana's green eyes were fixed on the scene.

Thank goodness for Daniel who'd just poked his head into the claustrophobic pagoda and suggested, 'Susie, accompany me on a gander at the garden before the evening takes over. It's Grade I listed you know . . . '

I was up and out before he finished his sentence, ' . . . and so well planned you'd struggle to believe it's eleven acres in total. What I'd do for all this.' His right arm cut a swathe through the scene in front of us and very nearly knocked my gin and tonic clean out my hand.

'Oh, do look,' he said as we popped out the end of a pergola walkway. 'Can you see the back of Stanley's head over there?'

I wasn't exactly sure where I should be looking.

'Above that hedge in the distance.' Daniel

pointed and I turned around. 'Archie will be pleased. He does like his visitors to jimmy riddle on the compost heaps whenever they can.'

I gave a small grunt of amusement.

I've witnessed it often enough to know the vast majority of country gents (thank goodness there's no evidence yet of women having caught on) like nothing more than to take a leak en plein air. Whether it be in the orchard, along the herbaceous border, on the compost heap as in the case of Stanley right now, or over a bridge into a river if you're lucky enough to have such an idyllic asset on your estate.

Daniel and I wound our way up paths, through rose tunnels and under water features. Daniel delighted in telling me the Latin name, 'Lathyrus odoratus', and the common name, 'sweet pea', of almost everything we passed. His enthusiastic knowledge spewed out in tongue twisters as I took in one name in every three.

'Where do you live?' I asked as we headed back in the general direction we'd come from.

'Oh, you know, mainly in London for the time being. I will of course move to the country when the old man kicks the bucket,' and then, Daniel's right leg, in an attempt to convey his words, shot out with an alarming lack of co-ordination and I had to try very hard not to laugh.

'So, you're the oldest son?'

'Only son, Susie,' he said insinuatingly (which I took to mean he needed an heir). 'You won't often find me in London. I travel a lot you know. Very comfortably too.'

I asked why — knowing in the nicest possible

way he wanted me to.

'I hire myself out as an overseas art history guide and, as it happens, most of my clients prefer to travel by private jet.'

'Nice!' I said, thinking if I wasn't an artist I'd love a job similar to this: swanning around Europe looking at masterpieces from the Italian Renaissance. That's the period I'd choose to cover.

'I try to keep it to twelve trips a year. Italy, Greece, Croatia and Turkey mainly. I give tours on foot, by boat or from a helicopter.'

'How wonderful.'

'Yes, my clients are looking for once-in-a-lifetime experiences. Eighty per cent is repeat business.' He smiled, as did I at the oxymoron in his marketing spiel.

When he asked me if I worked and I said, 'Yes, I'm an artist,' I imagined he'd want me to develop my answer further. But no, this man had a canny way of bringing the conversation back to himself, 'How lovely. The whole point of my job is bringing art to life. There's nothing quite like seeing pieces in their natural habitat. Wouldn't you agree? I particularly enjoy guiding people through the rubble of temples although there's a lot to be said for seeing a fresco in a church it was commissioned for.'

'There certainly is,' I said quickly before he began talking again.

I didn't actually mind Daniel monopolising the conversation as he had a lot of very interesting things to say. In fact, I liked him and felt that if his enthusiasm gave way to a two-way conversation over the weekend we'd quite likely, in such limited company, get on rather well.

'Now just look at that brute of a Hall,' he exclaimed as we walked down the lime-tree avenue. It was indeed a handsome sight at the end of the road.

'This is all so beautifully kept.'

'Yes, Archie's risen to the responsibility of keeping it intact, something that makes his father, Lord Norland, immensely proud. It's one thing inheriting nice things, Susie, and quite another having the business nous to keep it going.'

'What does Archie do?'

Maybe it was unintentional but Daniel deflected the question. 'Archie's a fine example to the likes of the Duke and me.'

'The Duke?'

'Yes, that's George who you met in the pagoda. He's the Duke of Thelthorp with one hell of an inheritance and between you and me I think he'd benefit from taking a few leaves out of Archibald's book.'

If stout George, who can't be as much as forty-five yet — although overweight people often look younger than they are — is a duke, it means he's the head of the family and, therefore, either his father died prematurely or married very late.

'What does George do?'

'He shoots!' said Daniel amused by himself. 'All I'll say Susie, is, it's never a good thing for anyone to rest heavily on their laurels.'

The garden tour ended when we turned the

corner with the front of the house and bumped into Hailey. Daniel told her he'd been talking me 'through Archie's bed life', at which point her eyes came out on stalks.

'Flowerbeds, Hailey!' he said as I, in an attempt to quickly distract them both, pointed at the plant by my side and asked 'What berries are those?'

'That,' said Daniel, proud of what he was about to tell us, 'is belladonna and those shiny black berries were very popular with the ladies of the Middle Ages.'

'Few years to go before you and I start liking them,' said Hailey, nudging my shoulder.

Daniel chuckled. 'Not middle-aged, Middle Ages. That's approximately 1100 to 1450.'

Hailey laughed with enviable uninhibited ignorance and I asked Daniel why it was called Beautiful Woman.

'Ciao Bella!' He winked, flattering my *very* basic knowledge of Italian.

'Well girls,' he said as his skinny, elongated fingers reached out and theatrically plucked a particularly dark berry. 'In the Middle Ages women rubbed these on their cheeks to create the reddish colour of a blush. Here,' he dropped it into Hailey's palm, 'you try. Susie your skin's too sunburnt.'

Daniel wasn't insulting me, it's just he's not the type to use the term 'tanned'.

Hailey rubbed the dark berry on her alabaster cheeks and as she did they flushed with warmth.

'Marvellous,' said Daniel clapping his hands. 'A truer English rose I never did see.'

Hailey and Daniel's attention swerved over my shoulder and I turned to see Archie's flat feet carrying him with sturdy gravity towards us as his middle-aged tummy wobbled under his Aertex.

'Glad to see you couldn't resist our gin!' cajoled Hailey noticing the glass in his hand.

Archie smiled at her. 'Charlotte wanted me to tell you she's going inside to get ready for dinner.'

'Lotty's calling,' said Hailey, helping herself to the drink in Archie's hand and giving it her best shot at draining it. 'Toodle-oo!' She raised the glass in the air, grasped the empty one from my hand and fled in the open front door. A fraction of a second later and she would have gone tumbling over the top of a lurcher, which was now coming out of the house in the manner of its name. Archie opened his short legs and the lumbering creature weaved between them and back through Daniel's.

'Och, there's a wee bit of Jock in him,' said Daniel with the most hopeless attempt at a Scottish accent.

'This is Yang,' introduced Archie as I patted the beautiful creature's narrow nose, but not for long: a tennis ball came firing over the top of us and off Yang went in its general direction. Then, narrowly avoiding a collision with the wall, the skinny dog leapt into the air and clasped his jaws around the yellow ball. Daniel ran towards him with his arms wide open in play and I turned to Archie and commented, 'Doesn't Yang's creamy coat look great up against that dark flint.'

'It does indeed.'

I found it odd that the wall was made of a different material to the house and Archie confirmed it had been built a little later. 'My family were friends with Henry VIII and in his fitful state of destroying the local abbey he gave my, great to the power of seven, Grandpapa enough flint to build a mile of wall.'

'How incredible.'

'Yes, it's rather splendid although some say as a result the house is haunted by clerical spirits.'

'Oh no!'

'I'm sure it's nonsense,' he quickly reassured me.

'Either way,' I said, 'I'd far rather be burgled in the night than wake up and see a ghost.' I'd always thought that a logical comparison.

'Really?'

'Yes. Explanations quell fear whereas the unexplainable can haunt your thoughts forever.'

'Give me a ghost any day,' he said with a resolute expression and then, oh no! it dawned on me how insensitive I'd been — Archie had a lot more possessions to worry about than I ever would.

Suddenly, the penetrating tone of a trumpet came blaring out the front door. Charlie Letterhead's lips were pursed to it and as he foolishly marched off the paving onto the lawn, his legs scissored as high as his waist.

I couldn't believe it; he was playing Handel's *Messiah, The trumpet shall sound, and the dead shall be raised.* Oh God, I prayed this wasn't some kind of cruel premonition.

31

Archie's eyebrows were raised. He'd clearly seen the act before. 'I'm so sorry, Susie,' he said. 'This behaviour must seem madness to an outsider such as you are. But, don't worry, they're a nice bunch. I've known most of them for years.'

'School friends?' I asked.

'Daniel, George and Charlie, yes.'

Of course, only the boys were . . . Single-sex education and all that.

'Oh look,' said Archie pointing at the black lab poking its head out the front door. 'Yin's reappeared.'

'Lovely dogs you have.'

'Well they do like to run off but I trust them. Pets are your business, aren't they? Horses at the minute, isn't it?'

My heart pulsed at the thought that eligible Archie had taken in something about me.

'I'm a painter really but yes, I do draw people's pets from time to time.'

'How are the racehorses going?'

'Right brutes to begin with, but we've been working on getting to know each other and they're much better at posing now.'

'I'm glad to hear it.' Archie laughed at the thought of a horse modelling and I paused for him to suggest I draw his dogs but he didn't volunteer a commission. Perhaps if there's time over the weekend I could do a quick sketch as a thank you and then he might bite. This tactic has worked in the past.

'Now,' he said. 'I must show you to your room.'

'I'll just grab my bag from the car.'

'Do let me carry it for you. I'm without a butler at the moment.'

I accepted his offer and we walked to my car, me hoping he wasn't going to spot his dog's bowl underneath it.

4

It wouldn't go in. As hard as I turned it, twisted it, lifted it up and down it just would not seal. This was an old-fashioned tower bathroom plug the likes of which I've rarely seen, and either I needed an instruction manual on how to insert it or the seal was in fact broken.

I really wanted to wash my hair and get it thick and bouncy in the way I know I can when clean, wet and dried upside down. I should have done it before I left Lucy's but I was seduced by the thought of the expensive products so often found in the bathrooms of smart houses, given as gifts by previous visitors. Here I had rose volume shampoo, rose sleek conditioner and rose satin body lotion all from Pretty Petals, a brand I could never afford.

I whipped off my clothes and got in to the cast-iron tub. I had to insert the plug in place as firmly as I could and then run both taps at top gush. The threshold of water the bath held as it drained was just deep enough to wash in. So, with foam flying onto the carpet I scrub-a-dub-dubbed in the most unrelaxing fashion but I was able to wash, and right now that was all that mattered.

My room, as so often happens when you're single and staying in a grand house, was on the top floor in what would have been the servants' quarters in the days when they lived in. It was made up neatly and smelt fresh but I was yet to come across any staff. Apparently, according to Daniel, who is clearly a bit of a gossip, Archie has recently sacked them all on grounds they'd become overfamiliar with his friends. Daniel had told me he was there at the crunch point when someone's girlfriend kissed the housekeeper hello, 'And after that, Archie sent them all packing on the spot.'

When I'd asked if that included the gardener he'd replied, 'Doug's whisked his wife Jasmine off for a week in the Borders.' I drew the line at finding out who was cooking dinner because, although I'd enjoyed being privy to these indiscretions, I didn't want to be full of prejudices before the evening got going.

With hair dry and make-up done, and wearing only a skimpy pair of French knickers and bra to match, the time had come for me to slip into my dark-blue lace dress and put on my mother's addition to my evening. Predictably concerned I wouldn't be smart enough for Archibald Wellingham's invitation, Mum, in good time, had parcelled up and sent recorded delivery a beautiful tiger-eye and pearl choker, which I was now wearing with pride. It's my favourite piece of her limited collection and reason to be glad I'm an only child.

I stood in front of the silvered armoire looking glass and agreed with myself 'legs brown enough to go without tights', so with a squish of perfume I left the room.

'Susie with an S!' said Hailey, seeing me come down the velvet-carpeted stairs. All eyes pounced and I wanted the bottom step to swallow me up then and there.

'Here's a glass,' said Archie handing me a flute of champagne.

'Maybe she'd prefer some of Primrose's punch,' suggested the overweight and undercharmed Duke, George, as he turned and ironically clinked his potent-looking blue cocktail with Hailey's.

'Champagne's lovely, thank you,' I accepted.

'I hope your room's okay?' said Archie as he offered me and Hailey a cheese straw from the table beside us.

'Yes, very comfortable. Thank you.'

'I'm so pleased,' he said as he turned away to top up others' glasses.

George plonked himself down, filling the closest chair to us, and Hailey enthusiastically asked me what my bedroom was like.

'It's at the top of the house, with a view over the courtyard.'

'That makes me feel very lucky. I have a four-poster bed with curtains and all.'

'Which way does it look?'

'What?' said Hailey. 'The bed?'

'No!' I couldn't help laughing, 'Your room, what's the view out the window?'

'Gee honey! I ain't been bored enough to look out the window yet!' and with that she frolicked towards the unlit fire and laid herself down on the floor next to cream-coated Yang.

George shuffled in his chair with pleasure as we watched Hailey's sequin dress ride up and down her thigh with every seductive stroke of Yang's back.

'Just because you're a duke,' called out Hailey, George now slapping his knee, beckoning her bottom, 'doesn't mean you have a free ticket to girls.'

I caught Stanley giving his wife a shocked glance and it made me wonder if George was married. Why else would they disapprove of his behaviour?

I glanced at George's left hand, he wasn't wearing a ring, but this doesn't necessarily mean he's unattached. Such fallal is frowned upon by the upper classes, and although wedding rings are creeping into the younger male generation, many gents continue to avoid them.

My father's not from the nobility and doesn't have a snobbish bone in him, but he certainly wouldn't wear a ring. He's a traditionalist, not a follower of fashion, and retorts that The Roman Ritual called for the blessing of only the bride's ring.

When I looked into this further, driven — as is often the case — by my love of getting to the bottom of things, I discovered there's no mention of wedding rings plural in the Book of Common Prayer either, and as far as I can tell the origins of the Double Ring Ceremonies came from a savvy advertisement campaign run by a dwindling jeweller soon after the end of the Second World War.

Much to George's delight, Tatiana swooped in and settled on his thigh. Her long green evening dress reminded me of an unforgettable comment once made to me from a leering toff, 'I'm more of a legs man than a tits man, Susie, and so I do wish you'd worn a shorter dress.'

George was clearly of the opposite opinion, as he couldn't keep his eyes away from her plunging cleavage. Although, in all fairness, even I was drawn in by the dangling diamond necklace that set it off so beautifully.

'Oi,' said Daniel as Charlie entered the sitting room from the hall.

He was looking, I thought, very smart in charcoal cords and a burgundy jumper, but Daniel didn't agree.

'Where's your velvet and slippers, me old chum? Thought we were having nursery supper did we now?'

Every other male in the room wore traditional country evening dress: velvet smoking jacket, cream (with definitely no sign of a wing collar) shirt, black bow tie and dinner-jacket trousers. The only difference in their attire being the various 'acceptable' colours of velvet (navy blue, burgundy or dark green).

'Would you like me to wear a tie?' asked Charlie pulling comically at the top of his shirt.

'We'll let you off wearing mufti just this once,' said Daniel.

'Tatty,' said Archie, interrupting her à deux with George. 'If you want to help with the first course now's the time.'

Tatiana rose elegantly from George's knee and headed, I presumed, to the kitchen.

'What's Tatiana up to?' said Primrose for us all to hear.

'She's gone to help Vicky prepare the mushrooms she picked this morning.'

'Vicky eh?!' said Charlie.

'She's the lady in the kitchen,' piped up Hailey.

'Woman,' corrected Daniel.

'How do you know her?' Charlie asked.

'I went to get the leftover punch from lunch and she was there unpacking the hamper so we got chatting.'

'What about?' snapped Archie.

'I was telling her how much I like you English. She's got that great accent too.'

Archie's smile returned, 'Yes, Vicky lives locally and has been doing some cooking for me recently.'

Thinking I knew the type, my mind drew a quick characterisation of well-spoken stand-in cook Vicky. Assuming she was 'on her gap year' and having recently completed a cookery course at great expense, I guessed she was now working for friends of her parents, earning her ticket to a developing nation. My ashamedly judgemental thoughts were interrupted by Charlotte, heading towards me with a flute in her hand, and pink of cheek.

'Fresh mushrooms for dinner, how simply deeee-licious.' Her glass shot up in the air as she exclaimed, 'It's such a marvellous blast to be footloose and fancy-free, Susie. My husband's a real old fuss pot and doesn't let me drink a drop now I'm pregnant.'

'Where is he?' I asked looking around the room and catching elegant Primrose, in a pale-yellow ruche dress, slip her arm into Archie's and lead him to the far sofa.

'Darling Hugh's away on business again.'

'What does he do?'

'Investments and what not.' She brushed off my question. 'Oh, do look at Hailey, she's soooo flexible.' Charlotte was laughing at her friend who was sitting cross legged with Yang's head fast asleep in her lap. 'I can't possibly keep up with those types of moves,' she said tapping her stomach.

'When's it due?' I asked.

'It!' said Charlotte, short and sharp. 'This is our darling Mini Mousey in here.' She rubbed her tummy, drawing in her kaftan to show off the enormous bulge. 'Fifteen weeks to go.'

'How exciting,' I exclaimed, astonished by the timescale. I was yet to see Charlotte without an alcoholic drink in her hand.

'It really is. I've spent months preparing the house and so wanted the bedroom painted for Mini's arrival that I've chosen a neutral colour and will get the estate to change it when we know if Mini Mousey is a boy or a girl.' With one last tap of her tummy she swapped her champagne glass into her right hand, held it up to her mouth and took a good slug. 'Where do you live, Susie?'

'East Sussex.'

'I've only ever heard of West Sussex.'

Too true I thought, as that's where all the smart people live.

'I live near Glyndebourne if you've ever been there?'

'Of course. We go to the opera every season but are you *sure* Glyndebourne's in *East* Sussex?'

40

'I'm certain it is.'

'And do you live alone, in the country?'

'Yes, just under the Downs, which I love.'

'So, you must have a doggy?'

'No.'

'What a surprise! My handful of unmarried friends all have a dog or a cat at the least. It can be company until you find Mr Right.' Charlotte gave me an uncalled-for sympathetic smile and tipped her glass at Charlie who was now the one with the champagne bottle.

He flung his arm around her shoulder. 'Isn't it tremendous to have Lotty on her own, so much more fun.'

'Charlie!' yelped Daniel striding across the room. 'You're about to fill up Susie's shoes.'

Without the slightest flinch Charlie raised the bottle and filled Charlotte's glass to the brim. 'It's like the good old times.'

'You've got to watch out for these two, Susie,' said Daniel. 'They're a naughty pair of pranksters.'

But Charlotte's attention was intent on Archie and Primrose sitting out of earshot, leafing through a leather-bound photograph album.

'Look at those two,' she said. 'I count myself as Archie's oldest female friend but if you widen the circle to professional relationships then I guess Primrose takes the title.'

George, who could have easily been mistaken for being asleep, lifted his slug-like eyebrows to join the conversation. 'I always thought they'd marry.'

'No way,' said Daniel, to which Hailey's ears

pricked up. 'Their childhood kiss and cuddle set that straight.'

Charlotte gave George an acknowledging nod, as if they too had fooled about together in the past.

'Right!' said Archie loudly from the other end of the room. 'Let's go through to dinner.'

5

One after another we followed Archie out of the sitting room, down the dusky corridor past the booze cupboard that initiated a 'help yourself to drinks in here if you want something other than wine', straight through the porcelain-stuffed drawing room and out into the garden.

I took in a breath of surprisingly fresh evening air and smiled at the elegance of the formally laid cast-iron table on the terrace in front of us. Each place had standing to attention: soldiers of silver and bone-handled cutlery, set either side (definitely not above) a melamine mat with a Norfolk landscape decoupage varnished on to it. Water tumblers had been filled up in advance and every place had two wine glasses, one for white and a slightly larger one for red. Stiff linen napkins rolled into silver rings separated the place settings one from another.

I was so glad to see we were eating outside, making the most of the daylight, which is more than can be said for the poorly lit house. Fontaburn Hall has a gloom to it that goes beyond the bad lighting and dark oak-panelled rooms. It stands like an only child who has no one to play with and the lack of family photographs inside erases any sentimental depth it could have. Even my parents, not known for public signs of affection, have their wedding picture in a dusty leather frame in the sitting room and at least two pictures of me stuck to the fridge. But Archie's gaggle of friends didn't carry this gloom and here we all gathered giddy with champagne.

As every well-mannered host would, Archie took the head of the table that faced the house, giving the person at the other end, 'Primrose you sit there,' a view of his expansive parkland populated with solemn oaks and lanky pines.

'Susie, if you'd like to sit on my right.' I felt honoured to be given the plummest seat around the dining table.

'Stanley you go next, then Hailey.' He paused. 'Hailey, where is she?' Charlotte shrugged her shoulders.

'Hail!' said Daniel throwing his arms up and drawing our attention to the unsteady character tottering towards us with a tray of shot glasses.

'I thought we ought to toast the Queen,' she said as Archie rushed towards her.

'Great idea,' said George and Charlotte as I began to dread having to take part. Shots have never agreed with my constitution and the outcome of any more than one is not something I wanted to suffer here.

'Right Hailey,' said Archie placing the tray safely on the table. 'You sit on Stanley's right, then you Charlie, do sit down Primrose, George go next to Primrose and Charlotte here.' Archie pulled out her chair. 'Glad to see you've made yourself comfortable, Dandy. Tatty will go between us.'

'Lotty,' said Hailey as Charlotte passed around

the shot glasses. 'Make sure you don't miss anyone out.'

My attention was then drawn to a woman striding towards the table with an undisguisable horse-rider's gait. 'Everyone,' said Archie. 'This is Victoria Ramsbottom.'

Victoria was much more attractive than her name gave away and, although young, she was well ahead of her gap year. How wrong I'd been. She drew a half-smile, took none of us in and with little grace placed the tray down next to George and handed out the plates.

'Tatiana's bringing yours,' she said to Hailey when the portions ran out, and without so much as a nod Vicky headed straight back into the house.

'Bit of alright,' chuffed George.

'Please be polite to Vicky, George,' said Archie. 'She's had a hard time recently.'

'Why?' squawked Primrose from the other end of the table, but any answer was cut short by Tatiana's arrival and announcement of 'I do hope you'll like my ceps on toast!'

Or '*Boletus edulis*', as you-know-who piped up to tell us.

'What's a cep?' asked Stanley.

'Oh darling,' said Primrose. 'Don't be such a fool. They're a type of wild mushroom we've eaten many times before. They grow in mainland Europe from June to September and are completely dee-licious.' Stanley turned to me and smiled as if I was the one who'd asked the question.

'Tatiana got up early,' said Archie turning to

45

look at the view of the park behind him. 'Picked a trug full under those pines over there didn't you?'

But just as Tatiana opened her mouth to confirm it, Hailey butted in, chivvying us all on, with a, 'Time to toast the Queen!'

There was a general lack of interest in where the mushrooms had come from and so Tatiana knocked back her shot, well before the rest of us.

'To the Queen,' coaxed Charlie, and in a matter of seconds even I had my head back and vodka trickling down my throat.

Dinner began in a reasonably civilised manner. All the men turned to their right and us women turned to our lefts and individual conversations paved the way.

Archie got stuck into berating social media and explained, 'Not one of my friends would ever dream of posting pictures from a Fontaburn weekend.'

'How can you be sure?'

'I trust them to know the form. Although occasionally I whisper in the ear of those outside the set.' He tipped his head towards Hailey with a forgiving smile.

'You didn't tell me,' I said with a cheeky grin.

'I knew I didn't have to!'

Archie and I were getting on well until I asked, 'How long have your family collected porcelain?'

'Quite some time,' he muffled as he stared at his mushroom. 'But let's not mix business with pleasure.'

I couldn't for the life of me think of anything to say.

Then poor Archie at the mercy of his good manners broke the silence between us, 'I deal in porcelain. My family have done for years. There's plenty of it around for you to look at but I'd really rather not discuss it over dinner.'

'Of course, I'm sorry.'

'Don't apologise. It's okay.' He leant closer towards me and under his breath let on, 'the topic caused a bit of a rift between some of us last night.' Then sitting up straight again, his tone rose and he asked if I'd seen his cousin recently.

'Well,' I blushed. 'The slightly embarrassing thing is, I've never actually met your cousin.'

'That *is* amusing as he gave you a frightfully good write-up and told me I simply must invite you to dinner.'

Oh crumbs. Whatever had Mum said on my behalf?

I wasn't quite sure yet whether I was pleased to have been invited or not. It was fun to be doing something different and I'd have a lot to tell Toby if he came to stay. But, having snooped along my corridor I now knew I was the only one sleeping on the top floor of this likely haunted house and I rather wished I hadn't accepted the offer of staying the night. Not to mention whatever shenanigans were to come later — this clique certainly seemed the type who'd be up for after-dinner games.

Daniel raised his voice, 'Take me with you next time. I'm very fond of picking mushrooms.'

'Tolstoy,' said George, with his finger on the buzzer.

'Full marks,' congratulated Archie who was shuffling his hand around under the table. He gave up. 'Charlie,' he said, 'please can you pour the red wine, as I'm just going to see where Vicky's got to.'

'I'll happily go if you want,' called out George in jest as Archie disappeared into the house.

I glanced under the table to see what he'd been fumbling for. There was a small white box with a grey button, a set-up I'd come across before — a remote bell to alert the kitchen that the plates are ready to be cleared. Either this one's batteries had run out or Vicky was elsewhere in the house.

Not that it mattered with Tatiana around as she'd already cleared the plates and was heading into the house in such a rush that I presumed (me being prone to use a similar tactic) she'd grasped the opportunity to accompany Archie.

Meanwhile Charlie had folded his napkin neatly over his arm and proudly taken on his role as stand-in sommelier. He had that last twist of the bottle down to such a fine art I was sure he'd played this joker before. Nevertheless, it amused us all.

'How do you know Archie?' he asked Hailey as he hovered at her side.

'Charlotte introduced us.'

'And how do you and Charlotte know each other?'

'We recently met in a KX Pilates class.'

'Oh, aren't you lucky,' said Primrose. 'I just can't bring myself to do it in the village hall.'

George's upper half wobbled as he suppressed

a chuckle at Primrose's unintended innuendo.

'What brought you across the Pond, Hailey?' asked Daniel.

'I wanted to meet some English people.'

'Men!' exclaimed Charlotte.

'I've only met married ones so far,' said Hailey.

'Hu hum!' said Daniel and Charlie together.

Hailey giggled and Daniel went on to ask her how she spent her time.

'I'm an assistant teacher at a school in west London.'

'Full time?' asked Primrose as she shot Stanley a look.

'Yes, at Lilac Pre-Prep.'

'Bodes well for pinching someone else's husband,' said Daniel.

'I'd *never* do that,' defended Hailey, which prompted an uncalled for (it was only a joke) apology from Daniel.

'I don't believe it,' perked up George. 'My wife's been bending over backwards,' he winked at Stanley, 'to get our son in there.'

Tick, George *is* married.

'Oh yes,' said Stanley. 'I knew I'd heard of it, isn't that where the young Prince is said to be going?'

'Yes, darling,' said Primrose curtailing the vulgar tangent of the conversation.

'Nothing like making friends with royalty from a young age,' mocked Daniel. 'You'd better sign your little one up soon Charlotte.'

'Yes, we must,' she replied tapping her tummy, and much to my surprise George reached out a stubby hand and rubbed her bulge — I think she rather liked it.

'I'm soooo . . . pleased,' purred Hailey, 'to be spending the weekend in a stately home.'

'This isn't a stately home,' corrected Primrose. 'It's a country house.'

'Oh, my darling don't be so finickity,' said Stanley.

'Well, darling, as Archie will be inheriting a stately home it's rather nice he can pass the time in a country house.'

'What's the difference?' asked Hailey.

To which George answered, 'A stately home is designed to dominate the landscape whereas a country house is deliberately designed to harmonise with the landscape.'

'Can't say that huge flint boundary adds to the harmony,' said Daniel.

'Don't mention the wall,' retorted Charlotte.

'Wooooo, Woooo,' warbled Charlie as he flapped his hands in a ghostly manner.

Primrose kindly tapped them down and assured Charlotte that she'd been staying here since she was a tiny tot and that 'There's not a single spirit anywhere other than the drinks cupboard.'

George roared with laughter.

'Did I miss a good joke?' asked Archie, who'd reappeared with a silver serving tray of green veg and a large bowl of game chips (something us ordinary folk would call hot crisps).

'Never mind the joke,' said Daniel.

'Go on.' Archie placed the tray in front of Primrose.

'It was about the Papist clergy in your house,' said George.

'Haven't you had it exthorthised?' lisped Hailey, the drink getting the better of her.

'Absolute nonsense pagan act,' said George, his tone firmly ending the conversation.

Archie sat down apologising for how long it had taken him to return, 'It's all Tatiana's fault for such a delicious first course. Vicky had no idea we'd guzzle it so quickly. I struggled to find her and you'll never guess what, she was upstairs turning down the beds.'

'You're so lucky,' said Charlotte, 'to have servants with initiative.'

'Well, I wouldn't call Vicky staff but it was good of her to do it.'

⋆　⋆　⋆

I had a strange feeling about this Victoria Ramsbottom. I couldn't put my finger on it but I did make a mental note that turning down the beds was a very odd thing to do if she wasn't staff. And for nothing other than my own peace of mind I set up a game with myself to get to the bottom of it. The thing is I have a fascination with people and what it is that makes us who we are, and when there is something amiss I can become rather obsessed with working it out.

⋆　⋆　⋆

Tatiana placed a platter of meat in the centre of the table and Stanley whispered 'grouse breasts' in my ear.

Primrose, who was filling plates with vegetables and passing them to her left, suggested Stanley serve the game.

'Susie first,' said Archie.

My heart gave a flutter of flattery, not attraction. Archie's charm lay in his generosity and laissez faire attitude, not his looks. He had an enchanting smile that knocked years off him but he was so rigidly English it was impossible to entertain the thought of going to bed with him. From his very first handshake, I would put him down as a pouncer or late-night leg humper rather than a man who has the gift of the gab for feminine foreplay.

Tatiana passed the large bowl of game chips across the table for me to dive my hand into.

'I love these,' she said. 'I had them for the first time when Archie took me to Rules.' She glanced flirtatiously to her right.

'Have you ever been to Rules, Susie?' asked Archie.

'No, never.'

'Oh,' said Tatiana, 'it's London's oldest restaurant, you *must* go.'

'Archie's showing off,' said Daniel. 'Barely a week since the glorious twelfth and we're eating grouse.'

'They are in fact my grouse,' said George whose neck disappeared when his shoulders leant in to the table.

'From your Yorkshire Moor or the Highland Moor?' asked Stanley who was spooning a breast on to Hailey's plate.

'Yorkshire.'

'You're so lucky to have *two* moors.'

'Yes, double the shooting and double the return invitations.'

'Always driven I presume?' said Daniel giving me a wink.

'Of course,' said George jumping at the bait. 'Why would one ever want a walked-up day? Nothing so exhausting as stomping through heather trying to shoot very few birds. I like to sit in a butt and have coveys sent over me. Driven, always driven.' George clicked his fingers at Stanley — he wanted two breasts on his plate.

'You're spoilt my friend,' said Daniel.

'You're jolly lucky I say,' said Stanley pausing with the dripping spoon in the air. 'Primrose's father sold his moor last year so my days of driven grouse have gone from thirty odd to sixteen at the most.'

'Stanley!' Primrose's voice came hurtling down the table. 'Watch what you're doing with that spoon and hurry up — the food's getting cold.'

Maybe it was the summer sun mixed with too much booze but suddenly I could detect an increasingly antsy atmosphere at the table.

'Charlie,' summoned Archie, 'you've left everyone dry. Fill up the glasses down that end will you.'

'Not my fault,' said Charlie. 'Every one of you is drinking like a fish, we'll all be blottoed in no time.'

'Speak for yourself,' said Primrose, the shoulder of her dress having slipped down her arm.

With plates full of food and glasses topped up

with claret the men turned to their left and us women turned to our right.

Surprisingly, considering I've dined in sophisticated company before, I've never eaten grouse, and as Stanley banged on to me about shooting in that way only the people who do it can, I took time trying to identify the flavour of my mouthful. The dark meat was unlike anything I'd eaten before. It was tough, which I suppose isn't unusual for an animal that has been living in bleak conditions, and there was a hint of sweetness in the first chew, most likely from heather berries I guessed, but this was soon overridden by strong earthy flavours. Luckily, it being rude to leave anything on one's plate, I liked it.

'Where do you live?' I asked when at last Stanley drew breath.

'Being the second son, I have had to fend for myself with regards to housing. We have a charming pied-à-terre in Chelsea and secured a country seat rather near here a year and a half ago.'

'Where is it?'

'Just outside the little town of Jiltwhistle. It's a sixteenth-century castle and has the most marvellous name of Mongumery. Primrose has been tremendously busy ever since we bought it, back and forth to Peter Jones with the interior designer.'

'It sounds lovely,' I said as I slipped a big-enough forkful of food into my mouth so as to avoid having to drop my rather smaller house into conversation.

'Well, we thought so. Bought it on the spot and although it came without land we shall be very happy there bringing up our family.'

'Do you have children?' I asked, focusing on keeping the conversation going rather than interesting.

'None yet but we're hoping for some soon.' Stanley turned his head and smiled up the table to his wife who for once had taken her eyes off him. She was watching Hailey who'd got up and was staggering down our side of the table.

'Charlie and I want to dance!' she said, clasping her hands on to Archie's shoulders.

'Hailey!' said Charlotte with a teasing tone that had a hint of command. 'In England, we stay sitting for the duration of dinner.'

'I want to be American again,' said Hailey thrusting her right arm in the air, Statue of Liberty style.

Charlie rose from his seat and pirouetted her into the house.

'I'm so sorry, Archie,' said Charlotte.

'What for? Hailey's great!'

George held forth. 'It does us all well to remember that although our fine selves and Americans both speak the same language, Americans come from a completely different cultural and social heritage. We get it so wrong when we criticise them as if they were British. The simple truth is they are all immigrants.'

'Quite right,' said Primrose.

I was worried for Princess Tatiana that George was going to continue on into foreign titles being two a penny but he lost his thread when

Charlotte began clattering the plates.

'Let me do that,' I said, standing up to relieve her, but Tatiana was already on to it. I sat back down and as my bottom touched the chair a din of dated pop music boomed from the house.

Charlotte finished the first lyric with a 'hmmm it's over now.' She had rather a good voice.

George mumbled something into Charlotte's ear that made her cast a cheeky smile back at him. Then suddenly, as if someone had flicked a switch, Primrose grasped the empty serving platters and strode inside.

My body physically shivered with the change in atmosphere and Daniel, thinking I looked 'a little cold', commented, 'It's getting parky out here. Arch, do you have any blankets?'

Ready and willing, Archie pushed himself up by the arms of his chair, pulled his creased smoking jacket straight and looked down at his hard-soled evening slippers. From the glimpse I got, they appeared to be embroidered with a boar's head eating a flower: the Norland family crest, I presumed, which had to be the only excuse for such an absurd design.

Many titled families use their crest, that's the bit above the helmet on their coat of arms, to decorate their possessions and it's not unusual to see it enamelled on china and engraved on the handles of silver cutlery — any junk shop will illustrate this. However, I've once come across a landed family who, I think, took the theme too far. They'd substituted all their outdoor tap handles with a brass replica grasshopper from their crest, leaving no one in any doubt they did indeed own a title.

'Another one bites the dust,' said Stanley, as Archie disappeared into the house.

'Sit tight,' said Daniel smiling at his quip. 'They'll be back.'

Charlotte filled up her glass and passed the bottle towards me. Gosh it's lucky, I thought, that Darling Hugo isn't here. I'm a hundred per cent on his side now, as hiccupping Charlotte really should not be drinking.

'Poor Charlie,' said Daniel indiscreetly. 'I do worry about him and what he encountered in Afghanistan.'

'Is he getting help?' asked Charlotte.

'Well he's left the army, which can only be a good thing, but until he finds a suitable companion I think he'll just plough on pushing his issues under the carpet and nulling his mind with gak.'

Stanley shook his head. 'My oh my, never a good idea to mix drugs and an unstable mind.'

'Or pregnancy,' joked Charlotte.

At which point George let out an amused grunt.

'Do you partake, Susie?' asked Daniel.

I paused, although not to think about the question. I've never been tempted or had the cash for a recreational drug habit, but I just couldn't believe Daniel singled me out.

'Don't be shy, there's often plenty around,' irritated Charlotte.

'No, no I don't take it.'

'Me neither,' said Stanley.

'Here you go, Susie.' Archie was back with rugs.

'Go on AW, place it around her shoulders,' encouraged Daniel.

'It's okay,' I said laying it across my knees.

Primrose, followed by Tatiana, reappeared.

'Victoria's left,' spat Primrose as if she were speaking about her own staff.

'What?' said Archie.

'She's left. Gone. Just like that.'

'What do you mean? How do you know?'

'There was a note,' confirmed Tatiana. 'It said she felt ill and has gone home.'

'Poor her,' said Stanley.

'Silly girl,' yapped Primrose, 'she left the oven on high and now the pudding's burnt.'

'Never mind,' said Archie. 'Thanks to all of you, there are plenty of chocolates indoors.'

George stood up announcing it was time for him to get the tremendous bottle of malt he'd brought.

'That's an excellent idea,' agreed Stanley.

Tatiana volunteered to make coffee and insisting she didn't need any help she turned on her heel and went back into the house.

'She's very willing isn't she?' said Stanley.

'I reckon she's trying to impress Archie,' said Charlotte.

'You could be on to something there,' grinned Daniel. 'Bachelor with no staff in need of a woman around the house. She's certainly doing her best to fit the role.'

'Told you so,' said Charlotte.

We all looked at Archie who sat at the end of

the table with an indecipherable grin on his face.

'Where did you find your help for this evening?' asked Primrose, who was hovering rather than sitting. 'Bit frosty, isn't she?'

'You didn't exactly give her a chance,' defended Archie proprietorially.

Primrose let out a faint huff, turned her back to the table and Stanley, without a word, stood up and followed her inside.

I agreed with Primrose. Vicky was a bit frosty, but what interested me most was how Archie had defended his cook almost as if she were one of his house party. His tone implied they had a relationship beyond that of employer and employee. Not necessarily sexual but definitely close. Note to self.

Daniel proclaimed it was about to rain, saying he could 'feel it in the air' and Charlotte agreed, her reason being, 'Mini Mousey is kicking, which is a sure sign something's up.'

'Let's have coffee inside then,' said Archie.

We all stood up and as no one else made any attempt to clear the table I, against my instincts, turned my back on it too. I was last through the French window into the drawing room and as I stepped over the ledge it banged shut behind me. A great shudder went through every pane and pregnant Charlotte practically toppled over on the spot. Thankfully a sofa within arm's length caught her bulging figure.

'Good God,' she let out, short of breath. 'Where on earth did that come from?'

'There's an almighty storm on the way,' said Daniel, who'd followed his nose to the window and was peering out at the rapidly diminishing daylight. 'I knew it, I could see heavy rain coming in this direction.'

This was good news for me, as I'd been told that stormy weather affected horses and so I knew Canny's would have been playing up again, meaning I hadn't wasted any precious drawing time by being here this afternoon.

Hailey had given up dancing for a seat next to Archie on the sofa, and so Charlotte shouted at Charlie to turn down the music. And by the time Tatiana entered the room with a tray of 'coffee!', Hailey was well and truly focused on removing the cellophane from a box of chocolates, giving Tatiana free rein to shoot Archie a coquettish glance.

The most almighty CRACK! of thunder sounded, the speakers blew and Tatiana's wobbling hands only just managed to settle the tray on the pouffe before the cafetière almost toppled over.

A deep rumble grumbled in the fading sky, the lights flickered and a spectacular silver sheen invaded the room. It struck against Tatiana's dangling diamond necklace and gave off a blinding sparkle as she made for the curtains.

'Tatiana? Are you okay?' asked Archie rushing to help her with the aged drawstrings.

'Yes, yes, I'm fine,' she brushed off his concern, and held her head high as she returned to the sofa.

'I simply love dramatic weather,' smiled Primrose who was puffed up like a grande dame in a long-backed armchair.

Archie nestled down on the sofa between Hailey and Tatiana and Charlotte said she was going to, 'go and find George, before he drinks all the whisky himself'. The onset of bad weather had sucked the heat of the day out the house so I moved towards the fireplace, which Stanley was fanning with bellows.

The mantelpiece was cluttered with exquisite tea cups and saucers and the intricacy of their foliage and bird design made me think they must've been hand painted. I wanted to go around the whole room but the fact no one else talked about the beautiful and eccentric display made me think it was not the done thing to draw attention to people's belongings. So, instead, feeling a pinch in my bladder, I nipped out of the room to find a loo.

6

When I passed through the sitting room on my way to the hall (where most country houses have a loo), I paused to have a nosey around. I wanted to get to know Archie a bit better without having to ask too many personal questions. This wasn't a dishonest thought — well, not totally, as my conscience dictates: anything I find lying around is free property, the owner clearly not minding if it's seen.

I took in two stiff invitations on the mantelpiece (or chimney piece as people here would refer to it). Both were in accordance with the upper-class format (any variation being considered pretentious): issued on stiff off-white engraved card, printed with curly-wurly raised type, one in dark blue and the other in black.

The first was a christening card of a chubby child in a Victorian lace gown. His name, Jonathan Michael Grant Fortismead, the only indication he was male. I bet Archie has several godchildren for the obvious reason parents like to pick their richest, most successful and well-connected friends.

Next to it was an invitation from Lord and Lady Loveday (what a sweet name) to the christening in two months' time of their daughter Violet Priscilla (VPL being unfortunate initials for a girl, I thought).

If I had a mantelpiece, which I don't, I hope I

wouldn't fall into this trap of displaying forthcoming engagements. To us mere mortals it's a brash show but there must be another reason, as everyone does it.

Propped up behind these was a large card from the auction house Sotheby's, inviting The Hon. Archibald Wellingham to a private view of the late Lord Fanbury's collection.

I shouldn't think Archie will be attending this one as, other than porcelain that he'd made clear to me was 'business', art doesn't appear to play a huge part in his life. All I'd seen so far were a couple of gloomy ancestors looming below the minstrel gallery and two stale Dutch still lifes hanging either side of my bed. But then again, maybe his father's castle has the majority of the collection . . .

Shriek! came sharp and loud, hurtling across the room, snapping me out of art musing, sending me spinning around, no time to wipe the guilt from my face. Hailey was crumpled in the doorway, her toothpick heels no longer holding her upright.

'Crumbs, Hailey. Are you okay?'

'Gee,' she took in a hiccup and second time lucky grasped hold of my hand. She was as light as a feather and as unsteady as jelly.

'Have you hurt yourself?' I asked, making sure to keep hold of her as she wiggled off her shoes. A very sensible decision I thought at the time.

'Nah, thankth Thuthie, I'm looking for Lotty.'

'I haven't seen her. She went to find George.'

Hailey's bare feet pranced silently up the

red-velveted stairs and with a now bursting bladder I went directly to find a loo.

★ ★ ★

Sitting on the seat, giving up on the doggerel about gun safety on my right, I turned to my left to scan the scroll of the Wellingham family tree. It was both old and hard to decipher, but clear that Archibald, Anne, Charles and Elizabeth had been popular family names. Our Archie was the elder of two brothers ... the younger, Humphrey, I remember someone mentioning was working abroad.

On my way back to the drawing room, I found Yin and Yang shivering under the hall table and stopped to give them a comforting pat. As hard as I tried to encourage them to follow me, they weren't for moving. Resolutely I stood up and then froze on the spot as I could hear voices up the backstairs.

'You go to bed,' George was saying, 'you're in no fit state to stay up.'

'But what do I do?' Charlotte's voice pleaded as the floorboards above creaked under the weight of them both.

'Leave it to me, I'll handle it,' said George.

And then, making sure I got well ahead of the footsteps above me, I made for the drawing room.

'Please help yourself to coffee, Susie,' said Archie with no sign of having wondered where I'd been.

'Thank you. But I'm okay.'

'You'd prefer this wouldn't you?' said Daniel pouring out a glass of champagne and thrusting it into my hand.

Why not! I said to myself as I took a seat on the sofa next to Charlie. I hardly ever drink champagne.

George trundled jovially into the room. 'Charlotte passes on her goodnights,' he said.

'Oh,' Charlie sounded surprised. 'Has she turned in already?'

'Well it is past midnight,' prompted Primrose, at which point shoeless Hailey entered the room, shot a death stare at George and wobbled her way in next to Archie on the sofa. Tatiana, on his other side, swung her legs away. I don't blame her. It's no fun competing with liberated women.

'Where's that whisky?' asked Stanley who was standing by his now roaring fire.

'Dammit, look at that,' said George. 'I forgot to bring it down.'

'Forgot?' said Primrose. 'But you've been gone *ages*.'

'No I haven't!' said George.

Charlie bounced up and crossed the room. 'Don't worry chum, I'll go.'

'No,' said George gruffly. 'My whisky's too good to drink at this stage in the evening.' His eyes then lit up, as he suggested absinthe instead. 'Arch I reckon you've got some in your cellar, that's where you keep it isn't it?'

'Now we're talking,' said Charlie, grinning at Archie.

'How do you know it's in my cellar?'

'We,' said Daniel, 'stashed it down there in the

spring when you brought a case back from Switzerland. Don't you remember that weekend? When George and I did all the heavy lifting.'

'Ah yes, I remember now . . . I'd just returned from a week-long après-ski bender.'

'Well,' Daniel turned to George, 'I think it's time we were rewarded.'

'Come on then George,' said Archie, 'let's go and get a bottle.'

'Mind if I come too?' I said. 'I love a cellar.'

Archie's face was full of surprise. 'No, of course not, do come.'

'Good call, Susie,' rang out Daniel as we left the room. 'Fontaburn's cellar is quite something.'

Archie led us through the front hall, into a stone-floored boot room where, hanging high up in glass cases, there were beautiful purple and yellow quartered jockey silks, the colours glowing despite the poor lighting. I held back to look at them as the boys went through a vaulted door below and, by the sound of things, down a stone staircase.

'Do you own a racehorse?' I called out, but no answer returned.

I followed after them, the air temperature dropping as I descended into the humid cellar. Wow! What a space. Dovetailing out in front of me were unbelievably impressive Tudor brick vaults. They went on and on, lit by dim orange mock-lanterns dangling just above head height. I didn't venture far in. It was the architecture, not the contents, I'd wanted to see. The dusty wine bottles stacked on their side meant very little to me, whereas the ecclesiastical character and true feat of structural engineering, holding up the vast weight above, really was quite something. I was so happy I'd asked to come too.

I could hear Archie and George shifting around boxes in search of what I'd call an evil spirit. I've only ever experienced absinthe in a sorbet and the effect it'd had on my behaviour then made me certain I didn't want to drink it neat tonight. Drunk Susie only comes out when I'm with my bestest friends, the ones who've seen me through my twenties and have remained by my side.

'Got it,' I heard Archie say and it wasn't long till I could make them out, coming towards me, George holding a bottle in the air.

'Chop, chop, Susie,' he said hurrying me up the stairs. No matter that I was blocking his exit, I stopped in the boot room to look up at the silks one more time.

'Nice aren't they?' said Archie who was right behind me.

'Do you own a racehorse?'

'I used to part own one but not any more. Sadly, my co-owner died.'

'Oh, I'm sorry.'

'Yes, well, no disrespect to him but it gave me an out. I never took to gambling.' Archie looked up at the silks. 'Topping colours, don't you think?' he said with a cheerier tone. 'We used to say 'purple and yellow he's our speedy fellow'.'

'Get a move on,' said George, and before any more questions could be asked he'd harried us back to the drawing room.

'Who wants some?' he asked, showing off the emerald bottle.

Hailey downed her champagne and held up her glass, 'I do!'

'Not in there,' said Daniel. 'Terribly uncouth.'

'Uncooooouth,' rang out Hailey much to Tatiana's conceited amusement.

Stanley jumped up and retrieved some shot glasses.

'Over here,' said Charlie who'd taken Archie's seat on the sofa.

'Tatiana?'

'Of course,' she said and Stanley handed her a glass.

'Susie?'

'No thank you.'

'Not for me either,' said Primrose.

Stanley plonked himself down on the sofa next to me, throwing his head back with alcohol-induced ease.

'Primrose tells me you paint. I'd love to see some of your stuff.'

Stuff you I thought, but then I considered what an ineffectual soul Stanley was, and knew he didn't mean any disrespect.

'Is there a regular class you go to? Primrose has a group she sometimes travels to Tuscany with — rather more shopping and sunbathing goes on I reckon, but then again it is a holiday.'

'I don't go to a class. I mostly paint outdoors or in the studio at home.'

'And how come you're in Norfolk?'

'I've been commissioned to draw a series of racehorses near here.'

'Fancy that! Who for? I love racing.'

'Aidan McCann.'

'Gosh, you must be good. He's a king in the racing world.'

'Do you know him?'

'Not personally, but I should think our paths will cross in time.'

'Do you own a racehorse?'

'No, no, although it's funny you should mention it as racing is the main reason we wanted to live here.'

I was under the impression they (or Primrose to be exact) had chosen this area so as to be close to Archie but maybe it was all rolled up into one. Who knows . . . this was a hard crowd to read.

'Are you planning to buy a racehorse?' I asked, trying to make sense of how his and Canny's paths would ever cross.

'No.'

'You just like it, do you?'

'Like what?'

Stanley was losing track of the conversation, probably drunk.

'Racing?'

'I love it.'

Thankfully I was saved any more chat by Primrose who dragged her husband up and announced to the room 'We're off to bed.'

George seized the moment to recite, 'Good night? ah! no; the hour is ill / Which severs those it should unite.'

Daniel joined him, 'Let us remain together still, / Then it will be good night.'

'Very good,' said Primrose with a sarcasm only ignorance could produce.

'We'll see you all in the morning,' said Stanley, tripping on the claw-and-ball foot of the sofa.

Then came 'Night,' in unison from everyone other than George who muttered, 'Very well then philistines,' his knowledge of the Romantics incongruous with his being.

Once Stanley and Primrose had left the room George suggested we all play 'a very English drinking game'. Archie nudged Hailey's shoulder as if to say 'this one's for you'.

No way did I want to play a drinking game. 'I'm going to turn in too, thank you so much Archie.'

'It's a pleasure,' he replied, attempting to push himself up.

'Sleep well Susie,' called out Daniel.

I scampered upstairs, thrilled to have been released from whatever chaos might follow.

It was all fine getting to the first-floor landing but I couldn't find a switch to turn on the lights for the second flight of stairs.

There was a mahogany console table along the corridor with a side lamp, which I switched on. Surrounding it were a collection of tortoiseshell photograph frames, each containing a single portrait of a smiling individual. All strangers to me, all different ages and grouped together like this they gave off a nostalgic air. I rubbed my finger on what looked like a stain on the table but was actually a small patch without dust. Surely the only explanation for this was that a frame must have been recently removed.

I looked along the wall for another switch but couldn't find one and my spooked heart beat heavy as I felt my way up the final flight of stairs. My room was first on the left. I grasped the knob, flung the door open and flicked on the light.

It was jolly chilly inside; the curtains hadn't been drawn nor the sheets turned down. Vicky must have missed me off the list. I stood at the end of the bed trying to fight off the unsettled feeling inside me but the tick-tock from the silver clock on the dressing table was making it worse.

My goodness, it's one o'clock in the morning. Well done Susie for lasting so late!

7

I drifted in and out of sleep, unable to completely nod off. Even the *Woman's Hour* podcast, usually my fail-safe method for sending me into a deep slumber, hadn't done the trick. I'd held back on absinthe but there was enough red wine in my system for me to be tasting it and breathing it in at the same time. My room was cold but the bed was huge, with a good old horsehair sunken mattress that had sheets so tightly tucked into the sides that I was building up quite some heat between them. The excess space around me brought on fantasies of Toby.

My mobile had no reception and I so wanted to know if he was coming to stay tomorrow. *Harrumph.* Perhaps there was hope at the window.

In a desperate schoolgirl manner, I put a towel over the sturdy radiator, heaved myself on to it and held up my telephone as high as I could. I peered out the window. It was almost four a.m., the rain had stopped falling at last but something sparked an outdoor light and its beam lit up the bottom storey of the wing opposite mine. *Crikey,* spread like a starfish across the inner bottom window ledge was a figure in a pair of pale-blue and pink stripy pyjamas. The type wives buy their husbands from mail-order magazines. I narrowed my eyes trying to get a good impression, but the middle bar of the long window was obscuring his head. *Zzzzzz* went my telephone out of my hands, me toppling after it on to the floor.

One new message, Toby Cropper.

Hi Susie, cracking walk. Would love to stay tomorrow. Thanks! Will text from Cromer. Toby

x

My heart skipped a beat and just as its rhythm was settling back an ear-deafening alarm pounded through the house. Damn drunken behaviour. I was now in a fluster, I didn't have my dressing gown with me and this lacy nightdress was not for sharing.

'Don't panic,' Archie's call travelled through the house loud and clear. 'All will be okay, please come down to the front hall.'

I slowly pulled on a jumper and my trainers, wound my way down the stairs and plodded through the sitting room with my fingers in my ears.

In the hall Daniel was standing with his back to the wall, staring at the floor, not speaking to anyone. George was in a heavy Tudor chair opposite, still dressed in his dinner clothes although bleary eyed as if he'd been asleep. Stanley, blasted Stanley, in stripy pyjamas, was leaning on the side table hugging Primrose who cowered in his armpit. Everyone, other than Daniel, acknowledged me but no one said a word.

Creeeek went the spare chair as I sat down. This drew an anxious look from Primrose. Her fringe was peculiarly damp and stuck to her forehead rather like a toddler's fringe becomes when parents in the midst of a dinner party are slow to pick up the wails coming down the monitor. Primrose had either had a nightmare or, I thought, was a tad overreacting.

'Finally!' came Charlie's exclamation as the alarm stopped and he and Tatiana stepped into the hall. I envied her linen dressing gown.

The shrill of the telephone sounded and Stanley, without a fraction of a pause for thought, stretched out his free arm and picked it up.

'Stanley Gerald speaking.'

'I think that's probably best.'

'No officer, not right here.'

'Thank you.'

He hung up and informed us, 'That was the police station. They're sending a community support officer down.'

'You fool Stanley,' said Daniel.

'Why?'

'You should have got Archie.'

'If there's a burglar in the house the police need to get here quick. No time for a conflab.'

'If it's a false alarm, you've wasted everyone's time.'

'Daniel, lay off him,' grumbled George.

A side door flung open. Archie was standing in its frame in the very same pyjamas as Stanley, his head nodding as he counted us. 'Hailey? Charlotte? Where are they?'

We all looked at each other. 'Stay here,' ordered Archie.

'Arch . . . ' whimpered Primrose but he'd gone.

'What the bloody hell is going on?' said George raising his head just enough for his bloodshot eyes to peer out from beneath his bushy brows.

'*Shh*,' said Daniel. 'It's Charlotte.'

Then the scream came loud and clear, hurtling down the back stairs, and into the hall, '*HELP*! Somebody, *HELP*!'

My immediate reaction was to tear upstairs after Daniel. We pounded along the corridor hurriedly looking in every room until we came to one with Charlotte standing in the centre of it, white as a sheet.

Daniel leapt to catch her wilting figure in his outstretched arms as she howled, 'Hailey's *DEAD*! She's *DEAD*! She's *DEAD*!'

Panic struck, I rushed to the bed. Hailey wasn't breathing. I grasped for a wrist under the covers. Good God . . . there was no pulse. I moved my shaking hand to her neck, and my trembling fingers confirmed the worst.

'She's dead,' I croaked.

Daniel let go of Charlotte and rushed around to the other side of the bed.

'She simply can't be,' he said, reaching across the mattress towards me. 'Let's prop her up with some pillows.'

'No!' I said rather sharply.

Daniel's head hovered over Hailey's mouth and when he rose up again there was no doubt in his expression. Hailey Dune was indeed dead.

She was lying on her back under the covers.

Her eyes, black with make-up, stared blankly up at the ceiling.

'We *must* call an ambulance,' I said.

Daniel sank to the floor and having chucked a sequin dress out of the way he reappeared with a mobile telephone to his ear. By chance it must have been lying at his feet.

I began to feel fuzzy, it was very warm in the room and as I took a step backwards my foot caught the strap of a stray bra. I toppled into the side table, knocking a small glass of water onto the floor.

Charlotte flinched and Daniel waved his hand as if to say just leave it.

I hung my head and stared motionless at a pair of lacy knickers lying on the floor — bare-shouldered Hailey must be naked under the covers.

Daniel's call had been answered.

'Fontaburn Hall. Yes. There's been a death. Yes, dead. No. I'm sure. No. No one.' He moved towards Charlotte and asked, 'Age? Surname?'

'Early thirties, Dune,' she mourned.

Daniel repeated the answers down the line. 'Yes. Archibald Wellingham. Yes. Daniel Furr Egrant . . . FURR EGRANT. Yes! Okay. Of course. Thank you.'

'Who are you talking to?' said Archie as he entered the room.

Daniel hung up.

'999. Hailey's dead.'

'Heavens above, you must be joking.'

Archie peered over at Hailey and then very quickly in a complete fluster he bent down to assure himself she wasn't breathing.

'She's DEAD!' cried Charlotte.

'This is absolutely desperate,' said Archie reaching to lay a small hand on Charlotte's shoulder. 'What on earth happened?'

None of us had an answer.

'ARCHIE! ARCHIE!' came Charlie's call. '*Where* are you? There's a Police Community Support Officer at the door.'

Until this moment I certainly, and perhaps the others, had forgotten all about the alarm going off.

'The *burglar!*' cried Charlotte in desperation.

Daniel shot a look at Archie, begging him to give us the answer, but instead he gave an order, 'We all have to join the others in the sitting room and wait for the ambulance.' He stood at the door ready to marshal us out.

'No,' said Charlotte firmly.

'It's best not to interfere at this point,' said Archie, taking my line on the situation. 'There's nothing you can do Charlotte.'

Daniel beckoned me over to help usher her out and as I held her trembling arm and walked her towards the door I felt hollow at the thought she'd lost her friend.

At that moment Charlie came rushing down the corridor at great speed. 'What's up? Charlotte?' he put his arm around her shoulder. 'What is it?'

Charlotte's voice cracked and a flood of tears came out on Charlie's chest, 'Hailey's dead.'

'What the fuck?' said Charlie at the top of his voice, pushing past us towards Hailey's room.

Archie failed to grab his arm and Charlie went in to see for himself. Then immediately, taking the situation into his own hands, he marched towards us insisting we go downstairs. The sharpness in his voice made Charlotte choke back her tears.

'Has someone called a doctor?' he asked.

'Yes,' said Daniel.

'What on earth is a plastic policeman doing here already?' barked Archie.

'It's Stanley's fault,' said Daniel. 'He answered the telephone call from the station, they'd got a message from the alarm system.'

'But it was a false alarm!' Archie took off ahead of us, downstairs and into the sitting room.

8

'Pleased to meet you Mr Wellingham,' said the PCSO with such bowed reverence you might be mistaken for thinking he was looking at his early morning round face in his shiny black shoes.

Archie, shaking his hand, apologised, 'I'm sorry. My friend answered the telephone before I had time to tell him it was a false alarm.'

'No problem, no problem,' said the PCSO.

Charlotte's grip tightened as I led her to the sofa opposite the ignorant others. She wouldn't sit down and I could tell in her stare she was trying hard to get George's attention but his heavy head wasn't lifting. At last with a bit of pressure from Charlie's hand on her shoulder Charlotte's bottom lowered.

Stanley, opposite, straightened his back and was just about to defend himself when the PCSO drowned him out. 'Better a false alarm than a burglar I'd say. Hello everyone, I'm Officer Wilson.' He wriggled his shoulders attempting to lessen the restriction of the high-visibility vest in his armpits. 'As I've been called here tonight . . . ' he stopped and looked at his watch, ' . . . or should I say this morning, it being almost 4.30 a.m. and all, I'll have to carry out the formal procedure.'

Archie crossed the room, flicked a switch and the chandelier above us lit up.

'Magnificent,' said Officer Wilson, holding his

hands up as if releasing a dove.

Archie's feet pounded on the floor as he strode towards the officer and whispered in his ear.

Wilson's cheeky-chappy face dropped. 'How absolutely terrible.'

I glanced at the others; simultaneously, fear grasped their expressions.

'I have some terribly sad news.' Archie drew in a sharp breath. 'We went to fetch Hailey, and, well, there's no easy way to say this. Somehow she died in the night. There was nothing any of us could do.'

'Dead?!' yelled George.

'Yes, I'm afraid so.'

'How?' asked Stanley.

'We don't know yet,' said Archie. 'There's an ambulance on the way.'

Primrose was shaking her head. 'It can't be true, it can't be.'

'It is,' said Charlie sympathetically. 'I'm afraid it is.'

Tatiana stood up. 'I want to see for myself.'

'No,' said Archie. 'We must respect Hailey's privacy.' I admired the integrity of Archie's comment. 'I am going to take Officer Wilson up there now solely because he is a member of the police force.'

'It just doesn't make sense,' snivelled Charlotte looking at George.

'You're telling me,' said Daniel.

'I reckon she drank too much,' said Primrose. 'Americans aren't good at holding their drink.'

'That's because their minimum legal age is twenty-one,' said Stanley.

'Not like us,' said George. 'I was allowed a glass of wine at dinner when I started prep school, that's what got me in training.'

'Was she ill?' Charlie asked Charlotte.

'I have no idea. She's a new friend.' Charlotte raised her head and cried out, 'I was the one who brought her here. This is all my fault.'

'No, it isn't,' said George firmly.

'Try not to think about it like that,' said Charlie. 'It's not anyone's fault.'

'It certainly isn't,' said Archie coming downstairs with Officer Wilson trailing behind.

The room fell silent. Archie sat down on the arm of the sofa and stared at the blue Peking rug onto which Charlotte was dripping tears.

Officer Wilson unclipped his mobile from his belt pouch, held it up and gently waved it at those of us watching him. He then left the room and disappeared into the hall.

Silence prevailed. I looked across at the other sofa. George's concerned face was fixed on Charlotte, Tatiana's head was bowed into her linen dressing gown and Primrose was curled up against her forlorn husband whispering something in his ear.

'Right,' said Officer Wilson coming back into the room. 'I called for an ambulance but they tell me one is already on its way.'

'You blithering idiot,' said George. 'Archie already told us there's an ambulance on its way.'

'Now, now,' said Archie. At which point thankfully the front doorbell sounded and he leapt up and ran out, followed at no great speed by Officer Wilson.

Two paramedics came rushing through the sitting room following after Archie up the stairs. Officer Wilson didn't reappear.

Charlotte shot up to standing, leaving me fearing for her bump. 'I must go too.'

Charlie reached for her hand. 'Stay here Lotty, it's better you don't go.'

'But I'm the only person who knows Hailey well.'

'I know, but they won't let you in.'

'How come Archie gets to go?'

'He's only showing them the way. He won't be allowed in either.' Hearing Archie come down the stairs everyone shut up as if he was their only hope for a miracle. He stood looking through us, motionless, the whites of his eyes leaving the others in no doubt — Hailey was definitely dead.

'What's going on?' asked Charlotte.

'The paramedics have confirmed Hailey's death and a senior police officer is on the way here.'

'What? The police?'

'It's only sensible,' said Daniel.

'Yes,' said Archie. 'They need to seal off the bedroom, and this is something a senior officer must supervise.'

'How ridiculous,' said Primrose.

'It's just how it is with an unexpected death.'

Officer Wilson appeared in the hall doorway, 'Best if I continue to wait here?' he asked, at which point the doorbell rang and Archie strode past him without answering.

'This way, Sergeant,' said Archie as he quickly

led a uniformed woman upstairs, no time for introductions.

'To call the police to the scene all sounds a bit suspicious to me,' said Stanley.

'Why?' asked Daniel.

'Well, wouldn't the paramedics just take Hailey to a hospital?'

'She's dead!' cried Charlotte.

'When someone dies,' explained Charlie, 'and they don't know how they died, the police are called.'

'Always?' asked Stanley. 'Even in the company of friends?'

'Yes,' said Charlie.

'How did she die?' asked Primrose.

'We don't know yet,' said Daniel.

'The mushrooms!' blurted out Charlotte.

'It can't be,' sniped Tatiana.

'I bet Vicky didn't cook them properly,' accused Primrose.

'*I* cooked them,' said Tatiana.

'Delicious they were too,' said George.

'Perhaps she ate one raw,' suggested Charlie.

Charlotte gave a great gasp. 'Hailey was in the kitchen before dinner, getting the leftover punch.'

'But you can eat them raw,' said Tatiana.

'Of course you can eat them raw,' confirmed Daniel. '*Boletus edulis* means edible.'

'Are you *sure* they were ceps?' asked Primrose.

'Yes,' said Tatiana defensively. 'Ceps have a brown cap, the flesh is white, the pores small and round. They have a faint white net pattern on the stem and when you cut them lengthways the inside remains white. They also have a distinct smell reminiscent of fermented dough.' Her knowledge of mushroom picking was deep rooted.

'Is anyone else feeling ill?' asked Daniel looking round the room. 'Well,' he concluded, 'it's not the mushrooms then.'

At which point the police officer, well ahead of Archie, hurried down the stairs and addressed us all.

'I'm Sergeant Ayari,' she said catching her breath, 'and I am sorry we meet in these circumstances but I'd like to help you all get through this as best I can. If I could please have your patience and co-operation for the time being I'd be very grateful.'

'Of course,' said Archie. Charlotte sniffed into the sleeve of her oversized cardigan and Sergeant Ayari began.

'Is this everyone?'

'Yes,' answered Archie proceeding to introduce us individually, as Sergeant Ayari wrote down the names in a small notebook.

Officer Wilson appeared in the doorway. 'And me,' he added.

'Come in,' said Sergeant Ayari.

He took a step forward, stopped, and clasped his soft podgy hands over his waistband.

Sergeant Ayari continued, 'The paramedics have confirmed Miss Hailey Dune dead but as of yet we're still waiting to hear any early information as to the cause.' She nodded at Archie, the only one of us privy to the goings on upstairs. 'I'm sorry to say that, right now, as insensitive as it may seem, I would like to deal with the question of the alarm. That's what brought Officer Wilson here.'

Other than mentioning his name Sergeant Ayari wasted no time in including Officer Wilson in her approach. She stood with her back to him, not remotely inhibited about hurting his feelings.

Why on earth was Sergeant Ayari focusing on the burglar alarm? Very odd, but I certainly wasn't going to try and pull her up on it. She clearly knew what she was about. Energetic, direct, she spoke in complete sentences and rapidly got to the point — obviously a very bright spark indeed. Maybe her unconventional approach was a cunning tactic to get people talking, and perhaps she suspected this had more to it than she let on.

'Now let's get to the bottom of this. A false alarm you say Mr Wellingham?'

'Yes, Sergeant.'

'How do you know?'

'I double-locked all the doors myself before I went to bed and none of them have been tampered with,' said Archie, eager not to waste her time. 'The alarm was isolated to the billiard room.'

'Who set foot in the billiard room?' asked Sergeant Ayari with a soft smile that took away any harshness in her tone.

'The Cotmans!' screeched Daniel.

'The Cotmans?' said Sergeant Ayari looking at the list of names on her pad.

'He's referring to,' said George, expanding his

chest, 'the largest collection of John Sell Cotman's watercolours in the country, which are kept in a plan-chest safe in Archibald's billiard room.'

'Nothing is missing,' confirmed Archie, much to Daniel's relief. 'Nothing has been tampered with and the safe is untouched.'

'Please take me to the billiard room Mr Wellingham.'

Archie got up, opened a closed door under the minstrel gallery and led the sergeant in.

'Whoever set off the alarm must have been in the house,' said Tatiana.

'I happen to know,' said Daniel, 'that all the ground-floor windows and external doors are alarmed at night so, if none were triggered, Tatiana has a point.'

Charlie suggested that the burglar might have come in earlier and could still be in the house. Primrose pulled Stanley closer and Daniel decided, 'If Archie's sure it's a false alarm then so am I.' Stanley reassured his wife that he did too.

With a good sense of my surroundings I knew my bedroom was at the top of the wing opposite the billiard room and I knew for sure there was a man in striped pyjamas in there when the alarm went off. Or at least I had been sure.

Archie and Sergeant Ayari came back into the sitting room, followed by a clean-cut paramedic, whose pockets rattled as he walked down the stairs.

'Sergeant,' he said. 'I'd like to have a word with everyone if I may.'

'Of course, please proceed.'

'My colleague and I have found an organic red substance on Miss Dune's cheeks. Can any of you explain this?'

I looked at Daniel, who answered without an ounce of hesitation, 'That was my influence doctor. I encouraged Hailey to rouge her cheeks with the berries of the belladonna plant on the doorstep.'

Archie gasped, 'You what?'

Sergeant Ayari and the paramedic exchanged a quick glance.

'Don't worry Archibald, I can assure you she didn't eat the berries.'

'Certain?' asked Archie staring at his friend.

Confidently Daniel flicked his fringe off his forehead. 'I'm absolutely certain, Susie's my witness.'

Archie turned to me and I nodded.

'What is this plant you're discussing?' asked Sergeant Ayari.

'It's on the doorstep,' said Archie.

'More commonly known as deadly night-shade,' said Daniel. 'Ingesting the berries can be fatal but no need to worry, Hailey rubbed them on her cheeks and none went anywhere near her mouth.'

Archie took the paramedic and Sergeant Ayari outside.

When they returned the paramedic went straight upstairs with the clipping and Sergeant Ayari told us she needed to make a call and that in the meantime we should, 'Get dressed but please no one enter Miss Dune's bedroom.'

Officer Wilson followed the sergeant out into the hall.

'Why was the alarm only set in the billiard room?' perked up Tatiana.

'Because you were all staying,' said Archie, 'I disabled the alarms everywhere apart from the plan-chest safe, the ground-floor windows and the external doors.'

'Was the door to the billiard room unlocked?' I asked.

'Yes,' said Archie.

'George,' said Charlie. 'Did you go to bed?'

'No,' he answered with coyness hard to believe he had. 'I passed out in that armchair.' He pointed at a chair under the stairs whose seat cushion certainly looked like it had been under a considerable weight for some time.

'Did anyone see George?' asked Charlie.

'I didn't,' said Charlotte. 'I went to bed first.'

'Primrose and I were next,' said Stanley. 'And Susie you followed us upstairs didn't you?'

'Yes, the clock struck one as I got into my room.'

Neither Charlie nor the rest of the late-night crew could remember when and in what order they hit the sack, but Tatiana assured us she had gone at 2.52 a.m. How she could be so exact I had no idea but it would do for now. After much discussion, it was agreed that Hailey was next, swiftly followed by Charlie, Daniel and then Archie, after he had taken Yin and Yang outside to the kennel. As for George, at what stage in the early hours of the morning he ended up in the chair, it is unknown.

'You were drunk, George,' accused Charlotte. 'How do you know you didn't open the billiard-room door thinking it was your bed-room?'

'When I woke that door wasn't open,' insisted George.

'Even if he had opened the door,' said Archie, 'the alarm wouldn't have gone off. In order for it to sound you must intercept the laser beam from the ceiling to the chest.'

'Did you?' Charlie asked George.

'No!'

'A moth,' said Stanley.

'What's that?' asked Archie.

'A moth could have set off the alarm. We were told this weren't we darling when ours was fitted?' He looked at his wife nestled in his armpit. 'Don't you remember, darling?' Primrose looked up and nodded at Archie.

'Enough of this speculating,' said Archie. 'Now we've got to the bottom of it I reckon we should all go and get dressed.'

I was first to stand up, eager to put my clothes on, but when Archie said, 'The paramedics would like a cup of tea,' I changed my mind and volunteered to make it — that gave me the perfect excuse to try and find out why they weren't taking Hailey's body away.

Officer Wilson and Sergeant Ayari were in the hall and as I passed through to the kitchen I caught the end of their fraught discussion.

'I was summoned here due to the burglar alarm,' grovelled Officer Wilson as I eaves-dropped from the other side of the kitchen door.

'But this young lady is *dead*,' said Sergeant Ayari.

'Yes Sergeant, that's why I called for an ambulance but one was already on the way.'

Sergeant Ayari huffed. 'You go now, I'll take it from here. There's a scene of crimes officer and a detective chief inspector on the way.'

I froze on the spot. I couldn't believe it. I can't believe it. A SOCO and a detective chief inspector — this means Sergeant Ayari suspects Hailey's death is criminal. But, surely not. Archibald Wellingham's friends might not be my type but I wouldn't ever suspect any of them capable of this level of foul play.

Bang! went the front door as Officer Wilson left without a word, and a split second later I very nearly let out a squeal as the kitchen door flung towards me and Tatiana entered.

'What are you doing?' she said.

'Oh! Silly me. I wasn't thinking straight, you caught me about to put on an apron from the back of the door.'

She grimaced and asked if I wanted some tea.

'I was about to make it for the paramedics.'

'Do you want some?' came her inflexible response as she took control of the kettle.

All I wanted was to be in Hailey's room but my discombobulation at the situation got the better of me, so I perched my bottom on the solid oak table and gave in to this haughty knyazhna. 'I'd love a cup, but I must make some for the paramedics too.'

'They can wait, we shall have ours first.'

'I can't believe what's happened,' I said.

'I want to leave,' replied Tatiana.

The kettle whistled.

'I'm sure we'll be able to soon.'

'I should never have come here.'

'Have you been here before?'

'No, and never again.'

'Are the rest of the house party friends of yours?'

'I haven't met any of you before.'

I thanked her as she put a mug in front of me.

'Not even Archie?'

'Yes Archie, but I don't *know* him.'

'Oh I see. How come you're here then?'

'I met Archie recently at a Sotheby's sale of Russian Modernist paintings. I was only there because it's a good place to search for a husband. He took me for two dinner dates in London and when he invited me for the weekend I accepted. He seemed so perfect: rich, single and shared my taste in art . . . ' (I applauded her honesty) 'but now I visit his house and there are no paintings anywhere. Absolutely none.'

'I've seen a few,' I said meekly, feeling sorry for Archie.

'None of any worth. He knew all about Russian Modernism when he took me out in London and now I see he has no taste.'

'You must have men falling at your feet,' I flattered her in an attempt to take the sourness out of the conversation.

'You too,' she smiled and briefly I warmed to her.

Time was short: I drank my cuppa as fast as I could in the hope that my tea-lady duty would give me a chance to revisit the scene before the detective arrived.

9

The paramedics hovering in the corridor outside Hailey's room gave me the impression that their work here was done.

'Here you go,' I said handing over the mugs of hot tea and making sure I got myself to a spot where I could see over the cordon into the room. 'I'm sorry it took so long.'

They both thanked me.

'Absolutely terrible isn't it?' I said.

'Yes, very sad to have such a young death.'

'So sad,' I found myself repeating as my eyes scanned the room as fast as they could. A dressing table of make-up and face creams, clothes hanging in the open cupboard and bath towels strewn over a wooden towel rack. On the far bedside table was a lamp whose shade was skew-whiff but other than this (and the glass of water I had accidentally knocked over) nothing appeared unusually out of place.

'Any news?' I asked.

'We're waiting for permission to take the body away.' The very fact they needed permission further suggested something was awry and if so I didn't want to be noseying around 'the scene of the crime' when the detective appeared, that's for sure.

In haste I turned to go, stopping for a moment as a loose nail on the outer doorframe snagged my jumper. Carefully, I wiggled it free. A strand of burgundy thread came with it and I rolled this between my thumb and middle finger as I went to investigate whose bedroom was next down the corridor.

'Knock, knock.' I put my head around the door, disregarding the thought that I might be about to intrude on one of the men getting dressed.

Charlie was packing his suitcase, Charlotte sitting in a chair nearby.

'Would either of you like tea? I can easily go and make some more.'

'No, thank you,' said Charlie.

Charlotte looked at me, her eyes pleading for something but I didn't know what.

'Is there anything I can do?'

'Tell me what's right,' she said in a small voice.

'Go on,' I replied.

'Must I ring Hailey's mother?'

'Of course, and her father too.'

Charlie dashed out of the room.

'She doesn't have a father,' said Charlotte, 'and she wasn't on speaking terms with her mother. Oh Susie, what do I do?'

'Pick up the telephone right now and call Hailey's mother. No question it's the right thing to do.'

'I've never met her though. I don't even know her name.' Charlotte pulled a phone out of her pocket.

'You must do it.'

I easily could have done it for her but I knew it wasn't right that I should.

Charlie returned. 'I agree with Susie,' he said,

'you must ring. Here,' he handed Charlotte a bit of paper. 'There was no lock on her mobile so the paramedic gave me the number for Mum.'

Charlotte's telephone quivered in her hand and my conscience got the better of my inquisitiveness and urged me to leave. I wasn't a good enough friend of either to hang around at such a grave moment.

I went to get dressed and shortly after a call from Archie brought everyone downstairs. In the sitting room there was a newcomer on the scene who, with one order, 'Please everyone sit down,' had us gathered on the soft furniture.

'Right, hello everyone,' said this nice-looking man with sandy hair that blended with rather than complemented his beige overcoat. 'I'm Detective Chief Inspector Reynolds.' He bowed his head and I wondered if it was because there was an Honourable, a Duke and a Princess in the room or whether policemen in the Queen's own county just have better manners. 'As you know, this is Sergeant Ayari.' He turned to his left and like an automaton clock Sergeant Ayari stepped forward and smiled.

'To bring you all up to speed,' DCI Reynolds continued. 'With negligible evidence and to be on the safe side Sergeant Ayari called me here.'

'Does this mean you think Hailey's death is suspicious?!' protested Charlie.

Neither DCI Reynolds nor Sergeant Ayari so much as flinched, both professional to the core. Although, I did think, at this stage, they could have shown a little more empathy towards us. Not that you want the police becoming overrun with emotion, but it was as if these two had completely forgotten that the young woman, lying dead upstairs, was in fact part of the house party.

'There's a colleague upstairs taking photos and possibly collecting evidence,' said DCI Reynolds. 'A routine procedure that all investigations adhere to. As soon as she's done Miss Dune's body will be removed for autopsy.'

'Autopsy?' squawked Daniel. 'Surely she died from alcohol poisoning?'

DCI Reynolds glanced at Sergeant Ayari who took on a more sensitive approach. 'It may be alcohol poisoning Mr Furr Egrant, but even so I'm afraid with the unexpected nature of the death of this young woman an autopsy is mandatory.'

'Golly gosh,' said Daniel. 'Do you really need to prod and fiddle about with the poor girl's body?'

'Yes, Sir, I'm afraid we must. For the duration, access to Miss Dune's bedroom will continue to be restricted.' He turned to Archie for confirmation that this would be adhered to.

'Right,' said DCI Reynolds hitching up his sleeves. 'I'm here to get an overview of what's happened and it would be very helpful if I could speak with you all individually.'

'Why?' spat out Tatiana.

'When a detective chief inspector, as I am, is called to the scene of a death, regardless of the circumstances, I must ensure proper procedure is followed.'

This, I knew, was so that in unforeseen

circumstances witnesses and evidence can stand up in court. But, as there was no evidence so far to suggest Hailey's death was malicious, I thought it quite right DCI Reynolds omitted this part in his explanation.

'I'll go first officer,' sniffed Charlotte.

'Of course, Madam, I'll conduct them in the billiard room so if you could wait for me in there,' he pointed at the closed door under the minstrel gallery, 'I'll begin very soon.'

Charlotte stood up and waddled across the room in her unflattering calf-length skirt. Nevertheless, all the boys watched as her voluptuous bottom moved up and down in a mildly alluring way.

'For ease let's say women first, then men please.' DCI Reynolds numbered us. 'And I'd like you all to remain here until your turn. After that you may do as you wish.'

'Of course,' said Archie.

'Right! This way Sergeant.'

Charlie, who quite likely experienced an unfortunate number of deaths in Afghanistan, stood up and paced around the room muttering caring words such as, 'The best go first', 'There is a reason for everything', 'A life lived is better than a life never lived at all.' Tatiana, who needed no comforting at all, stretched for the *Country Life* magazine on the side table next to her.

'I have a more up-to-date one here,' said Archie holding up a fresh copy, but she didn't react.

I turned to Archie and gave him a sympathetic smile.

'Do you really think she could have died from drinking too much?' said Stanley.

'Oh darling,' said Primrose, clearly feeling a bit more like herself again, 'alcohol can kill you know.'

'Maybe she was allergic?' said Stanley reassessing the cause.

'She would have known *that*,' said George in a tone that made me wonder if he felt guilty for initiating the drinking game.

Excessive drinking takes me back to my teens when, as underaged girls, we'd stand scantily dressed outside off-licences asking carefully targeted men to buy us a bottle of vodka. Unlike some of my friends I was lucky enough not to have learnt my limit the hard way. But it's thanks to them that I've sat in enough hospital waiting rooms to know stomach pumping is a good solution when you've drunk too much. In all *my* life, I've never heard of someone dying from an alcohol overdose. If Hailey was drunk enough to die, surely, she would have at least been sick before and I hadn't got a whiff of the undisputable smell either in her room or when I bent down to take her pulse.

I was third in line after Tatiana, and DCI Reynolds was as good as his word. The informal interviews didn't take long. Tatiana was out and my turn had come.

10

My interview began with the usual questions of Name; Occupation; Home address; followed by, 'What's your relationship to Mr Wellingham?'

'I met him for the first time yesterday. He'd heard I was working nearby so invited me for dinner and to stay the night.'

DCI Reynolds, who was looking mildly confused, turned to his left to make sure Sergeant Ayari was taking notes. 'How did Mr Wellingham know you were nearby and why did he ask you to dinner?'

'Well, my mother's second cousin once removed's goddaughter's husband's cousin is Archie. And when the cousin, who I haven't actually met, received a message that I was working nearby Fontaburn Hall he got in touch with Archie and suggested he should invite me to dinner.'

DCI Reynolds blinked several times.

'Did that make any sense to you Sergeant?'

'Yes Inspector, I've got it all down. Miss Mahl has a tenuous link to Mr Wellingham. She now knows him having been for dinner and the night but never knew him previously.'

'Okay, moving on then . . . ' DCI Reynolds's back straightened as he patted his tie. 'Where are you working and what is it you're doing?'

'I'm at Pluton Farm Stables, drawing six racehorses for Aidan McCann.'

'How long have you been there and how long do you intend to stay?'

'I've been there since Tuesday and I plan to leave this Thursday.'

'Thank you. Now, had you met any members of Mr Wellingham's house party prior to this weekend?'

'No, none of them.'

'So, if we were to do some digging we would find no connection whatsoever between you and Miss Dune.'

'Absolutely not.'

'It sounds to me, Miss Mahl, as if you didn't like her?'

'Oh no, I didn't mean it like that. She was a nice girl. I just meant you'd never ever find a link between us.'

'What makes you so certain?'

'I've never been to America, let alone New York. I don't live in London. I don't have a child in a private day school in Chelsea. I don't do Pilates and I don't often spend my weekends with this class of people.'

Sergeant Ayari attempted to hide her huge grin behind her small pad but I caught it all the same and smiled back.

'Did you notice Miss Dune drinking a lot of alcohol?'

'We all drank a lot, Inspector.'

'Enough to have forgotten elements of the evening?'

'No, no, I remember it clearly.'

'Would you say the same for the others?'

'I couldn't say I'm afraid.'

'Were there drinking games involved?'

'Yes.'

'Talk me through the game.'

'I went to bed before it started.'

'How did you know about it then?'

'George had suggested playing an English drinking game and just as he was about to organise it I left.'

'What drink was involved?'

'Absinthe I think.'

'Well that's not exactly English.'

DCI Reynolds was right and I suddenly realised that George had obviously wanted Hailey to take part in the game. Why else would he have put such emphasis on it being English? What on earth was he up to?

'Drugs?' asked DCI Reynolds.

'Not that I saw.'

'Did anyone have an argument?'

I thought carefully before answering. Several of the party were angsty with one another but that didn't qualify as an argument. I'm not sure what went on between Charlotte and George upstairs but something must have come about for Charlotte to go to bed and George to forget the whisky.

'No, Inspector, no arguments while I was still up.'

'Were you first to bed?'

'Charlotte went first, then Stanley and Primrose and then me.'

'Do you have any reason to believe Miss Dune was put under pressure to drink alcohol?'

'No.'

'Well I think then,' he turned to get Sergeant Ayari's confirmation, 'we can let you go.'

'Just quickly,' said Sergeant Ayari. 'Please can you give us a contact number for you, your address and your car registration if you have one?'

I gave her all she wanted and then rapidly, before I left, I took in a mental picture of the room. I wanted to be certain of its layout because, although these two had no interest in discussing the alarm, a tiny inkling in me wondered if it was connected to Hailey's death. There were three doors in here. The one I'd come through from the sitting room, another directly opposite it leading to the drawing room and one straight in front of me into the corridor with the drinks cupboard.

With the image in my head I went straight upstairs and drew a copy in the back of my sketchbook. It was confusing me why, if the person I saw in the striped pyjamas did set off the alarm, they hadn't admitted it. Maybe it was unrelated to Hailey's death but even so I wanted to get to the bottom of it.

I packed my bag and as I put my mobile in my pocket I was filled with a happy feeling that I would be seeing Toby later on.

The sitting room had emptied by the time I came back downstairs and I followed the breeze blowing up the corridor and soon heard voices outside.

The sun had risen, the sky was entirely blue and the air had a coolness that comes after a storm. Several of the glasses on the dinner table had smashed and ten waterlogged napkins lay strewn on the lawn.

'Oh, Stanley *please* get a dustpan and brush,' said Primrose. 'You'll cut your hands if you do it like that.'

Stanley looked at Archie who told him where to find one.

Daniel had appeared with Charlotte and a pile of rugs. 'I think we all need to stay out here and take in some fresh air,' he said.

'The ground's wet,' said Charlotte, scuffing the grass with her feet.

'Well that scuppers that plan then,' said Daniel, dumping the rugs on the dry paving stones.

Tatiana asked Archie how much longer we all had to stay, to which George replied, 'Not long I hope. I need to get to Northumberland by the end of the day.'

'Shooting?' asked Archie.

'Yes, with the Duke and his daughters.'

'Lucky you.' Tatiana tried again, 'Archie, do we really need to be here now Hailey's body has been taken away and the police have gone?'

'No one need hang around for my sake.'

Stanley was back to sweep the table and Primrose and I started gathering up the napkins.

'If anyone wants breakfast there's plenty of food,' said Archie, at which point Charlie came tearing around the corner with Yin and Yang yapping at his heels. 'These two are hungry.'

'Watch out!' said Primrose. 'There's broken glass on the table so keep the dogs away.'

'Thanks for letting them out,' said Archie.

'That's alright old chap. Can I have an egg before I go?'

'Of course. Anyone else?'

'Yes please,' said Stanley, who was then quickly put in his place by his wife, 'No darling, we can eat at home.'

'If you're leaving please can you drop me at the railway station?' asked Tatiana.

'Yes, of course. We'll leave in ten,' said Primrose heading into the house with a pile of soggy napkins, swiftly followed by Stanley and Tatiana.

'Can we have breakfast now Arch and come back and do this?' asked Charlie. 'My hangover's kicking in.'

'Me too,' said Daniel.

'Certainly,' said Archie. 'We've done most of it.' He put his arm around Charlotte but George intervened. He wanted her to hold back for some reason.

I followed Archie, Charlie and Daniel into the house and inconspicuously peeled off into the billiard room. It was perfect. I could hear every hushed word between George and Charlotte as they came slowly up the corridor.

'What were you thinking?' said Charlotte under her breath.

'I thought if she got drunk enough she'd forget what she saw.'

'But George, that means you killed her.'

'For heaven's sake,' said George raising his voice, 'don't be ridiculous. I'm truly sorry she's dead Lotty,' his tone hushed towards the end of his sentence, 'but you can't honestly believe I intended to kill her.'

'Of course I don't.'

'Please don't worry, no one will ever know.'

Their voices faded and when I couldn't hear their footsteps any more I sneaked out the far door of the room, into the sitting room and on upstairs. Not being part of the inner circle, I thought it time to pick up my overnight bag and be on my way. But, as I came downstairs, I heard Charlotte's voice in a room on the first floor and couldn't resist hovering on the landing to eavesdrop again.

'Darling I *had* to ring. Can't you spare a couple of minutes?'

'I'll be quick, it's just,' she stopped talking and I guessed she'd started crying.

'Yes, I'm okay, Mini Mousey's okay, it's just . . . ' the crying took over again.

'Why do you always say that?'

'It is serious, Hailey died.'

'Hailey, the girl from my Pilates class who I brought to stay with Archie.'

'Yes, she died here last night. Well, this morning actually.'

'No! Of course someone didn't kill her.'

'It was alcohol poisoning.'

'I thought so too.'

'I'm okay, yes. I wish you were here.'

'Quickly, before you go I must tell you I had to ring her mother. Oh, darling it was awful.'

'No, she didn't seem upset, just surprised. They didn't get on but I couldn't believe I had to do it.'

'Thank you, darling, that's so nice of you to say so.'

'I'll call tonight. Good luck today.'

'I love you too.'

I rushed down the final flight of stairs, plonked my bag on the floor and sat down in the armchair George had, supposedly, fallen asleep in. Before I left I wanted to work out what, if anything, he could have seen.

The unusually high-backed chair faced into the room and as hard as I tried and as much as I twisted there was no possible way anyone, under seven foot, would be able to turn their head and see the stairs. This meant, pyjama man could've easily crept down the stairs, turned back on himself and inconspicuously entered the billiard room from the corridor. Hence, leaving the door in the sitting room closed. But how, if the alarm had woken George instantly, could the person I saw in the striped pyjamas have gotten back past him without being seen? The only explanation I could think of was that portly George in his hypnopompic state must have missed it.

'Ah, George!' I said as he fortuitously entered the sitting room from the hall. 'When you woke who did you see first?'

'Archie, no Stanley, no Primrose. Why are you asking?' He walked on past me. 'I can't remember anyway.' George hadn't engaged me in conversation all weekend and his reluctance to do so now hit home as he marched on up the stairs.

I met Daniel in the hall. 'Is that you off Susie?' he said glancing at my bag.

'Yes.'

'Well it was a pleasure to meet you.' In came

his long thin neck for the *Mwah, Mwah* on both cheeks.

'And you Daniel.'

'God bless Hailey.'

'Yes, God bless Hailey.'

I went on through to the kitchen.

'I'm going to head off now, thank you so much Archie for having me.'

Charlie and Archie, the only ones in the kitchen, stood up and there followed a moment's silence. None of us quite knew what to say.

Archie reached to take the bag from my hand and moved towards the door.

'Bye Susie.'

'Bye Charlie.'

In came Charlotte as we turned to go.

'You're off?' she said. 'Thank you for being so kind Susie, I know we don't know each other well but you've been a great comfort to me.' I blushed as she kissed me warmly goodbye.

Primrose, Stanley and Tatiana were in the hall.

'Don't leave yet,' said Archie. 'I'm just going to see Susie to her car and I'll be back.'

'Arch,' asked Primrose. 'Where's your visitors' book?'

'In here.' Archie pulled out the drawer of the hall table. 'Let Susie sign her name first.'

'Lovely writing,' said Primrose, making up for the fact she was leaning over my shoulder taking in the names of those who had previously been to stay.

'Thank you,' I said. 'Bye everyone.' Stanley leant in to kiss me, followed by Primrose and then Tatiana.

'I'm terribly sorry for what you've been caught up in,' said Archie as we approached my car.

'It's okay, I'm just so sorry for what's happened. I'm staying very nearby at Pluton Farm Stables so please call me if there's anything I can do.'

'That's very kind.'

He put my bag in the boot and opened the driver's door. I kissed him on both cheeks and got in.

'Susie?'

'Yes?'

'I'm sorry to have to ask, but if anyone contacts you about Hailey's death please don't give a comment. The local press can be cruel.'

'Of course,' I said as the headline 'Affluent Local's Aristocratic House Party Comes to a Dead End', popped into my mind. 'I won't say a thing.'

I drove down Fontaburn Hall's drive and the insecurities of being amongst unfamiliar company that I'd had in my stomach over the same ground yesterday were now dampened by death. I felt tied to these people, their characters had left marks on my memories and I was convinced with a little bit of digging I could find out more than the camaraderie that lay on the surface of these childhood friends.

It can't be the first time since 1539 someone's died in one of these beds but I'll bet you it's under the most mysterious circumstances there's ever been.

11

I drove slowly down a Norfolk country lane with a huge weight on my mind and lack of direction as to where I was headed. In front of me the horizon dragged on and on, as if exhausted by the thought of never ending and I battled hard against the low skyline that was trying its very best to give me a flat feeling of depression.

I could never settle here. My two key prerequisites when choosing where to live (aside from good light for painting) were: 1. to be able to walk out my front door, straight up a hill and see the sea, and 2. nip in and out of London by train inside of an hour.

I feel so lucky to have found my dream home, Kemps Cottage, which came with the added bonus of no neighbours, allowing me the freedom to garden in last season's underwear. Privacy is something I hold close, a luxury people with big houses and land don't have. As soon as you introduce cleaners, keepers, farmers and handymen you no longer control your personal space. You just can't wander around naked, leave the bathroom door open, wear pyjamas all day, and let the washing-up pile grow.

Thoughts of home put me in my kitchen staring at an uninterrupted view of a particularly beautiful sweep of Down-land and I had a sudden urge to go for a walk. So, when a brown sign appeared up ahead, advertising the *UK's Largest Manmade Lowland Forest*, I took its turning.

The information sign in the wood-chip car park showed various 'trails' (yet another unnecessary addition of a US word into the English vocabulary) through 18,730 hectares of native trees. The one thing you don't want to do in a forest is get lost, so against my better instinct (which likes to roam free) I decided on the sensible option of a circular route with a café half-way. I popped a pencil and sketchbook into the pocket of my dress and set off, with a spring in my step for these tall trees had at last rid me of seeing the horizon.

There were an awful lot of other people on the path I'd chosen. It was a continual weave, in and out, of parents and pushchairs. My swifter-than-them pace was dictated by the speed of my thoughts.

I felt very sorry for Hailey's death, but there had been an intense tightening of my insides when I overheard Sergeant Ayari saying, 'There's a scene of crimes officer and a detective chief inspector on the way,' and a thrill of excitement had rushed through my body. It's not that I'd taken a dislike to anyone (other than maybe George) over the weekend, it was more, if my assumptions were right, that here was a mystery to be solved and I was perversely glad to be a part of it. Having once helped in the conviction of a murderer before, I rather fancied my chances at playing amateur detective again. I could exploit my skill as an artist; the acute observation needed in painting provided good practice in honing my sleuthing skills. Art would help investigating and vice-versa. Hailey's death had taken the struggle of drawing Canny's horses off my mind. So, as far as I could see, there was nothing to lose.

Shafts of daylight streamed down through the trees ahead and if it wasn't for the squealing children ragging around there'd be something rather mystical about this place. Instead I turned my mind to the mystery at Fontaburn Hall and began trying to identify some salient facts.

It worked in my favour that I'd been an outsider at the weekend, as I could freely observe each character unencumbered by never having met them before. Certain details came to mind: George's enjoyment when he rubbed Charlotte's tummy, Daniel's extraordinary knowledge of plants, Tatiana's willingness to help and how it juxtaposed with her title of Princess. However, it was Archie and Vicky's relationship that still preoccupied me most. I agreed with Primrose. Victoria Ramsbottom was a bit frosty, but what really made me think was, how come Archie had defended his cook as if she were one of his house party? His tone implied they had a relationship beyond that of employer and employee. Not necessarily sexual but definitely close. And this was something I was determined to get to the bottom of.

I had my sketchbook in my pocket to write down my thoughts at lunch. I never go anywhere without a sketchbook and have piles of used ones under the desk in my studio. All of them are full of scenes and objects that have caught my eye as well as thoughts I've had at one time or another. I'm sure if you flicked through some of my scribbles you'd say 'I could have done that'. But it's not just about the drawing; time spent with the subject allows one to capture sensual memories even in the simplest of sketches. And it's these emotional nuggets that spark an idea to pursue.

I don't have an answer to Hailey's death yet but I know if I keep tabs on my thoughts, record details of the atmosphere and individuals' reactions then much like my drawings, these 'emotional nuggets' could well 'spark an idea to pursue'. Exhilarated by the challenge that lay ahead, my speed picked up through the trees and I drifted into thoughts of Toby coming to the end of Peddars Way. I'm so excited he's coming to stay. If there's one person I'd choose to see right now it would be Dr Toby Cropper. I trust him implicitly and he'd tell me if my instincts were right. Putting his good looks and company aside, he's the best tried-and-tested accomplice I could hope for. He has all the medical knowledge to weigh up one theory or another and if it wasn't for him I doubt I would have had the confidence to get to the bottom of Lord Greengrass's murder in Dorset.

My telephone buzzed in my pocket.
One new message: Toby Cropper.

Hi Susie, hoping to be with you about
four p.m. if that's okay? X

I did a little jump for joy. Toby was coming to stay with *me*!

Great! See you later x

I knew him well enough to assume four p.m. meant more like five p.m., but I shouldn't dilly-dally just in case he was uncharacteristically punctual.

As I pounded the path I recalled conversations and observations from Fontaburn Hall and found myself coming up with two interpretations of every situation. Was Tatiana's willingness to help actually a disguise for something else?; did Stanley come across dull to deflect from his motives?; had the alarm been set off on purpose?; did George really fall asleep downstairs?; was Primrose in fact insecure?; had Daniel met Hailey before?; were Charlotte's emotions genuine?; could Charlie have had a fit of psychosis?; was Archie oblivious to it all? I was getting in a right tangle and knew the only thing for it was to reach the café and write it all down.

At the sight of the signpost my tummy began to rumble — immense hungover hunger had set in. The place was buzzing. Every table was occupied both inside and out with families taking advantage of the clear day after last night's storm. Despite pessimistic predictions as I joined a long queue, there was actually plenty to choose from at the counter. They even had my favourite: an egg mayonnaise sandwich made with bloomer bread.

'Cutlery over there,' said the broad-in-the-beam till lady as she pointed at a small stand to my left.

It was nice of her to show me but: who eats a sandwich with a knife and fork?

I held out my hand for the change.

'Don't hover around waiting for a seat,' she said bossily. 'You'll have to find an alternative outside.'

In view of the café, I perched at the bottom of a tree trunk on a surprisingly comfortable kerfuffle of surface roots. The sandwich needed salt but other than that it tasted pretty good. And the sour sweetness of my Sanpellegrino limonata did what it could for my system, suffering as it was under all the alcohol I'd drunk last night.

Turning over a fresh page in my sketchbook I began writing notes, knowing if I laid them out neatly they'd be easy to make sense of down the line.

Death by . . .
  — Alcohol
  — Unknown medical reasons
  — Poisoned: botanical; mushrooms; chemical
  — Drugs
  — Suffocated

Conventional motivations for murder . . .
  — Jealousy
  — Revenge
  — Harboured grudge
  — Love

— Lust
— Money

Things that I'd picked up on for better or worse . . .
— Daniel's knowledge of plants
— Daniel not answering my question of what Archie's job was
— Archie not wanting to mix business (porcelain) with pleasure
— Allusions to who had fooled about with who in the past: Archie and Primrose; George and Charlotte
— George's questionable faithfulness, tapping his thigh for Hailey and then Tatiana settling on it, rubbing Charlotte's tummy
— Archie's defence of Vicky
— Tatiana's willingness to help
— Vicky's initiative to turn down beds
— Vicky leaving early
— Tatiana overly anxious (thunderstorm)
— Charlotte going to bed
— George forgetting whisky
— English drinking game
— Man in PJs
— Burglar alarm

I turned the page.

Hailey's room . . .
— Lampshade skew-whiff
— Dress and underwear on separate sides of bed
— Very warm
— Water glass

Loose ends . . .
— The possible missing photograph frame
— George and Charlotte's secret
— Is it really alcohol poisoning?
— What made Sergeant Ayari initially suspicious?

Now the individual elements of the puzzle were down I knew I really should wait for what I was sure would come — revealing news from Hailey's autopsy. Nevertheless, on the route back to the car I couldn't stop myself picking over the disparate pieces, trying to identify a good-enough motivation for Hailey's death. But by the time I reached my car the thoughts and theories in my head were as tangled as the tree roots I'd perched on at lunch.

I thumped my fist on the bonnet, got into the driving seat and took off, wishing I'd come up with 'one sound theory'.

12

Back at Pluton Farm Stables the radio was playing some familiar pop music and Lucy was taking a baking dish out of the oven. 'Ah, Susie,' she turned and without a free hand to move the straight blonde hair falling in front of her face she spoke from behind it, 'it's nice to see you and good timing. I've been driving myself mad trying to remember Mr Wellingham's first name.'

'Archibald.'

'Archie, yes, that's it.' Lucy flicked her hair back. 'I knew it was something to do with a building.'

Statements like this are why I love Lucy's company.

'Dinner's done for when we want to eat it,' she said, and in surprise I exclaimed, 'But it's only three thirty.'

'I like to cook well in advance, so if it goes wrong there's plenty of time to knock something else up.' Lucy prodded her finger into the baking dish and tasted the red mush that came out. 'Looks like we're safe for tonight!' She grinned as I flopped down onto a chair and Red-Rum jumped onto the table.

'Did you have fun?'

I gave her a brief overview (without mentioning burglars or death) but Lucy wasn't actually interested in hearing about it. She was one of those rare people these days, what with Facebook, glossy mags and the trendy blend word 'Biopics', who genuinely couldn't care less about the aristocracy. Even the aristocracy like to know what their fellow aristocrats are up to. There had been a lot of it last night: Primrose obsessing over how so and so decorated their house, Daniel wanting to know the cost and landscaper of hoojamaflip's garden, Charlotte asking for the ins and outs of the latest scandal and George voicing his opinions on women sitting in the House of Lords.

The thing about posh people and those with buckets of money is most of us can't live with them and can't live without them. The very fact there is a high readership for a magazine titled *The Haves and Have Yachts* suggests within most of us there's a greedy sensation derived from dreams of owning luxury goods. And hand-in-hand with materialistic fantasies comes the enjoyment of reading about scandalous infidelity and glamorous rumours of entitled folk. I must admit, even I glance occasionally at the *Daily News*'s sidebar of shame.

'Want some tea?' asked Lucy.

'Yes please.'

The cat purred as I stroked the hyper-sensitive spot between his ears and slowly but surely his back legs bent as he sat down on the table.

'What about a crumpet?' asked Lucy, as she filled the kettle through its spout. 'I've been horsing around all day and am starving.'

'No thanks, I'm fine.'

'I like your dress by the way, and the one you

118

had on yesterday, never seen you before in fancy clothes.'

'Thanks.' I smiled at Lucy, who was wearing hip-hugging jodhpurs and a slightly too small blue T-shirt with the Eiffel Tower on it. Her pale white stomach winked at me without an ounce of self-consciousness.

'That was another topper of a storm last night; the horses were wailing in their stables — but you know what, Susie?'

'What?'

'They'll be as good as gold this week. No more storms on the way.'

'That's great news. I'm not sure I'd have coped if they continued like last week.'

Lucy didn't pay my comment any attention. She clearly didn't know what it meant not to cope.

'Lucy,' I said, steering my thoughts away from guessing what it was in her upbringing that made her so tough. 'You know I mentioned a friend might come and stay?'

'Yes,' she said generously.

'Well he's arriving this afternoon and I'm sorry I didn't let you know sooner.'

'Don't matter not telling me, my house is your house while you're here.'

'You're so generous. He's called Toby and he's very nice and easy to have around.'

'Ah yes. The man. How great!'

Not one bit of me wanted to go further into my personal life with Lucy, and as much as I really hoped Toby would be mine one day, I knew there was nothing I could do to ward Lucy off. 'He should arrive any minute . . . '

Knock, knock, knock came from the other side of the kitchen door. Red-Rum leapt up and my heart jumped.

'Speak of the monster,' said Lucy.

I got up and undid the latch.

'Toby!'

'Susie!'

He gave me a kiss on both cheeks. My heart was racing.

'Lucy meet Toby, Toby meet Lucy.'

Lucy stepped forward, I couldn't believe it, she pushed herself up on her tiptoes and yes, I was right, she reached and planted a kiss on Toby's cheek. He was thrilled. I could tell by that thing he does when he's flattered, he sort of smiles and dips his eyes at the same time.

'Welcome,' said Lucy. It was, after all, her house.

Toby had one small canvas satchel flung over his shoulder.

'Is that all you brought?' I asked.

'No! I've a bigger case in the car. This one smells better.'

Lucy giggled.

'Well if you want anything washed it's easy.' I immediately regretted sounding like a mother who's exchanged her light-hearted sparkle for a routine of forward planning and domestic tasks. And very quickly, before Toby had time to answer, I changed the subject. 'How was your walk? I wish I could have come too.'

'You would've loved it, Susie. It was completely beautiful. Great scenery for a painter.

You must go.' He pulled a chair out from the table and by the way he sat down I could tell his legs were tired.

'Who's this stripy ginger friend?' asked Toby and as he stretched to pat him Red-Rum shot out the door.

Lucy let out a laugh, 'That's my pussy Red-Rum, he's just letting you know he's the alpha male. He'll be back.'

'Lucy's making crumpets, would you like one?'

'No thanks, just tea for me please.' Toby smiled. His face was tanned and he looked even more handsome than I remembered. 'Lovely place you have here, and what a driveway, I've never been through such swanky gates in my life.'

'They're ridiculous aren't they, my boss likes to spend money and those were the latest addition.'

'I'd love a full tour tomorrow.'

'How long are you staying?' asked Lucy.

Toby looked at me to answer. I had no idea. We hadn't discussed it.

'How long can you stay?' I asked.

'Well I have a bit of time off and hoped maybe I could hang around for at least a day or two.'

'Stay as long as you like,' said Lucy. 'There's never anyone lodging here in the off season so the room's all yours for as many days as you want.'

'Thank you very much,' I exclaimed in unison with Toby's, 'Thank you.' I could hardly contain my happiness at the thought of, here's hoping, several days together.

When we'd all finished two pots of tea, gone through the entirety of Toby's walk and laughed until we felt at ease in each other's company, Lucy left to give the horses their final feed and I knew I had at least half an hour's grace to show Toby to his room and share my secret.

★ ★ ★

Toby plonked his satchel on the bed, swiftly followed by himself.

I sat down in the miniature armchair in the corner, trying to show a little but not too much leg as my dress rode up my thigh.

'It's good to see you Susie. I've missed you.'

'It's great to see you too. I'm so pleased you came.'

'You look tired,' he said. 'Are you okay?'

Either I looked exhausted or Toby (a man!) just had an emotionally perceptive moment.

'I'm very worn out and still a bit hungover.'

'Late night? You and Lucy hit the bottle?'

'Not exactly. I went to a dinner party and stayed the night at a beautiful house called Fontaburn Hall.'

'Check you out, sounds smart. I bet you were with your public-school friends?'

'Urggh! Toby! When you meet those friends I know you'll like them. Anyway, this weekend was different, the person who owns the house, Archibald Wellingham . . . '

'Archibald! Seriously? You have a friend called Archibald!'

'No! Let me finish. My mother in her well-meaning way found a tenuous link between our families and got me an invitation to dinner and the night.'

'Cooee, good on your mum.'

'They were all nice enough.'

'All? How many of you were there?'

'Ten including me. But, Toby,' I paused.

'Yes, Susie,' he mocked.

'You must swear what I'm about to tell you won't leave this room.'

'I swear. It sounds exciting!' Toby's blue eyes lit up.

'I need your help. I can't take it on without you.'

'If you're dragging me into another aristocratic death I'm with you all the way.' Toby laughed, he was joking.

'I'm so pleased!'

'Oh no. No, Susie,' he cupped his face in his hands, 'you can't be serious?'

'It's not that straightforward, but I really have to tell you.'

'Someone died and you think they were murdered?'

'Am I that predictable?'

'Only you could make such an unlikely turn of events predictable.'

I took this as a compliment and told him I didn't necessarily think it was murder but that Hailey, an American girl who was also staying, 'died early this morning'.

'She died? That's awful.' Toby looked genuinely sad. 'How come?'

'No one knows. Well, actually, everyone else thinks it's alcohol poisoning.'

'No surprise you look tired. A heck of a lot must have been drunk?'

'It wasn't though. Quite a lot was drunk but I just don't believe that's what killed her.'

'People have different thresholds you know.'

Yeah, yeah, I'd heard all this I thought but didn't say.

'You think it's murder don't you,' said Toby, 'I can tell.'

'I never said murder. But a policewoman on the scene called her detective chief inspector, the room was cordoned off, a SOCO arrived.' I drew breath, smiled at Toby and calmly said, 'they obviously thought something out of the ordinary was up and so do I.'

'I know you do! You're keeping your emotions out of it, which suggests to me you've been churning the details over slowly in your mind, looking for motivations.' He smiled at me. 'I'm right, aren't I? That sincere expression gives it away.'

My face relaxed, he'd hit the nail on the head. To think Toby could read me just like that — now there was a happy thought.

When I asked if I could tell him about it, it was more a matter of course than a question — I'd been dying to tell him.

'Fire away,' he said. 'But, just like last time, I'll be your sounding board, that's all. Okay?'

'Okay, sure.'

Careful not to influence his judgement I talked him through my stay from beginning to end. Just like it happened without adding any of my theories or prejudices. He was shocked they'd been drinking absinthe. 'It's lethal!' he said, 'with an alcohol content almost double that of whisky or vodka.' I told him I thought they'd been drinking it neat.

'Wow! That's hardcore.'

'Could it kill someone?'

'Well, she could have passed out, gone comatose and died.'

In this case it had to be George's fault. He was the one who wanted to play an English drinking game. A sure way of getting Hailey to join in. I reminded Toby I'd overheard George saying, 'I thought if she got drunk enough she'd forget what she saw.' This only confirmed my assumption.

'Well if they're both married and Hailey caught them smooching, it's no surprise George wanted to cover it up somehow.'

'But Toby,' I said, wanting to clear my conscience, 'if his intention wasn't to kill her I don't have to say anything yet, do I?'

'You can keep it to yourself until news on the autopsy. I doubt you want to make enemies this early on.'

I certainly didn't. I need the house party and the detective on side and if my accusations were false it would only make this harder. I must play the long game, win these people's trust first and then I'd be free to get under their skin.

I was so pleased Toby was up for working together. But when he suggested, as Charlie had, that Hailey might've been ill, I wished he'd begun with a more daring theory.

'But she was so bubbly, and quite frankly she was the life and soul of the party.'

'If it was a rare illness, it doesn't always show. All that alcohol could've covered up what really killed her.'

'So, you're saying it could be a perfectly natural death?'

'I can't say for certain as I don't know nearly enough about it, Susie.' Toby sounded tired and I didn't want to push it.

But, fortunately for me, he wanted to continue. 'Was Hailey's body warm when you felt for her pulse?'

'Yes.'

'Well, there's a slim chance she could have passed out from alcohol and died due to positional asphyxia.'

'What's that?'

'Restricted breathing that then causes cardiac arrest. Was she lying in a position that could have stopped her from breathing?'

'No, not at all. She was flat on her back staring at the ceiling.'

We both paused at the distinctive sound of riding boots on the kitchen floor tiles. Lucy was back and Toby and I had to change the subject.

'Just quickly,' I whispered. 'Maybe someone changed her position when they tried to resuscitate her?'

'Actually,' said Toby, 'either way the paramedics surely would have diagnosed it.'

'Yes, you're right,' I said, pleased I could at least cross one cause off my list. 'We mustn't ever let Lucy overhear us. Her room is through that wall,' I pointed behind me.

'Okay, noted.' Toby shuffled up the bed towards me. 'Do you think I could have a shower?'

'Of course. I'll show you where it is.'

I took him to the bathroom and, much like I'd been, he was thrilled to see there was a bath as well.

'If you do have a shower,' I thought I'd warn him, 'it has a bit of a dodgy temperature control but if you don't try and change it, it works okay.'

'Thanks, Susie. Also, you mentioned a washing machine. I could do with the use of that at some point.'

'I'll show you later. Unless you want to put it on now?'

'Later's fine.'

'We'll probably eat about seven thirty so we can do it then.'

I went to my room, which was at the end of the narrow corridor not so far away from Toby's. I was overcome with tiredness and lay on my bed, my limbs twitching as I unavoidably drifted into sleep.

13

Monday morning was here, and Lucy was right: the bright blue sky, cast with a blazing sun, didn't have a heavy cloud in sight. I left my room looking forward to a day of hard work.

My house-guest present to Lucy included some of my very own homemade marmalade and I really should have brought two jars as she was rapidly getting through it.

'You're amazing, Susie. I don't normally like things with bits in it but this is scrummy.'

I smiled at her between sips of tea. I never usually eat breakfast during the week. One of those theories that I'll keep in shape easier if I don't. Anyway, it's not like I needed anything to get me going today. I'm all-abuzz with the excitement of Toby being here AND almost more so, my anxious anticipation that there will be news on Hailey's death.

'Nice your friend, ain't he?' said Lucy.

'Yeah, Toby, he's great.'

'I hope he stays for a while. It makes a change to have a decent fella about. Jim and Rob could fair learn some manners from him.'

Lucy was referring to the stable lads who had leering eyes and potty mouths. Their confidence with women leapt way beyond their years. It amused me but wound Lucy up. I'm still not sure who it is she's slept with, although it could well be both. They're all at it in the horsey world

— it's as if the saddle provides the foreplay.

'Hey,' I said, 'where's Red-Rum?'

'Taking advantage of this beautiful day I think. Poor little munchkin didn't enjoy those storms. He's been cowering under the dresser for the last day or two.'

Lucy stuck her knife into the marmalade jar, drew out a large triangular chunk and smothered it on the last corner of her already-coated-in-marmalade toast.

If anyone needed sugar it was Lucy. I'd never seen such continuous hard labour as that which goes on in a trainer's yard. Starting with the first feed at 5.30 a.m., a strict daily routine is adhered to and there's no excuse for not turning up to work, hence why most of the minimum-wage twenty-five employees live on site.

'Hey Susie,' she said as a marmalade triangle entered her mouth, 'you should take Toby to a flat race, there's an evening meet tonight not that far away.'

'Are you going?'

'Na, someone needs to give these horses their last feed and tuck them up for the night and that someone is me. Especially if I want to be the head girl here one day.'

'Is that Francis's job?'

'Yeah, he's the head lad but when he retires I reckon I'll be in the running.'

'I hope you are, you certainly work hard enough.'

'You can put in a good word for me with Aidan!'

'Of course, I will,' I said, knowing full well it

would be several years yet before Lucy was experienced enough and Francis old enough for the tables to turn.

Although, it hadn't escaped me that Canny must favour Lucy somewhat, her having been given her own cottage when most of the other employees are left sharing accommodation on site. I'd pried a little into Canny's private life but hadn't got very much back. He's been married twice, the second one really not lasting long. Lucy fell in his favour both times, saying, 'These women like the money racing brings in but can't stick the hard graft that winning involves. Poor Aidan,' she'd put it, 'he's ace but not nearly appreciated enough.'

'Tell me about this meet tonight,' I said, thinking I really ought to go. I live right by Plumpton Racecourse and feel bad I've never been.

'It's on the flat at Ingle Park. The incredible speed's exciting but it won't be as good as watching a hunter in full flight over a flipping great obstacle.'

'What time is it at?'

'The first race is ten past six but you don't need to get there that early as the last is at ten past nine.'

'Is there a dress code?'

Lucy giggled. 'No. Well, you can't wear jeans and trainers, but you don't have to dress up. This course ain't a patch on the likes of Ascot, Epsom or Newmarket but it's a good place to start.'

Thoroughly practised in our routine, Lucy went to get Great Knockers into the cordoned-off part of the paddock and I ran upstairs to collect my basket of drawing materials. There wasn't a stir from Toby's room. He must still be fast asleep.

I walked up the fence line of the horses' field and the air buzzed with bees pollinating the purple sprouting clover. I felt so happy. A cloudless sky and bright sunshine gives the best light to work in. The clarity cuts a crisp outline of the horse and the contrast of bright light on its body and intensely dark shadows in its sockets makes it so much easier to achieve volume in a drawing. Today should be a doddle.

'There you go, Susie,' said Lucy, undoing Great Knockers's headcollar. 'She's a lovely mare this one and a very promising point-to-pointer.'

'Aidan's quite successful isn't he?'

'He's brilliant. Although this one's owner ain't giving any slack. We're under pressure for her to beat the record of five Gold Cups in a row.'

'Is that possible?'

'We believe anything's possible. We just have to work hard at fitness and hope she doesn't get injured.'

Even I knew now, due to the continuous occupation of the walkers in the paddock, just how frequent injury amongst racehorses is.

'Shall I stick around for a bit?' asked Lucy. 'I've got fifteen minutes spare before I have to meet a lady who's coming to the yard.'

'That would be great. Thanks so much. I want to start by taking photographs so if you wouldn't mind reattaching the headcollar and encouraging Great Knockers to walk with you it'd be perfect.

But, keep at least a head in front of her as otherwise your shadow will get in the way.'

Lucy was brilliant. She had a special knack of getting inside a horse's head and making it do whatever she wanted. I snapped away from every angle as Great Knockers followed after her in a figure of eight, never once overstepping Lucy's shadow. As they passed back and forth in front of me I became utterly mesmerised by the muscle movement on such a fit horse.

Photographs are very useful for reference but when it comes to a full understanding of the skeleton, and how joints work, drawing is the only thing for it. So, when it was time for Lucy to leave I settled into sketching, exploring the horse's form, making many drawings as Great Knockers moved around the field.

It was such a hot day the charcoal rubbed off on my fingers even more than usual and when Lucy came back to get me for an early lunch she laughed at the, as she put it, 'gothic make-up all over my face'. I'd obviously been rubbing my nose and wiping my brow, oblivious to the mess coming off my fingers.

I wiped my face with a rag before we headed back to the house, 'Is that better?'

'All gone!' she smiled.

'Have you seen Toby?' I asked, slightly miffed he hadn't come to find me.

'Yeah, he's been up a while, we've just got back from a lovely walk.'

This took me by surprise.

'I gave him the full tour,' said Lucy and then I remembered Toby had requested it last night.

'He asked me if you'd mind him coming to see you and I didn't know what to say.'

'What did you tell him?'

'I told him you were working. Come,' she said, 'mind if we go through the stables, I just want to say goodbye to someone.'

I didn't mind at all. It's not often I take the shortcut through the yard as I'm conscious of not wanting to get in anyone's way. Also, I don't like to draw attention to my art and fear if I get too friendly with the crew they'd all be coming to see what I'm up to. This was an interruption I really didn't want.

It was quite a sight entering the first quad and seeing thirty or so enormous animals being washed and brushed down after exercise by an army of thick-thighed girls and boys, all in love with horses and/or each other.

'Susie,' said Lucy as we approached the netted bun of a woman with her back to us, 'Meet Mrs Ramsbottom.'

Goodness gracious me! I was now standing, staring into the eyes of Archie's cook. She nodded 'hello' with no recognition.

'Hello again,' I said, already having gathered enough to assume Victoria Ramsbottom couldn't have been that ill on Saturday if she was now standing here in riding kit looking and sounding absolutely fine.

'Do you know each other?' asked Lucy.

'We met at the weekend.' I grinned, at which point the penny dropped and Vicky's face fell.

'Yes, so we did,' she said. 'Don't let me hold you up, you look like you're off somewhere.'

133

'Thanks for coming today,' said Lucy. 'I'll let you know when we're short again.'

Before there was time for me to ask Lucy any questions we were outside her cottage having a laugh at Toby trying to single-handedly squeeze a trestle table out the front door, Red-Rum doing his very best to get under his feet.

'Lucy and I thought it'd be nice to eat outside,' he said as I dumped my stuff and shooed away the cat.

'Great idea. How did you sleep?'

'Like a log.'

I helped steady the table.

'Who were you drawing today?' he asked and I blushed.

'Great Knockers.'

'Seriously? That's its name?'

'Hers is mild in comparison to some of them.'

Lucy excitedly reeled off the other five and we had a good laugh at the horses' expense. A ploughman's lunch was already prepared on the kitchen table and Red-Rum was having a good sniff around. Lucy and Toby carried out the cutlery and sauces and I dashed upstairs to take a look in the mirror. I'm not usually so vain but in Toby's presence I acted on impulse.

'Susie!' Lucy shouted up the stairs. 'Your telephone's going.'

I reached across the banister and grasped it from her hand as she fled back outside.

'Hello?'

'Miss Mahl?'

'Yes.'

'Detective Chief Inspector Reynolds here.

May I have a word?'

My heart missed a beat.

'Of course, Inspector.'

I went into my bedroom and shut the door.

'I understand my call may come as a surprise but there are a few questions concerning the weekend that I'd like to ask you.'

'Yes,' I replied.

'As you are still in Norfolk I was hoping you might be able to pay us a visit at the station this afternoon.'

'Oh,' was all I said, nothing else would come out. For some unknown reason I felt guilty. It reminded me of telephone calls with Mum when I was a teenager and she would finish with, 'your father would like a word', which was code for, 'here comes a telling off'.

'If it's difficult for you to get here,' began DCI Reynolds, 'we can conduct the questions on the telephone but if possible I'd rather not.'

'No, no. I can easily come to the station. When would you like to see me?'

'As soon as it's convenient for you.'

I glanced at the clock, 'I could get to you for one thirty?'

'That would be most helpful. Thank you. We'll expect you then. Norham Police Station, NF2 3XX, sat nav brings you to our door.'

I will never let sat nav into my life. It gives me pleasure remembering where I've come from, what I've passed and where I've arrived and GPS would only take away this pleasure.

I live on a single-track lane in Sussex, a straight one-and-a-half-mile stretch, no turnings, just two T-junctions at either end. Yet delivery people ring me from sixty yards away asking for directions. I rush out on to the road and wave at them. Only to have them arrive furious that my eighteenth-century cottage is not where sat nav says it is, and I find myself assuring them the house hasn't moved.

I knew how to get to Norham and I was fairly sure the police headquarters wouldn't be hard to find. Half past one could hardly come quick enough. I ate lunch longing to give Toby an update but there wasn't a moment without Lucy. I was preoccupied by my thoughts and my company paled in comparison to hers but right now I didn't mind.

'Are you off to the races later then?' Lucy asked Toby and he looked at me with a bewildered expression. I'd completely forgotten to mention it.

'There's a meet tonight not far from here. Shall we go? It could be fun.'

'It'll be fun,' said Lucy fluttering her eyes at Toby. 'You should go if you've never been before.'

'It'd be a first for me and I'm keen if you are Susie?'

'Very keen.' I smiled.

'You're coming too aren't you Lucy?' Toby's voice carried far too much enthusiasm for my liking.

'Na, not tonight, I've got work to do.'

'Poor you.'

'Not poor me, I love my job, nowt better than a horse you know. They're the most beautiful, exotic and incredible beasts that live on the planet.' She glanced at Red-Rum basking in the sun, 'A cat comes close second of course.'

'And with a name like his you obviously know your stuff, so come on, how do we tell a winner from a loser?'

Lucy went into a rhapsody, 'Every horse is very different. I look for one who really uses himself, his tail swinging like a pendulum.' Her right arm was going mad with excitement. 'If you visit the enclosure before the race you'll get a good look at the runners. Mind and take note of the trainers' outfits. Smart suits and silk ties tell you their horses have won in the past.'

'Brilliant,' said Toby. 'We'll celebrate our winnings with you when we get back.'

Lucy told us if we were in any doubt we should put our bet on a horse wearing a sheepskin noseband. She said it 'helps keep their head down so they don't get spooked', which sounded sensible enough to me. Toby asked if I was 'up for giving him a drawing lesson this afternoon', and I was pleased he'd worked out a way of us doing something together. Of course, I'd give him a lesson!

'I just need to nip into town first,' I said, standing up and clearing my plate. Toby looked bewildered but didn't ask. 'Sorry to rush, I don't want to waste this lovely day. I won't be long.'

I popped upstairs, quickly changed into a summery dress and rushed off to my meeting with DCI Reynolds.

14

'Miss Mahl,' said DCI Reynolds, this is 'Sergeant Ayari, who you'll remember.'

'Yes, hello,' I nodded. 'Please call me Susie.'

We were in a box room with no windows. The usual scene: empty table, bucket chairs and two police officers with pads and pens.

DCI Reynolds pulled out a chair for me. 'If you'd like to take a seat then we can begin.'

I tucked my legs under the table and sat upright, eager to proceed, uninhibited by the fact that I must currently be a suspect.

'Now, Miss Mahl. Susie!' he corrected. 'Before we begin I just want to make clear, this is an informal interview and you have the right to leave at any time.'

'I understand,' I said deferentially.

'Sergeant Ayari and I are looking for clarity.' DCI Reynolds's eyes were fixed on mine. 'We would like to go through with you the events of Saturday evening and the early hours of Sunday morning at Fontaburn Hall.' A sharp nasal inhale finished his sentence.

I glanced at Sergeant Ayari. Her poised silence made me feel uneasy.

'In order to get you up to speed,' said DCI Reynolds, 'I must inform you that Miss Dune's standard post-mortem has given us reasonable cause to confirm that her death was not, as the house party presumed, from alcohol poisoning.

A full forensic post-mortem has been requested and a police murder enquiry triggered.' It was Sergeant Ayari now whose eyes were fixed on me.

'M-u-r-d-e-r,' I let out ever so softly.

'Yes,' said DCI Reynolds, turning up the volume. 'This morning an inquest was opened in Norfolk Crown Court and the identity of the deceased has been confirmed.' He nodded for Sergeant Ayari to continue the point.

'Miss Hailey Dune, aged thirty-one, assistant primary school teacher at Lilac Pre-Prep, in London. American citizen on a work visa in the UK. Residency in UK totals eleven months. The inquest has been adjourned until investigations are complete.' She spoke without an ounce of compassion, which was (hopefully) probably mandatory in these circumstances.

DCI Reynolds cleared his throat. 'The investigation into the cause of Miss Dune's death has begun. Due to the circumstances, there is pressure to gather evidence as quickly as possible, and for that reason the pathologists' medical tests and my team's Fontaburn Hall investigations will be carried out simultaneously.'

I took in a sharp breath and nodded in agreement. Yesterday, with his dull beige exterior and nonsense questions, DCI Reynolds had aggravated me but today, despite the fact he was again dressed in varying shades of the anodyne colour, he intimidated me.

'Good, good,' he said, pushing the end of his pen against the table to release the nib. 'A few questions, some of which are repeats from last time.'

At last Sergeant Ayari smiled at me, and I wondered if it was her way of compensating for her boss's uncompromising manner. It did the job. I relaxed and smiled back, wanting her to know I was on side, ready to work as a team — if I should be so lucky.

'How long have you known Mr Wellingham?' asked DCI Reynolds.

'I'd never met him or any of his guests before Saturday night.'

'I see. Yes, I remember now.' He looked at Sergeant Ayari for her confirmation. She had yesterday's interview in front of her but I didn't doubt her memory.

'When and what time did you arrive at Fontaburn Hall?'

I recalled Hailey's announcement of gin o'clock. 'About five to six on Saturday evening.'

DCI Reynolds and Sergeant Ayari exchanged a knowing glance.

'Other than the names on my list,' DCI Reynolds pushed a piece of paper across the table towards me, 'Was anyone else present?'

'Two dogs, Yin and Yang.'

'Mm-hm,' agreed DCI Reynolds. 'Anyone else?'

'Yes, Victoria Ramsbottom.'

'A guest?'

'No, she was doing the cooking.'

'Had you met her before?'

'No.'

'Did she have any interaction with the guests

asides being the cook?'

'No.'

'Was she staying at the Hall?'

'No.'

'How long did she spend there?'

'I'm afraid I don't know.'

'Did you see her leave?'

'I didn't see her but I know she left.'

'How do you know?'

'She left a note in the kitchen saying she'd gone home because she felt unwell.'

'Did you see this note?' DCI Reynolds was far more perceptive than I'd previously given him credit for.

'No,' I said, realising my mistake: I could have so easily checked for the note but had missed the opportunity.

One thing was clear, DCI Reynolds wanted evidence and this linear approach made me think better of mentioning the burnt pudding and how peculiar I found it that Victoria Ramsbottom, an experienced cook (she wouldn't have tackled grouse breasts, not to mention game chips if she wasn't) had failed to take the pudding out of the oven before she left. Thinking on my feet for a second, if the sick note was a veil for a quick exit then perhaps something ominous had been playing on Vicky's mind, preoccupying her and causing her to make such a foolish mistake.

DCI Reynolds, busy making sure Sergeant Ayari was getting this all down, didn't think to ask me if I'd seen Victoria Ramsbottom since Saturday. Lucky for me — if I had to tell him she'd been at Pluton Farm Stables it might drag

Lucy into the whole thing, and I really didn't want to bring all that upon her. As it was I could now indulge in a little bit of discreet snooping myself before putting him in the picture.

'Moving on to meal times,' said DCI Reynolds. 'Please can you give us a full list of what you drank and ate during your stay.'

'One glass of gin and tonic, three glasses of champagne, several glasses of red wine, a small cup of coffee, quite a few glasses of water and a cup of tea.' I took a breath avoiding a yawn. 'I ate a cheese straw, two cheese straws in fact, ceps on toast, one grouse breast, a handful of game chips, leeks, broccoli and a Bendicks bitter mint.'

'All taste normal?'

'Yes. Of those I've eaten before.'

I should think DCI Reynolds would have run a background check on me by now and therefore must know that mushroom picking and grouse shooting didn't go hand in hand with an artist's income and south London upbringing.

'Any digestive side effects since your stay with Mr Wellingham?'

'Nope.'

'Now,' he said with a hint of self-consciousness, 'I would like us to turn our attentions to the bedroom. At what time did you, if at all, first enter Miss Dune's bedroom?'

'I don't know what time but it was soon after the burglar alarm stopped sounding. Daniel and I rushed upstairs when we heard Charlotte's cry for help.'

'What was her cry?'

I racked my memory for the exact words.

'Susie?' he asked, impatient for my answer.

'I'm very sorry Inspector, but I can't recall what she said. It was alarming, I remember that, because her voice carried all the way down the back stairs into the hall.'

'Why did you take it upon yourself to answer her call?'

'It was my immediate reaction. I didn't make a conscious decision. I heard a scream for help so I ran.'

'And Daniel?'

'You'll have to ask him.'

'Did none of the others follow on?'

'No.'

'Mr Wellingham? Where was he?'

Good point! Where on *earth* was Archie at that moment? He'd come into the hall when the alarm stopped but why hadn't he run straight to his friend in distress?

'I don't know, Inspector. He did come to the bedroom but after Daniel and me.'

'Would you say Daniel and you were the spriteliest of the bunch?'

'Perhaps, yes. Although I think it's worth taking into account how different people react in tense situations.'

'I think it'd be best Susie if you let us decide what and what not we take into account.'

DCI Reynolds was quite right, I'd spoken out loud and out of turn and although *I* felt I'd make a good co-detective he'd firmly reminded me, I must earn my place first.

'Please describe Miss Dune's bedroom to us as it was when you first entered. Objects, persons, clothes, toiletries . . . now don't feel inhibited and make sure not to miss anything out.'

I had to be careful here as I have a visual memory. I knew I could give an almost perfect description of the room and although it may well work in my favour if I did, it could alternatively lead DCI Reynolds and Sergeant Ayari to the conclusion that I was a key suspect. So, omitting the colour, pattern and material of all soft furnishings as well as the period style of the furniture, height of wall-light fittings, type of beading on the skirting board and wording from the magazine poking out of the top of Hailey's handbag, I launched into a concise description. 'Looking into the bedroom as if from the window, Charlotte was standing in front of the dressing table staring over the chaise longue at Hailey, who was lying on her back on the left-hand side of the four-poster bed. Hailey's eyes were open and as far as I could tell she wasn't wearing any clothes.'

'Was Miss Dune wearing clothes or was she not, Susie?' interrupted DCI Reynolds.

'Her dress and underwear were on the floor and her shoulders were bare.'

'I see. Go on.'

'The duvet was ruffled on both sides of the bed and the lampshade on the right side of the bed was skew-whiff.'

'Right side? Still looking at the scene with your back to the window?'

'Yes, all this is as if from the window.'

I had a strong visual in my mind and it

suddenly struck me that Hailey's underwear, her bra having got caught on my foot, was on the opposite side of the bed to her dress, which Daniel had chucked out of the way. This threw up two options. Either Hailey, drunk and disorderly, could have undressed around the room, tipped the lampshade herself and ruffled up the entire bed. Or someone else was in there too.

'This, Susie, is the most detailed account of the scene we've received so far and it's particularly helpful to us that you were in there very early on.'

DCI Reynolds looked again towards Sergeant Ayari and I wondered what, out of all I had said, was most interesting, or whether in fact I had just dropped myself in it.

'Please go on,' he said with a genuine smile and I now saw him in a different light. His far more relaxed demeanour showed he was in fact a kind man. He had those soft eyes that would be hard not to trust and his mouth held a smile even in repose. I assumed this pair was looking on me favourably so I continued my description, across the dressing table and into the open wardrobe. I spoke exactly how I'd seen it; I won't drag you through it, there was nothing of any note, other than to say I did in the end admit to knocking over the glass of water.

'Having made us aware of your acute attention to detail,' complimented DCI Reynolds, 'I would be interested to hear your interpretation of the evening's events.'

I froze and gulped. 'I'm sorry, Inspector, I

would rather not share anything at such an early stage. Not that I really have anything to share.'

Niggling at my conscience was the man I'd seen in the billiard room, the one in stripy pyjamas. I wanted to bide my time before introducing a possibly coincidental tangent. So as DCI Reynolds hadn't yet drawn a parallel between the alarm and Hailey's death, I didn't mention it.

Without the slightest bit of animosity, he said, 'If at any point you want to come and see either me or Sergeant Ayari for a further chit-chat please do.' And with a sincerely rigid (and now familiar) forefinger he pushed a business card across the table. 'This has my direct line and mobile on it.'

'And here's mine,' added Sergeant Ayari, as it dawned on me they may well already know I'd played amateur detective before and, if so, I thought I'd chance my luck and provoke a discussion.

'Inspector, how come the pathologists are so sure Hailey didn't die of alcohol poisoning?'

DCI Reynolds glanced at Sergeant Ayari who gave a rapid sharp nod.

'Not enough alcohol showed up in her blood or her urine. In fact, unlike most inebriated patients, she had not urinated.' DCI Reynolds pulled his chair out from the table and clasped his hands in his lap.

'Between you and me Susie, alcohol poisoning would have been a satisfactory explanation for all involved, but it's certainly not looking to be the case.'

Sergeant Ayari nodded in agreement.

'As for drugs, they would have given us an alternative explanation but there was no trace of recreational substances in Hailey's system.' DCI Reynolds stood up to show me out, 'Just one final word.'

'Yes, Inspector,' I said as I rose from my chair.

'As I'm sure you're aware, Mr Wellingham is quite the public figure in these parts and I ask you please, on his behalf, to keep this business under your hat whilst we carry out our investigation. It makes our job a lot easier if we can act in privacy without the press or busybodies spouting nonsense along the way.'

'Of course, you have my word,' I said as I slipped their cards into my handbag and left.

15

'There you are Susie!' Toby was lying on the small patch of grass outside Lucy's cottage reading Delia Smith's *Summer Collection*. 'I thought I'd cook for you both tomorrow night.'

'That would be excellent.'

He jumped up onto his feet and the earnest look in his eye as he came towards me suggested he was eager to know where I'd been.

'Not here,' I said. 'I'll fill you in in the paddock.'

'Drawing-lesson time, hey?'

'Yup. I'll just change quickly and pick up my things.'

★ ★ ★

Toby and I walked up the fence line to Great Knockers, him carrying a spare canvas chair of Lucy's.

'Do you always sit down to work?' he asked.

'Not if I'm painting landscapes but always if I'm drawing big animals.'

'Why's that?'

'You'll see, but it's important to have your eye line midway up the animal's body. If you don't, it makes it very difficult to draw them in proportion.'

'I've been thinking you should draw Red-Rum for Lucy,' said Toby in a particularly cheerful voice that aggravated me.

He was taking advantage of my profession (unless he was going to commission me — no — that would be even worse). And why was he thinking up such a thoughtful gift for Lucy?

'I could do with the practice,' I said flippantly.

But he took it literally. 'Surely you've drawn lots of cats?'

'For some reason few cat owners employ me.'

'But people are mad about cats, I reckon I could get you a commission or two.'

I smiled at him, he was back in favour.

★   ★   ★

Once we were out of earshot, I told him he'd been right, 'Hailey didn't die of alcohol poisoning.'

'I *knew* you were off to see the police.'

'DCI Reynolds asked me to come in. You don't think I would've gone voluntarily do you? I'm far more level-headed than that.'

'I know, I know. I'm just teasing. Now though,' he said unfolding his chair, 'you can tell me all.'

Toby sat down, glued his eyes on me and didn't once look away as I told him all about the forensic post-mortem and the police murder enquiry.

'I thought something was up,' I said, 'but, I hadn't wanted to believe it was murder.'

'My goodness,' Toby sounded excited, 'Pet Detective strikes again.'

'*Shhh, Shhh.* You never know who's listening around here.'

149

He recoiled into his chair.

'Just quickly,' I said, 'did you meet the woman Lucy was with this morning?'

'I saw her with someone but I didn't meet her. Why?'

'I've never seen her here before, that's all.'

Toby sat up. 'So, what did the police tell you?'

'Nothing. I was being interviewed formally.'

'Oh, come on Susie, I know you, you *must* have got *something* out of them, you were there for at least half an hour.'

I gave a conceited smile, and repeated DCI Reynolds's exact words in his formal voice, 'Not enough alcohol showed up in her blood or her urine. In fact, unlike most inebriated patients, she had not urinated.'

Toby's eyebrows raised and I knew he was impressed.

'What do you think it is?' I asked.

'I've no idea. Let's go through her symptoms.'

'There weren't any other than drunkenness.'

'Still, talk me through them.'

'First her speech became slurred, then she got energetic and keen to dance and at one point she fell over on her way upstairs.'

When Toby said, 'We can pluck several possible symptoms out of all that', I picked up my sketchbook to write them down.

'Hey, let's see that,' he said, taking it out of my hands and flicking through the pages. 'Of course, you've been recording it.'

'Now,' he handed it back to me. 'Make a note of slurred speech, energetic, dizzy, thirsty . . . '

'Thirsty?'

'I know she was drunk, but maybe she drank a lot because she was thirsty.'

'But DCI Reynolds said she hadn't urinated.'

'Surely, he meant she hadn't urinated after death, not all evening.'

I blushed. 'Yes, good point.'

'Add it to your list, it's an interesting one.'

'What does it mean?'

'It could be that Hailey's kidneys weren't working properly.'

'Really?'

'Yes, and if the investigation is running along these lines then I think DCI Reynolds's team will have gone on a hunt for poisonous mushrooms and the pathologists will be carrying out a post-mortem kidney biopsy testing for orellanine toxin.'

'Orellanine toxin?'

'You said the Russian Princess picked and cooked ceps didn't you?'

'Yes she did.'

'The world's most poisonous mushroom is deadly webcap and a small one of those can easily be mistaken for a cep. Deadly webcaps contain the highly toxic compound orellanine, which destroys our liver and kidneys.'

'You know your stuff don't you?' I grinned at him. I love that Toby has a brain and, between you and me, I find it surprisingly attractive when he rabbits on in work mode.

'Tatiana couldn't possibly have made a mistake,' I exclaimed, suddenly realising what Toby had been saying, 'You didn't hear her on mushrooms. She knew everything.'

'Did she help in the kitchen?'

'Yes . . . ' I went silent. It had struck me that Tatiana had carried the two remaining first-course plates into the garden, one for her and one for Hailey.

Toby said exactly what I was thinking, 'In that case she could have picked and fed Hailey a webcap on purpose.'

'No,' I didn't believe it, 'Tatiana might have been jealous but, there's no way she killed Hailey.'

Toby spoke softly, 'Susie, if you think someone killed Hailey then why not Tatiana?'

'Oh crumbs. When you put it like that I wouldn't confidently say any of them killed her.'

'Well that's what you're up against so you better take a deep breath before you dive back into another police investigation.'

This made me feel mildly guilty for indulging in Hailey's death.

'Listen,' reassured Toby, 'put it out of your mind. Don't start looking for reasons to suspect any of these people until you hear if the pathologists have found orellanine toxin in Hailey's system. I'm sorry for mentioning it.'

'No, don't be sorry. It's wonderful you're a doctor. I'd never get anywhere without you. And you could be right. Maybe Tatiana did do it,' I sighed.

'Honestly, it's dangerous to stew over your thoughts before you have evidence to go on. Our minds are very good at tying the wrong ends together when we want to make sense of things.' Toby smiled at me, 'Time to start drawing.'

I rooted around in my basket, putting our drawing materials together and Toby got up to give Great Knockers a friendly pat.

He was struggling to make friends. Great Knockers' ears were back, her head going whichever way his hand wasn't and, giving up, his long face sauntered back towards me.

'Time for drawing!' I said, handing him a stiff board that he held flat as I taped a large piece of paper to it.

'What about you?'

'I'll use this sketchbook, it has a hard back.' I handed him a thin stick of charcoal, 'You may want a pencil but I'm not going to let you have one. Now, copy me.'

We both drew a large black rectangle an inch inside the edges of our paper.

'This box helps you remember you're doing a drawing not a sketch.'

'I can't draw. Maybe a sketch would be easier.'

'Everyone can draw. It's just another way of expressing ourselves.'

'Really?'

'Yes, but you have to let go of your inhibitions and not worry about making it good immediately as this takes a lot of practice.'

'Okay, I'll try.'

'Think of it like this: if I said stir a pot you wouldn't jump the gun and say I can't cook. It's the same here, I said draw a box and you did it.'

'But that part's easy.'

'Trust me, if you take the same unselfconscious approach we'll get there.'

Toby raised his eyebrows.

'You need to find a part of Great Knockers's body that draws your eye and then put a mark on your paper, like this.' I turned my sketchbook to him. 'I like her underbelly so here's its curve.'

Toby put a line on his paper for her tail.

'Now look really hard and see what and where things intercept her body.'

I demonstrated on my drawing by putting in the fence post that I could see under her belly. 'To understand the shape, you need to focus on the objects around her and draw your picture, starting at the tail and working across the frame.'

'I'll give it a go!'

'You must look with your eyes twice as much as you draw with your hand and never let the process be interrupted. This intense engagement with the subject will bring out your best work.'

Toby had begun and taken my word for it. He was absolutely silent. Easy-peasy to teach.

What fun it was sitting side by side in our own worlds, the sun shining, butterflies fluttering past and the occasional dragonfly buzzing into sight.

'Great Knockers looks like she's floating,' said Toby, upsetting the atmosphere and staring with frustration at his drawing. 'How on earth did you manage to get such weight into your picture?'

'Yours is great!' I said, it being a reasonably good start.

'No, it's not. It looks nothing like her, or yours.'

'I'm well practised.'

'Help me!' he pleaded.

'You have to draw the shadows not the animal. Look where the light falls and see the way it gives definition in some places and not in others.' I reached across and smudged the charcoal line beneath his horse's jaw. 'See, her face is now much lighter and pops out at us.'

'That's so clever.'

'If you make her underbelly darker, it gives volume.' I rubbed his picture with my mucky fingers. 'Go on, you work your way down the legs.'

Toby went for it, his desire to finish getting the better of him.

'Be careful,' I said. 'You mustn't make it up. You have to look very closely and only put in the shade you see.'

I handed him a rubber, 'Use this to make the outline of her back crisp. There's no dark there.' I pointed at his drawing. 'Now you see, charcoal's much easier to move around than pencil.'

'Isn't it just.'

'Key thing is not to overwork it, so I think it's time to call it a day.'

'Thanks so much for my very first lesson,' he said, clasping an arm around my shoulders. 'Can I have another one tomorrow?'

'Same time, same place if you're keen?'

'Mad keen!' He gave me a squeeze and I felt my body tense. I haven't been intimately touched since Geoffrey, my last failure of a relationship, and I felt nervous of letting someone else in. Although, deep down, beneath my reservations, I was longing for something to happen between Toby and me. He is pretty wonderful.

16

'Susie!' I heard called out above the crowd and swung around, wondering who on earth I knew in this rabble of people.

Toby and I were in the commoners' enclosure of Ingle Racecourse. There were short men everywhere, which made me think if you can't join the jockeys you back them. Retro IBM screens with neon blue and red columns of confusing names, numbers and symbols flashed above head height.

Toby had a cobbled-together-at-the-last-minute look, which I liked. The linen blazer he was wearing was blue, I suppose, but had that purplish shiny tinge of something that needs redying or replacing, and although crinkled it was clean (one thing I mind about).

I'd squeezed into a tight pair of, I thought, sexy black trousers and a too long to be a T-shirt, too short to be a dress, red top. My wedged espadrilles, aside from the fact they brought me to a perfect height to peck Toby on the lips if I should be so lucky, were chosen to stop me sinking into the soft ground as I walked.

'Susie!' came the call of my name again across the crowd and I spotted the frantically waving hand of a smartly dressed man standing at the bar. Oh, my goodness! 'It's Stanley Gerald, from the weekend,' I whispered in Toby's ear as we squeezed through the posse to join him.

156

'Susie! What a marvellous surprise to see you.' Stanley pecked me on both cheeks, which I guess is what these types do at occasions like this. Toby stood behind me, reticent, until Stanley's right arm shot out above my shoulder and he announced 'Stanley Gerald,' with a pride only the upper classes can muster.

I moved to one side as they shook hands and I asked, 'Is Primrose here too?'

'She's gone to the bathroom, shouldn't be long. Would you both like a drink?'

'That's so kind,' charm rolled off Toby's tongue, 'I'll get ours.'

Stanley double-clicked his fingers in the air and lickety-split he'd summoned the bar lady.

Unfortunately for Toby, Taittinger was the only thing on offer up this end of the appropriately named 'Long Bar' and without the slightest flicker of a quandary he went ahead and spent a small fortune on two flutes. Champagne again, aren't I lucky!

'Darling,' said Stanley raising his arm to his wife. 'Look who I've found.'

'Susie, how lovely to see you,' she smiled, and I followed form, kissing her on both cheeks.

'This is Toby Cropper,' I introduced, and Primrose's right hand shot out at the same speed at which her head withdrew. This put Toby firmly in his place.

Stanley, having forgotten the conversation we'd had in the early hours of Sunday morning, expressed his surprise at meeting us here, 'I didn't know you were from these parts.'

'She's not,' corrected Primrose. 'You're here with work aren't you Susie?'

'She's here with me,' said Toby in a gentle tone that took the sting out of his words.

'Are you local?' asked Stanley as he handed his wife her glass.

'No, just visiting.'

Then with a gift for the gab Toby asked how we all knew each other.

'We were acquainted last weekend at Fontaburn,' said Stanley. 'Archibald's a terribly generous and affable old friend of Primrose's, isn't he darling?'

'My oldest and best,' she grinned.

'Is he here too?' I asked.

'No!' said Primrose rather sharply.

'It's just I saw beautiful jockey silks in his boot room, so I thought he might be.'

Primrose turned to her husband. 'I think the queue for the premier enclosure will have subsided by now.'

'Come on then, let's scoot,' said Stanley with a silly wobble of his head.

'Not us,' I said, 'we went for the course enclosure ticket instead.'

'Oh well then, you'll have to put up with the smell of hotdogs down there,' smiled Stanley.

'It's Susie and my first time at the races, so, we thought we'd start at the bottom.'

'Right then, I better set you straight,' said Stanley, genuinely trying to be helpful. 'In the parade ring you want to look for a lean horse that has good muscle definition, alert eyes, and a calm and relaxed walk.'

'We often win,' said Primrose. 'Stanley knows what he's talking about.'

'Thank you,' said Toby raising his glass, but Stanley recoiled so he turned to me instead, 'Here's to a winner!' and our glasses clinked.

'Darling,' beckoned Primrose, 'I think we *must* head to our enclosure now. It was lovely to see you again Susie and meet you Toby.'

'Bon courage,' said Stanley as Primrose pulled him through the hoi polloi.

'Well, there you go.' I turned to Toby. 'My nickname for her is Snoberina.'

'They seemed nice enough to me.'

'Really? You liked them?'

'People like that don't mean to be condescending, they just can't help it. I thought Stanley was a bit thick but a nice bloke and Primrose was pretty so I liked her.'

'Oh, Toby!'

'Not nearly as pretty as you though.'

I couldn't help smiling.

'Come on,' he said. 'Let's get to grips with this racing malarkey.'

★ ★ ★

The racetrack curved in a big circle towards the horizon. The grass had been scorched by the summer sun and the white rails sparkled as if they'd been freshly painted. To our right was Stanley and Primrose's stand, awash with pastel colours. Ladies in floaty dresses and tall men with quiffy hair. In our enclosure the crowd felt much more familiar. Flat caps that had seen

159

better days on old-time racegoers with grumbling mouths looking as if they were yearning for rolled-up cigarettes in their corners. Bookmakers shooting out the tic-tac signals, and pairs of old ladies who'd been bitten by their husband's gambling habits. Included in this mishmash were some marvellously dressed girls on the go. Stiletto heels shivering under enormous figures squeezed into strappy numbers. Perms, topknots, peroxide and buns — you name it every type of hairdo was here, accompanied by boys in shiny suits wearing pointy-toed shoes and laying claim on the souped-up vehicles in the car park.

Shut Up Boot Up Giddy Up, Ingle Park Racecourse EST. 1783 was on the front cover of the text-heavy programme. Neither of us could make head or tail of the contents and, thankfully, unlike some men I've known in similar situations, Toby didn't object to me asking a fellow racegoer to help.

The hard-to-age particularly cheery-faced man I chose was a scruffy soul and had somehow sailed through the entrance gate in jeans and trainers. His plastic cup of lager wobbled about in the crook of his elbow as he flicked back and forth through the pages of our programme, excitedly wittering on about trainers, jockeys, past performances, current fitness and betting odds. Thank goodness Toby looked like he was listening, as I was completely absorbed in the extraordinary length of this man's fingernails.

When he continued burbling mumbo jumbo

about placing accumulative bids and doubling our stakes, I really did switch off, having already decided just to back one to win. This seemed to me by far the easiest way to place a bet. 'What's your best tip?' asked Toby when the lesson was over.

'Don't gamble,' said our companion with a Cheshire grin.

'Thanks mate,' said Toby as the man tapped him on the shoulder and disappeared into the crowd.

Toby turned to me. 'Wasn't he nice?'

'Yeah. But, did you see his fingernails? They were extraordinary. I reckon he's a gamer.'

'A computer gamer?'

'Yeah, he was pale and those nails look to me to have grown at double speed, which is a sure sign of a high caffeine intake.'

'Well, you are the sleuth after all.'

I grasped the opportunity, seeing as I was making arbitrary judgements, to ask Toby if he thought Primrose or Stanley struck him as the murdering type.

'Susie!' his tone surprised me. 'I did wonder how long it would take you to bring that up, but you're not serious are you?'

'Why not?'

'One, we're in public, and two, you *must* wait and see what DCI Reynolds tells you next. It's not right to start suspecting what seemed to me a perfectly nice couple.'

'But speculating is so much fun.'

'That comes from being an only child.'

'What?' Toby had thrown a serious curve ball.

'I didn't mean it unfairly, it's just that an only child spends more time alone than the rest of us.' He gave me a that's-not-necessarily-a-bad-thing smile but I wanted to know more. He'd just pinpointed something I'd never ever considered before: the effects of being an only child and how it had shaped my character.

'And?' I said.

'Therefore you live much more in your own head, speculating on the world around you.'

'Fair point. Although, I've never thought about it like that.'

Until this very second, I'd always thought my fascination in individuals' characteristics and obsessive observation go hand in hand with being an artist. I hadn't considered it something I'd nourished due to the fact I don't have brothers and sisters. If this *is* the case it dawned on me perhaps I'm comfortable being an artist, leading a solitary profession, because I'm an only child.

'Hey,' said Toby, 'there are lots of positives to being an only child. You, for one, have a content nature when you're alone.'

'Really?'

'Yeah, and, you never had to fight for your parents' attention.'

'You don't think I'm spoilt, do you?'

'No, you're not spoilt.' Toby put his arm around my shoulder. 'Come on, let's go to the enclosure and seek out the silkiest ties and fittest horses.'

As we walked, tight together, Toby's arm made for going around my shoulders, we both agreed we'd follow Lucy's advice, Stanley's having been startlingly obvious.

17

It looked set to be a dead heat from where we were standing, right up against the outside fence of the last furlong. Toby's Thunder Bolt and my Triumphant Terrance were flying towards the winning post, side by side on the straight, whips thrashing as the crowd erupted and little flags the colour of jockeys' silks waved madly in the grand stand. Neither Toby nor I made out a word of the race call until it was over, and the judge raised his voice, loud and clear.

'I don't believe it!' said Toby staring at me with excitable surprise. 'Your horse blooming well beat mine.'

'I told you he was a winner.'

'You and Lucy with your sheepskin nose-bands.'

Toby did try to persuade me to back a horse with better odds but Triumphant Terrance with his 33/1 had just made me one hundred and sixty-five pounds off a fiver. 'Not bad,' I boasted. 'Let's quit while we're ahead.'

'You're ahead.'

'Drinks are on me then.'

'Let's eat something too,' said Toby who was driving.

'What about a jumbo sausage?' I pulled him towards a Portakabin with the most revolting looking long smooth sausages turning on a grill.

'Not today thanks.' He pulled against me.

'Let's walk a bit, there must be more stalls around the corner.'

This was an ideal moment, I thought, for Toby to take my hand, but he didn't. And what followed scuppered any plans he may have had in doing so. We'd paused to take in the unavoidable sight on the plasma screen. A wanton colt had been, let's just say, turned on, and the camera man was thoroughly enjoying sharing this young horse's smutty state with us all.

'Bit below the belt,' said Toby.

'Guess he was forced to collaborate willy-nilly.'

We both laughed and walked on to find a converted horsebox selling 'Honest Burgers' and when I said, 'I guess that means there's no horsemeat in them', Toby was alarmed, '*Shhhh*! you *can't* say that out loud. You're so naughty Susie.'

We approached the hatch and one of the two Elizabeth Street WC1 Christmas market Indian-style tweed waist-coated boys, in the most polite manner of any stallholder here I'd bet, asked, 'Sir. Madam. Would you like Chinese water deer or beef?'

Chinese water deer is not as it sounds, an MSG flavour-enhanced meat from a deer that swims, it is in fact a stumpy runt of a deer found in high numbers racing across the flat (yes, very flat) arable estates in Norfolk. Their legs, unable to cope with the slightest undulation, restrict them ever escaping the county. Consequently, landowners in this south-eastern bulb of the British Isles have monopolised the market and

165

this common meat has become a premium product. As delicious as it is I wasn't prepared to pay over the odds for it.

'Beef, please,' I replied.

'Make that two, please,' said Toby sifting through his wallet.

'I'm paying.'

'No, you're not, this one's on me.'

The serving boy with good old-fashioned manners plucked the note from Toby's hand before I had time to wrangle.

'Caramelised onion and tomato relish, in that tray if you'd like it,' he said, handing Toby his change.

Yum. I put a large dollop into my sesame brioche bun.

'In here too,' said Toby. 'Let's go sit in that stand, it looks like there are plenty of empty seats and we'll get a good view over the racecourse.'

★ ★ ★

Once we were comfortably settled and one delicious mouthful down I told Toby how pleased I was he'd come to stay. 'I was finding drawing really hard last week. It was much more fun doing it with you today.'

'Well, it's not like you could visit me and join in with my job.'

I giggled (Toby's a mortuary clerk), 'I would be fine in your office.'

'I'm afraid it isn't just office work. There are grim bits like overseeing the preparation of the dead and the autopsy department is also under my supervision. But, it beats being a heart surgeon, which is what I was before.'

'Why did you stop?'

'The enormous responsibility that the patient's life hangs in the balance became too much for me. I had recurring nightmares that I'd never be able to save anyone.'

'I bet you saved lots of people though.'

'Yes, but it made no difference if I carried out a successful operation, I still dreaded failing the next one. The strain of operating on children, teenagers and young adults, affected me far more than medical school ever prepared me for, and without putting too fine a point on it, in the mortuary you don't have any of this.'

'Well, I think it's amazing you were a heart surgeon even if you aren't any more.'

'Thanks Susie. What about you, do you miss being a PA to the celebrities?'

'Never. It was fun knowing the truth behind the glossies but the sad fact is a lot of them are lonely and unhappy.'

'Are you in touch with anyone you worked for?'

'Not close touch. If I bumped into someone I'd of course say hello and be pleased to see them but their lives are on a different level so our paths are yet to cross.'

'I hope I'm with you if they ever do.'

I smiled. Little did Toby know I hoped he'd be with me a lot.

★ ★ ★

The sun was ever so slowly melting in the sky, taking its time to go down as it does on a really beautiful summer's day. We didn't stay at the races much longer, as we'd decided to get out of the car park before the rush.

'Jiltwhistle,' I called out as we whizzed past the sign. 'That's where the Geralds live. I'd love to see their house. I reckon it's a pile.'

'Probably,' agreed Toby. 'They looked the type who'd live in nothing short of a pile.'

'I wonder why Primrose didn't marry Archie.'

'Because she married Stanley.'

'But Stanley's so dull and not half as smart as Archie, and he may be better looking than Archie, which isn't saying much, but I'd have thought Primrose would marry for money and a title over looks.'

'Like most girls?!' said Toby.

'Not me! I fall in love with people for who they are not what they have.'

'But you're an artist Susie.'

'What do you mean?'

'Your whole being is romantic and I know it's not money you're after.'

'How do you know?'

'You wear it on the outside, you wouldn't be painting and living in the country if it's a rich man you want.'

'You make me sound like a spinster.'

'You might be one day.'

'Oh, Toby stop it!'

The journey back was swift. We were home by nine and had walked through the front door to find Lucy painting her nails at the kitchen table and Red-Rum curled up on her lap. It struck me as an odd combination, manicured hands and stable work, but I didn't draw attention to it.

'Who wants a dram?' asked Toby. 'I have a bottle of Scotch upstairs.'

'Whisky?' I said, alarm bells ringing — my ex-boyfriend Geoffrey was rather too fond of the stuff.

'Yeah, I took a small bottle in my rucksack and hardly touched it.'

All was okay. Geoff certainly would have finished the bottle on day one.

Lucy pulled a face as soon as Toby left the room. 'I don't like whisky.'

'He won't mind if you don't have any.' I smiled. 'How was your afternoon?'

'Great thanks.'

'The woman I met after lunch . . . '

Lucy butted in, 'Yeah, Mrs Ramsbottom, you knew her?'

'I don't know her but I met her at the weekend.'

'Yeah, she's posh too.'

'Did Mrs Ramsbottom say anything about the weekend?' I asked, thinking it unnecessary to point out she was the cook not a guest.

'No.'

'Nothing at all?'

'No. But like I said, she's posh so we don't chat socially and it's not my place to ask the questions. Oh shite,' Lucy's fist thumped the table as Red-Rum shot off her knee and out the door, 'Mrs Ramsbottom left her sleeve-less

Puffa thing in the yard and I bet she forgot to pick it up.'

'I'll take it back to her if you want.'

'I've got so much on tomorrow and I want to help you as usual. Maybe Ruth can take it.'

'Honestly, I don't mind at all.'

'If you really don't mind, I'll leave it on the table for you.'

'Great, I'll do it first thing.'

'Thanks so much Susie.'

'What's this?' asked Toby returning with his bottle.

'Lucy was riding with a woman today and I was asking about her.'

'The one you asked me about earlier?'

Damn it Toby! He'd dropped me in it.

But, thankfully Lucy seemed totally unfazed and told me, 'Her husband was a friend of Canny's and when he died she took up being an exercise rider.'

'Poor woman,' I blurted out, 'I can't believe her husband's dead. That's wretched.'

'Yeah, she's young ain't she?'

'Far too young to be widowed.'

'Fair went for it today so she did.'

'What's an exercise rider?' asked Toby.

'A proper one rides the horses out every morning and keeps them fit for race meets. They do the same hours and distance each week but Mrs Ramsbottom just covers when our trainers are on holiday. She's an experienced rider and I think going at a pace helps with her grief. That's what the other exercisers say.'

'Did her husband die recently?' I asked.

'Yeah, he was in the army.'

'Afghanistan?' asked Toby.

'No, someplace beginning with H. Had the word hell at the beginning. Haven't forgotten that.'

'Helmand,' said Toby who was fiddling around finding glasses and pouring out the whisky.

'Yeah, that's it,' said Lucy.

'How long ago?' I asked.

'Well, she's only been coming here for three months so not that long ago.'

'Do you know how he died?'

'I think they call it friendly fire. He was shot by mistake.'

Toby turned around and plonked three glasses on the table. Whether it was politeness or a desire to impress, Lucy said nothing when he pushed one her way.

'You okay, Susie?' he asked. 'You suddenly look rather tired.'

'I'm okay, I just feel really sorry for Vicky and war makes me so angry.'

I didn't want to talk about it any more. I couldn't bear to think of Vicky's grief. Heaven knows how you come to terms with accidental death. No wonder Archie had stuck up for her.

'Americans,' said Toby. 'Stupid bloody Yanks. We shouldn't have ever gone to war with them or at least we should have left as soon as we knew we were sending lambs to the slaughter. Our politicians can be so pig-headed at times.'

'How do you know an American shot him?' asked Lucy.

'It's most likely if it was friendly fire.'

Good god! My insides felt as if they might cramp up and seize. Could Vicky have killed Hailey just because she was American? Would her loss have been motivation enough to take out her anger on an innocent woman?

I took a long slow sip from my glass, shunting the theory to the back of my mind until bedtime where, alone in my room, I could then think it all through.

Toby was nursing his glass of whisky in both hands and Lucy was waiting for him to speak again, hanging off his every word regardless of the subject matter. I don't honestly think she realised the alluring jiggle her bosoms gave every time she giggled but, if that's what worn underwear does, I really ought to keep mine on the go a bit longer.

As the evening went on I became more and more agitated by Lucy's natural ability to flirt, and before I got competitive about winning Toby's affections I took myself off to bed with a large glass of water to clear my head.

Red-Rum was curled up on my pillow. I really had won his favour and I felt bad nudging him off the bed but I draw the line at sleeping with pets.

I closed the bedroom door behind him and I did wonder if I was being a bit cold-hearted. It's not a thought I've ever had about an animal before but Toby's mention of my being an only child was making me question all sorts of things . . . if I'd had to muddle in with siblings in the past, would I be more willing to share my personal space now?

The room was hot, the air having cooked in today's sun, and as I lay in bed reciting an evening prayer I became curious as to why my parents, both Catholic, only had one child. I suppose it's odd I've never asked them, but this let's-analyse-Susie and speculate on what-makes-her-how-she-is wasn't a game I'd ever played before. And I didn't really want to start now.

I took a sip from my glass and focused on Victoria Ramsbottom instead, the woman whose name, when Hailey first mentioned she'd been talking to her in the kitchen, had caused Archie to snap, 'What about?' Vicky's husband I now knew was killed by an American so no surprise Archie had been sensitive to Hailey and her meeting.

I was remembering the heat of Hailey's room and the glass of water on her side table that I'd sent tumbling to the floor. This, combined with the fact my bed had not been turned down, now led me to conclude: when Archie went looking for Vicky during dinner, she had in fact been in Hailey's room, yanking up the heating and putting a glass of poisoned water in place — killing the American in revenge for her husband. And having almost been caught in the act, it's no wonder Vicky completely forgot to take out the pudding.

As I fell into sleep, settled by my perfectly sound chain of thought, I desperately hoped I'd wake to find Vicky's gilet on Lucy's kitchen table — it would give me the perfect excuse to meet Mrs Ramsbottom one more time.

18

I'd followed Lucy's amusing little map to Vicky's house and was standing on the doorstep, gilet in hand, banging her knocker.

The door opened with such gusto that if it was coming the other way it would have whacked me smack bang in the face and left me flat out on the ground. And as I tried to reconstruct my let's-make-friends-as-quickly-as-possible face, which had been wiped with an expression of dumbfounded shock, I was caught short; Victoria Ramsbottom's lips snapped a curt 'Yes?'

'It's Susie,' I said, tightening the grip on her gilet, which as long as it remained in my possession gave good reason for me to be on her property.

'Of course, sorry, third time in four days in yet another place, had me for a second there.'

'Oh,' I said, spotting a dog basket behind her under the hall table, 'you have a lurcher too. Isn't he sweet?'

Vicky absorbed my compliment of her pet with pride, me thoroughly well practised in the art of getting an owner on side.

'Yes,' she said moving back into the hall, 'this is Lance.'

'Good boysies,' I said as I bent down to pat him. 'Fine choice to have a name that doesn't sound fierce when you shout it.'

'We called him after my husband's regiment.'

I looked up. Vicky turned her head away and at the same time a ray of sunshine cast its lengthy span through the front door and across the floor, sparkling off an object on the chair by my side.

'Wow,' I said reaching for whatever it was without a thought.

Vicky's head turned, her hand grasping for what was now in mine, a tortoiseshell photograph frame — no time for me to look at the picture inside.

'That's *personal!*' she snapped and placed it face down on the chair.

'I'm so sorry,' I said, now shaking. 'That was incredibly rude of me. I'm an artist and the play of light got me so excited. I wasn't thinking.'

'My husband's dead,' said Vicky plaintively. 'That's a picture of him and it makes me very sad to look at it.'

'Oh gosh, how terrible, I'm so sorry. I'm such a fool. Here . . . ' I handed her the gilet, 'I only came to return this.'

'Oh, thank you. That's very kind of you but really, you shouldn't have.'

'It was no trouble for me to bring it back.'

Vicky stood holding the door wide open and I got the message, time to leave.

'Thank you,' she said as I said 'Bye'.

The heavy door banged behind me, its big brass knocker reverberating as I dilly-dallied reading the stickers cluttered on her Volvo bumper: CLA, Fight the Ban, Help for Heroes and then last, a jockey silk decal, purple and

175

yellow quarter no less. Archie's slogan rolled off my tongue, 'purple and yellow he's our speedy fellow'.

Then . . . it hit me. I don't know much about racing but I do know colours relate to owners and not trainers, and therefore if this sticker has been put on a Ramsbottom car by a Ramsbottom, then it's highly likely Vicky's deceased husband was the same person Archie co-owned a horse with.

I jumped into the driving seat. Finally I was getting to the crux of Archie's close relationship with his cook.

I drove slowly, back to Pluton Farm Stables, ruminating on the tortoiseshell photograph frame. It was exactly like the ones I'd seen at Fontaburn Hall . . . could this mean Archie's nostalgic collection was a table of homage to dead friends? And if Vicky's husband's photograph was as good a mugshot as the others, did she nick it on Saturday night? Is that why she was upstairs or had she spotted it when she was already upstairs supposedly turning down the beds?

I don't want to accuse her of stealing, she really didn't seem the type, but, her sudden waspish reaction when I picked up the frame definitely had connotations of shame and guilt.

I paused the car at Canny's electric gates and, as they swung open, my emotions swung back, leaving me feeling incredibly sorry again (about time too) for Vicky having lost her husband. Suddenly I despised myself for thinking I could, without any evidence whatsoever, accuse a woman in such a vulnerable state. Of course, I wasn't going to call DCI Reynolds and share my theory with him just yet, as that would be incredibly cruel.

I was back by nine o'clock and it was no surprise Toby was still in bed. He'll have a thick head today if his and Lucy's late-night giggles coming through my floorboards are anything to go by.

I carried a strong cup of black coffee outside and sat on the bench, my head against the wall, eyes shut, the summer sun warming my face. Procrastinating, that's what I was up to. Using Lucy not being here to help get High Maintenance into the field as reason enough to take things a bit slower than normal. I breathed in a deep breath of early morning Norfolk air and opened my eyes.

Where on earth *was* Lucy? It was very unlike her not to be here at this time of day and I could hardly bear to let myself think she and Toby might be curled up together. The thought made me feel sick. I wanted Toby to like me. Like me properly. But I knew, if it's a fling he's after, I stood no chance with Lucy around.

I took a furious sip of hot coffee and *Ow!* I burnt my tongue. I laughed at myself. Nothing like reality to snap one out of indulgent self-pity and I made a mental note not to be jealous of Lucy, it's a terrible sin. *James, Chapter 4, Verse 2. You desire but do not have, so you kill. You covet but you cannot get what you want, so you quarrel and fight.*

I know this verse, and many more from the

Bible, off by heart. Detention at school (which I was given at least twice a term for minor tomfoolery) involved writing out the same verse fifty times. I spent hours in the library, my hand cramping up but this punishment had no effect on me. The fun in breaking rules, whether that be passing notes in class, fumbling around with boys on Lover's Lane or waking up very early and climbing over the Astro Turf caging for a spot of dawn tennis, always outdid detention, which wasn't so bad with a friend there too.

Bzzzz. My telephone vibrated in my pocket, *bzzzzz, bzzzzz.* I recognised it, it was the same number from yesterday.

'Hello.'

'Susie, Detective Chief Inspector Reynolds here.'

'Hello, Inspector.' My voice sounded as thrilled as I was to receive his call.

'Are you alone and can I have a word?'

'Yes.'

'I wanted to let you know that your name has been cleared.' My stomach plummeted with relief, an overreaction but one that happened nonetheless. 'Evidence proves that whatever Miss Dune ingested you can't have been the one who gave it to her.'

'Oh?' I sounded surprised, in the hopes he would continue talking.

'Are you there Susie?'

It hadn't worked. I'd have to take the direct approach instead . . . 'Yes Inspector, I was just wondering what it was that killed her?'

'We suspect it was a toxin and as you were neither involved in the cooking or the serving we can safely remove you from the list of suspects.'

This is crazy. Hadn't anyone mentioned I'd mixed the gin and tonics with Hailey? I wasn't going to bring it up but it did make me think two things. Best-case scenario: DCI Reynolds was looking for a reason to get me off the hook. Worst-case scenario: his investigation had gaps in it and I couldn't rely on anything he said.

'Have others' names been cleared?'

'Not for the time being. The duration of everyone else's stay has put them in the kitchen at one time or another.' DCI Reynolds took a breath. 'Susie?'

'Yes, Inspector?'

'Sergeant Ayari has been carrying out some background checks and there's one thing on you I'd like to confirm.'

'Yes, Inspector?'

'Are you *the* Susie Mahl?' he asked.

I smiled so hard I nearly let an inappropriate sound travel down the telephone.

'Possibly, I haven't met another.'

'Was it you who had a part to play in the unravelling of that murder in Spire? The Earl of Greengrass?'

'Yes, that was me.'

'Well, aren't we lucky to have you on board. Quite a reputation you've made for yourself.'

'That's so nice of you to say.'

'Well, regarding Miss Dune's case, if there's anything you've picked up on or want to draw our attention to, my door is always open.'

'Thank you, Inspector. Do you think Hailey was poisoned?'

'Not by those mushrooms, none of my team came across a single deadly webcap amongst the ceps in the parkland and the pathologists didn't find any orellanine toxin in her body.'

I really had won his trust!

'What do you think it was?'

'We're looking into it.'

I didn't push my luck to get an answer.

'Keep in touch Susie,' said DCI Reynolds.

'Of course. Thank you for your call, Inspector.' I hung up.

I'd walked the distance to the yard and I can't tell you how happy I was to see Lucy sitting on a bale next to Jim. As soon as she saw me she jumped up. Jim pinched her bottom and in turn she gave him a swift slap on his hand.

'Susie, are you ready? If so I'll get High Maintenance now.' Lucy bounced towards me eager to help.

'You must've been up early,' I said.

'Rob ain't here today so I had to give Jim a hand.' She turned to smile at him but he'd scampered. 'Thanks for taking Vicky's thingy back.'

'That's okay. She has a very nice house.'

'I ain't ever been.'

'Also, I saw a jockey silk sticker on her car bumper and I wondered whose colours quartered purple and yellow are.'

'You're joking right?'

'No. Why?'

'There are thousands and thousands of

registered silks, I wouldn't 'ave a clue which colours belonged to which owners.'

'But if it was Norfolk I thought you might know?'

'Norfolk's probably got the most silks of all,' Lucy laughed. 'I'd know if it was one of the very best racers but nope, purple and yellow quarters, I 'ain't ever seen them. Can't tell you the stable neither. Do you have to know?'

'No, I'd just like to because Archie Wellingham had the same silks in his house so I assume they must be connected?'

'Definitely connected, the pair of them could've been in the same syndicate or co-owned a horse but you can't be sure they owned it at the same time.'

'Are owners very rich?'

'Not always, but usually the more money they have the better the horse. Makes sense don't it!'

'Yup.'

'Say they did share a horse and Archie sold his half when Mr Ramsbottom died.' Lucy's small cogs were turning. 'It means either the horse weren't any good or it's so good Archie's not wealthy enough to buy the other end. But,' Lucy shook her head, 'I don't recognise purple and yellow so it can't be a real star.'

'Right,' I was wasting precious drawing time on this silk tangent, 'I must get to work.' It was so hot I knew I'd have to stop during the midday sun.

'What would you like me to do with your last and final model?'

'Yeah! We're almost done. If you could cordon

her off while I get my stuff, that would be brilliant.'

'Sure thing. I can stay with you and walk her round if you want?'

'Nah not today but thank you.'

'Well if you do need me just shout as I'll be in the yard mucking about but only until midday. Jim and me are going to test-drive a lorry this afternoon.'

'Okay will do. Thanks so much.'

Lucy had gone by the time I got back and High Maintenance was a legs-collapsed panting lump on the ground. I softly nudged her back haunch with my foot, which got her up alright, but after a brief wobble on all fours maddeningly she was straight back down again, hooves tucked under her.

I let out a fed-up cry and stared glumly across the paddock, which stretched for acres in front of me. It was the most luscious, largest field you could imagine, brushed blades of green grass and broken swathes of buttercups.

Annoyingly, I'd been working so hard this last week I hadn't yet found time to fully explore the estate, but as far as the eye could see it left one in no doubt that Pluton Farm Stables was beautifully maintained. Five hundred acres in total, a grid system of dusty tracks, wide enough for livestock lorries, fenced off by chestnut post and rail (a popular choice for those with deep enough pockets).

There were window boxes on Lucy's cottage but no other domestic garden arrangements. As for Canny's house, it was out of sight, encased within a beech copse to one side of the gallops. I was longing to sniff it out but Lucy's warning of security cameras had stopped me prying.

Grrrr, my patience was running out. High Maintenance's reluctance to stay up for any length of time was driving me mad so I gave up on drawing and got my camera out instead. This motionless collapsed lump made it easy to photograph her features, something that would come in handy for the final picture.

My favourite thing about photography is, unlike with drawing or painting, you can think of two things at once and for the rest of the morning my mind wandered over Hailey's death. If the pathologists hadn't found any orellanine toxin in her system, yet they think she's been poisoned, then what was it the investigators were now looking for?

19

'Susie!' cried out Toby.

I panicked and ran towards him. 'What is it?'

I stopped short of the paddock fence, realising in his swagger that it wasn't an emergency.

'It's only the phone for you, no need to look so frightened.'

'Sorry, I was alarmed by your shout.'

'Well the *chap*,' said Toby with a hint of irritation, 'didn't want to give me his number, said he'd hold on. Lucky for him I've found you. The telephone's off the hook in the kitchen.'

Toby took my drawing things and I ran to the house and picked up the receiver.

'Hello?'

'Good morning Susie, it's Daniel Furr Egrant. Would you like a moment to catch your breath?'

'No, I'm fine thanks,' I said trying not to let on how surprised I was to hear from him. 'How are things?' I asked, realising maybe he'd just rung for a chit-chat; he was the person I'd got on best with at the weekend.

'Things?' reiterated Daniel.

'I was just wondering how you are?'

He remained silent. What on earth was Daniel playing at? He rang me.

'What can I do for you?' I asked.

'I know this call is out of the blue but you're the only one of us not a suspect in Hailey's death.'

'How do you know?'

'DCI Reynolds told me and therefore you're the only person I feel I can confide in right now.'

Surely the only reason DCI Reynolds told Daniel was in the hope a call like this might come my way.

'Did *he* suggest you get in touch?'

'No, no. That would be out of the question but I need to tell this thing to someone and you appear to be the safest bet.'

'Okay . . . '

'You seem a good egg, Susie, and taking into account your profession, what I'm about to say shouldn't come as a shock.'

'Go on then.'

'I'm trusting you implicitly.'

'Yes, of course.'

I was now in a muddle . . . Should I appear easy going and unshockable? Or, serious, which in turn may well stop him talking?

But, I had no need to worry, Daniel's confession, 'Archie wasn't in his bed the night of Hailey's death', came in one sharp shot of breath down the telephone as if he was glad to be rid of it.

'How do you know?'

'Well, I, . . . *I* . . . *I* . . . *I*,' he stuttered, '*I* . . . *I* . . . *I*.'

'Don't worry Daniel it's okay, just tell me.'

'I went to his room and he wasn't there.'

'What time did you go to his room?'

'Shortly after I went to bed.'

'Did you and Archie go upstairs at the same time?'

'Archie put the dogs in the kennel first.'

'So, he may have been yet to come upstairs?'

'He'd definitely come upstairs but he wasn't in his room.'

'How can you be certain he ever came upstairs?'

'His clothes were in a pile on the floor.'

Of course they were, I *should* have jumped to this conclusion. I'd seen Archie in his PJs, which obviously proved he'd been upstairs.

'Maybe Archie was in the bathroom when you went to his room.'

'Not possible. He has an en-suite.'

The brevity of Daniel's words gave the impression he was trying to catch me out. This was immensely aggravating.

'Maybe he came back to his room once you'd left.'

'That's exactly it, Susie, he didn't.'

'How do you know?'

'I slept in Archie's bed. He wasn't there when I drifted off or when I woke to the alarm.'

'Why are you telling me this? Surely you've told the police?'

'No!' he said firmly. 'Amongst you arty types,' — I hate this expression — 'no one bats an eyelid but in the circles I move in people simply don't accept being homosexual isn't a choice. I'd never survive if this got out.'

Even though Daniel was overreacting I did feel sorry for him, knowing there are still some posh gay men who to this day marry a woman to follow form and have an heir. Nevertheless, far more prominent in my mind than Daniel's sexual orientation was whether he was suggesting Archie had something to do with Hailey's death.

'Just to be clear,' I said. 'You went into Archie's room soon after you'd gone upstairs to your bed. You got into his bed and were there until the alarm went off?'

'Yes, that's correct.'

Daniel then told me, 'It wasn't Archie who killed her,' which was an odd thing to say considering I'd never accused Archie.

'Did you see him?' I provoked.

'See him what?' Daniel's voice was panicked.

'You said Archie didn't kill Hailey, I don't think he did either but I wondered how you knew.'

'I know Archie and he didn't do it.'

I took charge of the conversation. 'You have to tell DCI Reynolds what you know. Keeping quiet to protect a friend may incriminate you.'

'But I told them I was in bed when the alarm went off.'

'A half-truth's a lie. You *must* say whose bed you were in and be prepared to answer why.'

'Heavens above, what about . . . ' his voice died out.

'I wouldn't think twice about that. They'll be pleased to have the other information.' I knew now all Daniel needed from me was reassurance and encouragement.

'Susie, you're marvellous.' He sounded giddy and I could picture him flicking his floppy fringe off his brow with relief. 'It was quite the right thing to call you, thank you kindly for your sound advice, I shall ring DCI Reynolds right away.'

'Any time, Daniel.' I meant it.

'Toodle pip.'

'Bye.'

I knew Lucy was out but I hadn't for the life of me expected to see Toby hovering in the kitchen when I turned around. He'd been as quiet as a mouse.

'How come that man has your number?' he asked.

'He had the house number not my number so he probably looked it up in the book.'

'One of your posh friends, was it? Sounded *awfully* formal with me.'

I was thrilled to see Toby's reaction. I think he likes me!

'Isn't his voice hilarious? He'd never get a job with the BBC.'

'Who was he?'

'It was Daniel, from the weekend, ringing to basically confess he's gay.'

'You're not serious?'

'I am. He was worried about telling the police he'd been in Archie's bed. Isn't that sad.'

'Archie's bed!'

'Yeah, but Archie wasn't there.'

'Quite risqué of Daniel to get into his bed.'

'Maybe, but maybe not. Anyway, where was Archie?'

'In the Russian girl's bed?' said Toby. 'Or yours?' he quickly added.

'Toby! He wasn't in mine, and I can't believe he was in Tatiana's considering what she said to me about him.'

'When did she say it?'

'On Sunday morning.'

Toby pointed out that Tatiana could have been putting me off the scent of thinking Archie was in her bed. But, I reckon this was a bit far-fetched.

'Why did Daniel ring you?'

'I assume he wanted a final push to go and tell the police.'

'Or,' said Toby, 'he could have been jealous of Hailey flirting with Archie and fabricated the whole story to cover up the fact he killed her.'

'Which would mean Archie was in his own bed all along.' I let out a huff. 'This is *so* complicated and even more so that Archie was wearing the same PJs as the man I saw in the billiard room.'

'So that's why he wasn't in bed.'

'Not necessarily as Stanley was also in the same stripy pyjamas. But, if we buy Daniel's story there'd be enough time for him to get into Archie's bed and fall asleep before the alarm went off.'

'And was the alarm connected to the death?' asked Toby.

'I just don't know. The police haven't brought it up again so I guess I'm the only one who thinks it might be.'

'Maybe it's time you told them about this man in the PJs?'

I had very little mental energy left to consider doing this right now, and anyway, if I shared my theory of Vicky with Toby, it could eliminate the PJ man altogether. But, I wasn't going to tell Toby about Vicky. I didn't want him to think of me as a cruel person and it would be hard for

189

him not to if he knew I was accusing a woman in mourning. Toby had a soft spot for women, I'd seen it before and I didn't fancy the struggle of trying to convince him of my point of view. So, it came as a great relief when he changed the topic and suggested we needed to eat some lunch.

'I don't think there's much in the fridge,' I said pulling it open, 'but I could make us some tuna mayonnaise as there's plenty of bread for sandwiches.'

'Sounds good to me.'

Toby began buttering the bread and I hunted in the larder for some tins.

Much to my joy I also found my favourite, a packet of salt and vinegar crisps, which perked me up.

'I spoke to DCI Reynolds this morning,' I said, our conversation uninhibited in the knowledge that Lucy was far away test-driving a lorry. 'He told me Hailey didn't die of orellanine toxin or deadly webcap but they do think she was poisoned.'

'By what?'

'They don't know but the good news is I'm no longer a suspect.'

'Glad to hear it. Are you happy to sit outside and eat these?'

'Sure,' I said and we left the kitchen. 'Hey, Toby, how do you think Hailey died?'

'Crikey Susie, I have no idea. I hate to disappoint you but,' he paused, 'she might have died from kidney stones.'

'Nonsense,' I said as his plate wobbled on his knee. 'You can't die of kidney stones.'

'You can, Susie, I know.' He spoke gently. 'I'm a doctor and DCI Reynolds said her kidneys were malfunctioning, didn't he?'

'Yes, but what are the signs of kidney stones?'

'Usually a high fever, vomiting and intermittent unbelievable pain.'

'She certainly wasn't in any pain I can tell you that and I don't think she was sick or feverish.'

'Well, maybe the stones were still in her kidney. Pain only comes when they travel to your bladder.'

Toby, having finished eating, popped back into the kitchen and it upset me he felt he could break our flow of conversation like this. We weren't talking about a casual matter here, and although I really didn't mean to sound resentful when he came back outside I said, 'What makes you think she had kidney stones?'

'Thirst and the fact she hadn't urinated, that's all, don't worry.'

'So, you're not actually certain?'

'Not certain but there is a chance she could have died of kidney stones.'

'Okay,' I said, reluctant to agree with him but I opened my sketchbook all the same and added it to my list.

'Hey, you don't want to come with me on a trip to the supermarket, do you?' Toby's enthusiasm for something so mundane immediately picked up my mood.

'Of course! It's too hot to draw in the midday sun so let's go.'

20

Toby and I were in his car travelling through Canny's elaborate gates on our way to the supermarket, me scratching the end of my nose even though there wasn't actually anything making it itch. Every time I put my hands down it would irritate me again, and so the process went on until Toby said, 'Perhaps you should give DCI Reynolds a call and take him up on his offer of a chat.'

'Why?'

'Firstly, I think you want to,' he looked across at me and smiled. 'And secondly, he might have some new information, you never know. And we've got to do something to get you back on form.'

'I'm sorry. It's really eating away at me and it's so unfair when you've come to stay.' I shuffled around in my seat, sorted out my posture and getting a grip of myself I looked across at Toby and said, 'I'm going to try hard to block it out for a bit.'

'As if. Go on, give him a call.'

Thrilled by Toby's encouragement I immediately dialled DCI Reynolds's number. And although he was happy to talk, 'It's hard to tell at this stage what killed Miss Dune. But the team at the hospital are working all hours and are trying to narrow it down as we speak', his ability to explain the situation without giving specific details was immensely frustrating.

'Was Hailey's liver intact?' I asked knowing I was grasping at straws but I had to provoke him somehow, and I was after all talking to a policeman not a doctor.

'I'm in no doubt they know what they're up to,' was all he said.

'If I came to you would I be able to see a copy of the autopsy?' Toby glared at me and I knew I was overstepping the line, even before he prodded my thigh.

'The autopsy report is only available to next of kin or other authorised individuals. I'm sorry, Susie, but that doesn't include you.' It was unnecessary but nice of him to apologise.

'Perhaps I could come in and have a chat anyway?' I'd decided to take DCI Reynolds at his word.

'Do, I'll be in my office until late so turn up when you want.'

Within minutes Toby had dropped me outside Norham police station and gone on to the supermarket.

DCI Reynolds's personal space was a closed-off glass cube in the corner of an open-plan office. The rows of other desks all faced away, their sitters' eyes glued to computer screens, helpfully giving us a little bit of privacy at least.

As soon as I'd been welcomed in, together with Sergeant Ayari, DCI Reynolds nipped off to make me a cup of tea. I didn't want one but it was an easy way of getting him out. Something I needed right now as I wanted privacy to share my theory on Mrs Ramsbottom with Sergeant Ayari. It'd then be in her hands whether to tell the boss at this stage or not.

'Sergeant,' I said. 'I've seen Victoria Ramsbottom recently, the woman who did the cooking at Fontaburn Hall.'

'Oh yes, the one who left midway through dinner because she was feeling ill.'

'You know?'

'Of course, we know Susie.' She smiled. 'We've been over and over the events of the evening and this is an important detail. Her departure put us on high alert that perhaps she'd been poisoned too.'

'Oh gosh, she hadn't had she?'

'No, which opened up a whole new avenue of investigation. I don't know how well you know Mrs Ramsbottom?'

'Not well at all.'

'But you've seen her you say?'

'Yes.'

'Where?'

'Yesterday at the stables where I'm working and then this morning I went to her house to return an item of clothing she'd left behind.'

'I see. So, you'll now also know she wasn't very ill.'

'I didn't think she looked ill.'

Sergeant Ayari went on to tell me Mrs Ramsbottom didn't object to any of the tests ran on her to ensure she had no toxins in her body, and amongst the clear results, there were no traces of flu or a cold.

'That's good but why weren't we all tested?'

'Mrs Ramsbottom was the only person who said she felt ill and therefore the only one we were afraid could have been infected if there was poison on site.'

I didn't a hundred per cent believe this but I respected Sergeant Ayari for telling me as much as she felt permitted to tell, and I concluded for myself that medical tests can be expensive and perhaps they felt it was a wasted expense at this time.

Sergeant Ayari continued, in the same matter-of-fact tone, to tell me that DCI Reynolds is, 'conscious Mrs Ramsbottom has had a very sad time recently and he's inclined to think her illness was psychosomatic'. If it wasn't for Sergeant Ayari's next sentence, 'You'll understand it must be hard for Mrs Ramsbottom to be around happy couples of her age,' I'd have said her words denoted an uncompromising core. Something that would give her great advantage in this line of work.

When she finished with, 'Nevertheless, any successful investigation must not be influenced by human empathy and she therefore is still a suspect on our list,' I was pleased to hear it, thinking Sergeant Ayari was in the making for a mighty fine investigator.

'Does Victoria Ramsbottom have a connection with Archie beyond being his occasional cook?'

'Yes, her husband and Mr Wellingham jointly owned a racehorse. Over the last year they formed a close friendship although following Mr Ramsbottom's death the racehorse was sold.'

'Ah ha!'

Sergeant Ayari's face was full of surprise. 'Were you on to this Susie?'

'I had my suspicions.'

'And do you have any others? You know you can confide in me.'

I thought hard before saying anything.

'Please Susie,' Sergeant Ayari pleaded.

'When I entered Hailey's bedroom in the early hours of Sunday morning I noticed it was far warmer than mine and that there was a glass of water by her bed. The one I told you I knocked over.'

'Yes, don't worry about that.'

'Well, based on nothing other than my own thoughts, I wondered whether Victoria had used the excuse of turning down the beds, bearing in mind mine wasn't, to enable her to turn up the heating in Hailey's room and put a glass of poisoned water in place.'

The dumbfounded expression on Sergeant Ayari's face worried me.

'Please don't think I'm heartless,' I said.

'Let's not worry about that. You're telling me Mrs Ramsbottom could have been the one who poisoned Miss Dune?'

'Yes, I suppose I am.'

'On account of her being American?' Sergeant Ayari looked troubled. 'From our background checks we do know about the friendly fire incident and it is awful how her husband died, but do you really think it's motivation for murder?'

'That's the only motive I can think of.'

In skipped DCI Reynolds with three cups of

tea. 'Here you go Sergeant, I knew you'd want one.'

'Thank you, Inspector.'

'Susie, no sugar, right?'

'That's right, thank you,' I clasped the mug.

'What did you want to discuss?' he asked as he strolled around to his side of the desk.

'Well, I was so pleased when you rang to tell me I'm no longer a suspect and I wanted to come in and have a chat.' I spoke nonchalantly, despite feeling terribly guilty inside that I was doing exactly what I'd told Daniel off for: telling a half-truth is a lie.

'Of course,' said DCI Reynolds. 'The sooner you knew the sooner we hoped,' he looked at Sergeant Ayari who was lost in her own thoughts, 'you'd be in here to help us.'

He ruffled around his desk, picked up a notepad, underneath which I saw a green file with Miss Hailey Dune written in bold diagonally across it. My eyes lit up. 'Don't worry Susie,' said DCI Reynolds, misinterpreting my expression, 'my notes are for me and I promise nothing you say will be held against you.'

Phew!

As he sat down I caught his glance and realised the low-cut dress I'd put on for Toby's benefit could actually come into play here.

I leant forward. 'Perhaps we could both share what we have so far?'

DCI Reynolds shuffled back in his chair. 'There are very few things I'm permitted to share but you *must* tell me all you know.'

'Inspector,' said Sergeant Ayari breaking her

pensive silence. 'Can you and I have a brief word in private please?'

DCI Reynolds looked at me, sitting comfortably sipping hot tea, and asked if I'd be alright left alone for a moment or two.

'Yes, very happy.'

Out the room they went, on through the open-plan office and out of sight. I couldn't believe my luck. My body trembled as I quickly and carefully stretched across the desk and flipped open Hailey's file. The third divider down was labelled 'Autopsy'. I glanced through the glass, no one was looking. I'd stopped breathing, and quick as a flash with my mobile firm in my hands I took photos of the three relevant pages.

It was seamless. I flipped the folder shut, pushed it back into place and no one whatsoever had caught me in the act. I have no clue how I would've explained it but that necessity was irrelevant now.

'Very, very interesting your theory on Mrs Ramsbottom,' said DCI Reynolds entering his office with Sergeant Ayari's broad smile coming in behind him. 'Are there any more thoughts you've had that you'd be willing to share with us?'

'It depends who your key suspects are,' I said, shocked at my own presumptuousness.

DCI Reynolds gave a chuckle. 'This is classified information that with the intuition you've shown us thus far probably matches up to your list but often in suspected murder cases the motive is hard to find, sometimes it's an impulsive act and in others a carefully thought out revenge.'

I finished his sentence for him, 'Giving us two separate avenues to explore.'

'Exactly. The only concrete evidence we have, Susie, is kidney failure, and I'd go as far to say that this has led us to assume Miss Dune may, and only may, have been poisoned.'

DCI Reynolds took a long sip of tea and I wished Toby was here. Without him I couldn't possibly suggest kidney stones. It's not a diagnosis I would've ever come up with alone and if I threw it in to the pot right now, it'd be perfectly obvious to these two I'd been discussing the case with someone else.

Instead I asked whether he thought Hailey swallowed something by mistake.

'Our primary concern is to determine cause and manner of death.' DCI Reynolds's delivery was crisp and uncompromising. 'The pathologists are carrying out tests to determine the effects of chemical agents on Miss Dune's vital organs and my investigators are at Fontaburn Hall searching for any trace of domestic or unfamiliar chemicals.'

I decided, in the hopes it may lead me to get something specific out of this 'chat', that the time had come for me to give a little bit more from my side. 'I don't want to introduce a false lead,' I said. 'Which is why I didn't tell you this earlier but I saw a man in stripy pyjamas through the window of the billiard room moments before the burglar alarm went off.'

'Shoot!' let out DCI Reynolds. 'I thought we'd

put that scenario to bed.'

Sergeant Ayari looked at him.

'Can you give us any more information, Susie?'

I wavered as to what to say. My mind cast back over the scene.

'I'd looked out of my bedroom window; an outdoor light was on and it lit up the bottom storey of the wing opposite mine. It was then that I saw a figure in pyjamas spread like a starfish across the inner bottom window ledge.'

'Who was it?' asked Sergeant Ayari.

'Unfortunately, I don't know. The middle bar of the window obscured his head.'

'Didn't you see when he got down?' asked DCI Reynolds.

'I'm afraid I'd carelessly fallen off the radiator onto the floor by then.'

'I do hope you were okay?'

'Absolutely fine. I'm sorry.'

'Why were you on the radiator?' asked Sergeant Ayari.

'I was trying to get reception on my mobile telephone.'

'I see.'

'Both Archie and Stanley were wearing the same pyjamas as the man I'd seen.'

The conversation halted, DCI Reynolds was violently jotting down notes, then, lifting his head he ordered Sergeant Ayari 'to act immediately'.

She stood up. 'Yes, Inspector.'

'Take a colleague with you right now and conduct a thorough search of Fontaburn Hall billiard room, paying particular attention to the window ledge the figure was standing on. Footprints, fingerprints, DNA — that's what we're looking for. Please keep the information Susie has given us under your hat for the time being. If Mr Wellingham raises any objections then you can tell him we've broadened our search to cover all bases. I want you to pay close attention to his reaction, it could be of great value to our investigation.'

'Okay.'

Sergeant Ayari moved towards the door and DCI Reynolds got up. 'Off you go and report back to me as soon as you return.' He closed the door behind her and paced slowly across his office to the window.

'Someone, Susie, is covering something up. Of that I can now be sure.' He double-tapped the window glass and turned back to his seat. 'For your own peace of mind, you should know that in their statements Mr Gerald said he was in bed when the alarm sounded and Mrs Gerald in the adjoining bathroom, each acting as an alibi to the other.'

'So, Stanley wasn't in the billiard room?'

'If the hard evidence doesn't support this belief, the theory must be held suspect. However, the three people we know who were not in their own beds are the Duke, Mr Furr Egrant and Mr Wellingham. Only the latter wearing the pyjamas you describe. This leaves me wondering,' DCI Reynolds leant on his desk, his knuckles turning white under the strain of his forearms, 'is it Mr Wellingham or Mr Gerald who's playing me for a fool?'

'If I took a guess Inspector . . . '

'Guesses are unhelpful,' he interrupted. The speed at which DCI Reynolds dipped his head and sat in his chair suggested he was as surprised by his tone as I was.

'I'm sorry,' I said.

'Please don't be. I forgot myself for a moment. In this line of work, we must always test theory against evidence and avoid making any assumptions no matter how logical they might seem. But, Susie, you are free to speculate and I'm now intrigued to hear.'

'After the alarm went off and we gathered in the hall I noticed Primrose was far more attached to her husband than she had been earlier in the evening.'

DCI Reynolds raised his forefinger to his mouth. I'd piqued his curiosity.

'Her fringe was peculiarly damp and stuck to her forehead, which makes me think something had made her anxious, well before the burglar alarm went off. And Stanley, of course, was in the same pyjamas as the man I saw in the billiard room.'

DCI Reynolds's face looked up towards the ceiling and I sat hoping Toby had a book in his car. This 'chat' was going on far longer than a supermarket shop, but I couldn't exactly walk out now.

DCI Reynolds's forearm stretched across his desk and his fingers briefly drummed. 'I like you, Susie, and I could really do with your help, so for that reason and that reason only,' he drummed once more, 'I'll let you in on a private matter between Mr and Mrs Gerald.'

'Thank you. I really appreciate your trust in me.'

'Mrs Gerald suffers from bipolar disorder. Are you familiar with it?'

'A little,' I said knowing Toby could fill in the gaps later. 'Was her anxiety related to this?'

'It could have been a side effect of her condition, yes.'

'Don't you think the timing was rather fortuitous?'

The expression on DCI Reynolds's face said it all — where was my empathy? He paused and his eyes left mine. 'The Geralds are trying for a baby and therefore Mrs Gerald has come off her medication.' He looked back at me.

'I understand,' I said quickly and apologetically. DCI Reynolds's telephone began beeping, he raised his right hand. 'Just one moment.'

'Hello?'

'Yes.'

'Very helpful indeed.'

'Thank you, Margery.'

'Well, Susie, there's something else to knock off the list. Our visit to the contract cleaners has eliminated any possibility that they could have introduced hazardous acid to Fontaburn Hall as this company, Sparkles, pride themselves on their organic products — which in this case has saved their bacon.'

'That's good.'

'I'm sorry to cut you short,' he said, 'but I have a visitor coming in so I must see you on your way.'

'No, no, that's fine. I've taken up enough of your time. Thank you for speaking with me.'

'Do keep in close touch with us.'

'Yes, I will.'

DCI Reynolds walked me to the lift.

Clu clunk, it went as it reached the ground floor and I did a double take at the youthful figure in black leather trousers standing with her back to me. *Cooee*! It was a hot day for such heavy clothing.

Hearing my step, she turned to face me and I don't know what startled me more: the aged face coming towards me or the reflection of my startled expression in her silver shades.

'Gee,' she said, 'is there nowhere to get a cup of coffee in this place?'

'I should think there's a machine in the foyer.'

'Thanks lady, I really need it.'

I headed for the station exit but she kept pace muttering under her breath, 'Alcohol's the only answer but coffee will have to do for the time being.'

I think this woman thought I was going to serve her and as I was too embarrassed to point out her mistake I ended up leading the way to a machine I'd just spotted, by the toilet sign of all places.

Once I'd set it to fill a hopelessly thin plastic cup, and knowing that for better or worse Americans will tell you anything if you give them a prod, I turned to her and said, 'I'm sorry for what you're going through.' It came straight out just like that and was received by shoulders that shot back with a huff as if to say

'I'm better than all this.'

'You don't need to be sorry sweetie, it's my runaway daughter who should be but that ain't happening now.'

This was said without the slightest bit of sorrow, and even though I was finding it very hard to believe a mother could speak of her dead daughter with such resentment, I was sure this *must* be Mrs Dune. And as I didn't want to put myself in a compromising or dishonest position at this time I knew — right now — I *had* to get out of there.

'I hope you sort it out okay,' I said handing her the cup.

'Thanks, nice meeting you.' She turned to go but I could tell by the hesitation in her hips that she'd forgotten where the lift was.

'That way,' I pointed and she sashayed off towards it.

21

'You look shell-shocked,' said Toby as I got into the car.

'I think I just met Hailey's mother.'

I was staring straight out of the windscreen, focusing on the diminishing white wall of the police station as Toby reversed the car.

'Not that woman in drag I saw going into the station a few minutes ago?'

He was joking.

'Yup, the one in the leather trousers and silver sunglasses.'

'Come on?!' Toby braked hard as he'd only just noticed the light at the junction was red. 'That's unbelievable.'

'It's more unbelievable that she didn't show an ounce of emotion considering her daughter has just died.'

'Well it can't be her.'

'It was, I know it was. She mentioned her runaway daughter and Charlotte told me Hailey wasn't on speaking terms with her mother.'

'Maybe you're right then.'

'Isn't it wretched? I don't think I should ever mention I've met her.'

'It's probably best.'

Once we were out of Norham, back on a two-lane country road, I asked Toby to pull over when he could. Immediately, without even questioning it, he swung his car off the road into a large empty lay-by.

'Everything okay?'

'Yeah, I just want to tell you in private what DCI Reynolds said.'

'Go on then.' He turned the ignition off and I opened the passenger door. It was hot and I needed air. 'What did you find out?'

'The pathologists are testing Hailey's vital organs for unusual things and there are investigators at Fontaburn Hall searching for domestic or unfamiliar chemicals.'

'At the same time?'

'Yes.'

'Well that means they must've uncovered *some* evidence that has led to another search of the house.'

'The only evidence they have is kidney failure.' I'd decided to keep my discussion with Toby purely medical. It was where he could be most useful.

'Well there must be something else they're not telling you and my guess is a toxin of some kind.'

'DCI Reynolds was frustratingly vague but,' I took out my telephone, 'I've got photographs of the autopsy report.'

'Susie!' A disapproving smile swept across Toby's face, 'I won't ask.'

Then, saying nothing, he plucked the telephone from my hands and began zooming in and out of the pictures.

I did try to justify my actions, '*Any* inquisitive person would have looked. I was left alone in DCI Reynolds's office and the folder was just lying on the desk,' but Toby wasn't listening. He was completely engrossed in the autopsy.

Very quickly, I ran out of patience. 'What does it say?' I asked.

Toby, totally unaware I might have been longing for him to speak, popped out with, 'There was calcium oxalate in her urine alright and they've found kidney stones.'

'So, she did die of kidney stones?'

'No, she couldn't have.'

'Why not?'

'They were only in one kidney, you need them in both to kill you.'

'Was her other kidney healthy?'

'Yes.'

Toby's eyes were straining at the screen and I wondered if he wears glasses. I hope not. I've never found it easy to kiss a spectacled person passionately and taking them off can spoil the moment.

He was now talking to himself. His lips were actually moving even though no sound was coming out.

'What else does it say?' I asked.

And without raising his head Toby answered, 'It's confusing. This shows a very high concentration of oxalate in Hailey's system.'

'From something else?'

Finally, Toby looked at me and said, 'When fats and nutrients aren't absorbed properly calcium may bind to the unabsorbed fat instead of oxalate, and this causes a build-up of oxalate.' His head reverted straight back to the telephone and although he was talking to himself again I didn't mind. His jargon had gone over my head and I was quite happy to wait for a simpler explanation.

'Interesting,' he said. 'This report shows a much higher concentration of oxalate than would ever build up from stones in one kidney . . . Yes!' he exclaimed, 'I knew it!' he looked at me. 'Irritable bowel syndrome is mentioned here.'

'Fat lot of use that is.'

Toby laughed and went silent again.

It was time to throw in my own suggestion, 'I think Hailey had filler in her face. Could this have poisoned her?'

'Nah, but to be fair, with IBS as severe as hers it's no surprise she had filler in what would otherwise be a severely drawn face.'

Toby reached across to hand me my telephone but accidentally dropped it in my crotch. 'Sorry about that,' he said giving me a cheeky smile.

'So, you reckon it was IBS?'

'*Hmmm* . . . IBS causes a build-up of oxalate but Hailey's system had far more in it than I would ever expect.'

'Where else could it come from?'

'It can come from drinking or eating anything with oxalic acid in it; could be bleach, metal cleaners, floor polish, stuff for getting rust off metal, plants or even rhubarb leaves!'

'Rhubarb leaves?'

'It sounds ridiculous but it's the truth.'

'How funny.'

'There's your answer anyway. They're searching the house for a product containing oxalic acid.'

'I doubt they'll find any.'

'Why?'

'I overheard a call between DCI Reynolds and the contract cleaning company. They only use organic products.'

'That doesn't mean they won't find old products or rhubarb leaves in a cupboard.'

'I wish *we* could visit the house.'

'Well we can't!' said Toby as if he didn't trust me not to come up with a way of having a sneaky peek.

'What do we do now?'

'Well, if toxic acid *is* found the police can't prove anything without evidence that it links to someone. You can busy yourself with that for the time being.'

'What do you mean?'

'It's clear you've won DCI Reynolds over and therefore you know he'll fill you in as things progress. In the meantime, you can search for the motive to murder and be all ready to complete the circle.' Toby sounded genuinely confident in me.

'I'm so pleased you're in on this,' I said, immediately wanting to stretch across the gear stick and kiss him, but I've never been the forward type and wasn't going to try now.

'I'm just here as a sounding board, you're the one who gets fired up about playing super-sleuth.'

'It's the attention to detail I enjoy. I can't help it, I'm an artist!'

'And being a visual person is what makes you not a bad detective.'

'Not bad,' I joked. 'I have a hundred per cent hit rate so far.'

'Well, the pressure's on to maintain that.' Toby nudged my shoulder with the back of his hand. 'C'mon, pull that door shut, you owe me another drawing lesson.'

Toby and I had a very amusing afternoon joking around drawing High Maintenance. His suggestion of laying a trail of straw finally got her trotting around the field and while he went in circles dropping clumps I got a lot more work done than I'd achieved that morning.

When Toby's concentration lapsed he left me to it and took himself off on a walk. I longed to go with him but if I was ever going to get home this week, which I must as I have a friend coming to stay for the weekend, I knew I had to stick at it.

Other than the fact Toby wouldn't be with me, I was looking forward to returning home and getting back to my studio. It's daunting to have such a big project, six horse portraits, in front of me but there's also the excitement of starting something new. I've already decided I'll begin with the geldings. They're such gargantuan animals.

I have a huge sheet of MDF in my studio, waiting at the ready, for me to pin my preliminary sketches on. And when I get home, I'll load all the photographs on to my computer, ready to use as a reference for the overall drawing.

Mel, my friend who's coming to stay, has horses of her own and I know she'll be a great help in advising me on all sorts of things a non-horsey person such as me doesn't know. Is a horse sitting down acceptable? Do they even sit down, or do they only lie down? Does it really matter if their ears are forward or back? Can I draw a tail in the air? I need answers to all of these before I can choose a pose for each. Every drawing must be different; it'd be a dull collection if not.

In a way, it's a shame Mel's coming alone. I'm godmother to her second child, Henry, and I'd like to see him. He is after all one of only two godchildren I have. It surprises my mother I don't have more but I tell her it's because I'm Catholic, not unpopular. 'Well maybe you should've made more Catholic friends then,' comes her uncompromising reply.

Oli, Mel's husband, is one of those great hands-on dads who can cope without her. And I know part of the reason Mel likes a weekend with me is because I don't have the distraction of children — not to say I wouldn't like to be a mother one day.

Mel and I will workshop my situation with Toby I'm sure. All my married friends like to live vicariously through my romantic escapades. I think it's because when I ask them for relationship advice, it makes them still feel part of the scene.

At last! This final sketch had High Maintenance's hefty behind down on paper. I stood up and placed the drawing on my chair. It looked good. I'd done it! The enormous horse was bursting out of the page and I was filled with that great sense of achievement you get when you look at something you can't believe you drew.

I hummed with happiness as I packed up my things and I would have skipped out of the field if I hadn't been carrying such a load.

I dumped my stuff at the stable-yard gate and, as I couldn't see anyone around to ask, I went in to look for Lucy. Red-Rum was the only being about, licking his paws — a clear sign he'd recently caught a mouse. On seeing me he attached himself to my heel and I was pleased to see we were friends again. Ever since I shooed him out of my room I've been making it up to him. Feeding him tit-bits under the table and tickling his belly, proving to myself I'm not harbouring cold-hearted instincts from being raised an only child.

I felt sorry for High Maintenance being separated from her friends, so went back to the field and wound up the cordon on my own. The horse was so lethargic she didn't even move when I patted her nose nor when Red-Rum playfully paraded around as if he was boss. I thanked her for modelling and turned away. My work here was done and it was now time for a long rewarding soak in the bath.

Six horses in seven days wasn't bad, although you'll have come to understand why most artists never make much money. If we charged by the hour no one would ever believe it.

22

Knock knock came through my bedroom door.

'Can I come in?' asked Toby edging it open.

I shifted around in the vanity-table chair. I was in my dressing gown, all clean and red in the face. My fresh underwear was on full display in the corner and I spotted Toby's eyes drawn towards the ivory silk lace. He quickly looked back at me with a coy expression.

'Great cast-iron bath here isn't it?' he said.

'The best.'

I patted the bed. 'Sit down.'

Both of us giggled as his bottom almost toppled off the very soft edge.

'Whoops!' He shuffled back a bit more.

'I love a bath at any time of day,' I said as I checked my dressing gown was tightly done up.

'Me too. Although what I really like is when someone comes to talk to me. Our family always had communal bath time.'

'I talk to my mother when she's in the bath but I wouldn't like my father to come and join in too. That would be odd.'

'We don't still do it,' laughed Toby at the thought. 'Anyway, sorry for disturbing you but my phone's completely out of juice and I was wondering if you have a laptop I can use to check my email?'

'Of course, help yourself, it's there on my pillow. The battery's dud so you'll have to keep it plugged in where it is.' This being the best excuse I could think of to stop him leaving the room.

Toby stretched backwards and I got a flash of the tight black band on his boxer shorts. I love this style.

'I just need to make sure there's nothing urgent from work,' he said.

I turned to look in the mirror and caught him having another glimpse of my lingerie in the reflection. Part of me was pleased, the other part wishing he'd come across it another way.

Am I silly to be thinking there's something developing between us? I really fancy Toby but if he fancies me too then why haven't we got any further? The impossible first move doesn't get any easier with age. In fact, it becomes harder. The lunge is no longer excusable. Although I wouldn't mind AT ALL if he lunged at me right now.

The romantic ideal of a sweet sober kiss, the man holding your cheeks in the cusp of his hands, lovingly gazing into your eyes before softly pressing his lips against yours, is far from a British man's capability. I knew I'd have to go to the Continent if this is what I was after. Right now, I have Toby sitting on my bed and surely, although small, it must be a step in the right direction.

'Toby,' I said and he looked up from the screen. 'I just realised I don't know much about you.'

'Where did that come from?'

I dismissed his defensive tone. 'Well I don't know where you live or where you grew up and I like to know that about my friends.'

'You *do* know where I live. In the West Country. And I grew up in Bath.'

'Seriously, you grew up in Bath?'

'Yes, why?' He seemed a little uptight.

'It's just you were saying how much your family like baths. It's funny that's all.'

He smiled.

'All okay with the email?' I asked, thinking it better to leave off any more personal questions for the time being.

'Yup, they seem to be coping without me. Mind if I Google a few things?'

'Not at all. When you're done you should look up Fontaburn Hall, it really is a magnificent place.'

'Will do.'

'I never told you about visiting Vicky today.' I'd thought better of keeping it from him. I was now happy to risk my own reputation to get the knowledge I needed.

'Vicky?'

'Yeah, the woman who exercises the horses, the one whose husband died.'

'Don't tell me, you think that poor lady's a murderer.'

'Just let me ask you one thing. *Pleeease.*'

'Okay . . . '

'What could you put in a glass of water that would kill someone without them knowing it was in there?'

'Google says . . . ' he waited for the results to show, 'drinking too much water can kill you.'

'Do *you* know anything?'

'Arsenic's the only thing I know of.'

'Well that's not it.'

'Not what?'

'If Vicky suddenly decided to kill Hailey, with no pre-planning, what could she have found in Archie's house that would have enabled her to poison a glass of water by Hailey's bed?'

'Does the water have to stay clear?'

'Yes.'

'In that case my best guess is she could have rubbed the rim with a poisonous plant, but this is an immensely sophisticated way of going about it and you'd have to be an expert botanist.'

'Arghh, Toby. This shifts the blame to Daniel . . . he knew all about plants.'

'Well, investigating Daniel first seems kinder to me than putting all your efforts into poor Vicky.'

I asked Toby what kind of plant it could have been and he reverted to Google again.

'It says here if you crush the beans of a castor plant you get ricin, which can kill. Ingesting it can make you vomit and therefore it leaves your system but inhaling it causes stomach pain, dehydration and destroys the main internal organs.'

'Perhaps it wasn't the glass of water. Maybe Daniel or Vicky put it on her pillow?'

'If so that would mean Archie would have to have a greenhouse to grow it in and a tall one at that, these plants are huge.'

'If it was Daniel he could have brought it with him?'

'But, why would he bring a poisonous plant to the weekend? You said he'd never met Hailey before and, to be honest Susie, the investigators would have found it on her pillow by now.'

'Yeah, you're probably right. I don't want to think Vicky's guilty but why if she was the cook, would she have been upstairs?'

'Are you saying you wouldn't chance your luck of having a nosey around a big house?'

'Toby! You're right and if she was caught having a snoop she might well have told Archie she was turning down the beds.'

'That it?' asked Toby swivelling the computer towards me. Fontaburn Hall was on the screen.

'Yeah, that's it.'

He read out the strap line, 'Grand sixteenth-century Tudor country house with notable porcelain and ceramic collection,' and then added, 'it looks rather spooky in this picture.'

'I have a good sense for bad spirits and I didn't see any.'

'Not all ghosts are bad you know.' He smiled. 'Hey, maybe the man in the stripy PJs was actually a ghost.'

'Can't be, Archie told me the house was haunted by clergy and I doubt they wear stripy pyjamas.'

'You think they sleep in their habits?'

'Probably!'

Toby was typing Fontaburn Hall into Google Maps and now with a bird's-eye map of the location I could see the village of Fontaburn. It was east of the house and, as I'd approached from the west, not to mention the fact the perimeter wall shielded any view, I had missed it entirely.

'Looks like there's a museum in the village,' I said pointing at the symbol on the screen.

Toby clicked it and up popped a picture of a wattle-and-daub building. 'Local museum tracing the history of the Norland family.'

'We should visit!'

'It's still open, so we could pop down there now?'

'Do you really want to go?'

'I know you're keen. And I'm interested in ancient British families so definitely, let's go.'

'Ancient British families?'

'Yeah, they've given us our architectural and social history, it's always interesting to learn more about them.'

'Great.'

'We should invite Lucy too,' said Toby and my heart sank.

He got up.

'Just before you leave,' I said, our conversation of families reminding me of the Geralds, 'DCI Reynolds told me Primrose suffers from bipolar and is currently off her medicine as they're trying for a baby.'

'That was indiscreet of him.'

'It is, isn't it, although I think he kind of had to tell me when I accused Primrose of being so anxious about the burglar alarm.'

'Weren't you anxious?'

'I thought it was a false alarm. Primrose was much more worked up than the others, and remember Toby, Stanley was in the same pyjamas as the man I saw in the billiard room.'

'Well, from a doctor's point of view, it would

be unfair to interrogate Primrose on account of what they know to be bipolar symptoms.'

'What is bipolar?'

'It's not something that leads someone to murder, that's for sure. And if you're attempting to draw parallels between Primrose's symptoms and the events of Saturday night, I'd hold back.'

'I'm not drawing parallels any more I just want to know what it is.'

Toby bounced back down onto the bed. 'It's a mental disability caused by a hormonal imbalance. Its effects include very low self-esteem, which is a psychological state far away from that of a murderer's.'

'But she didn't appear withdrawn at the beginning of the evening, and she's not exactly unconfident. I reckon something must have happened that changed her state of mind.'

'You're drawing parallels, Susie.'

'But I want to fully understand it.'

'Well, people with bipolar can be absolutely fine one minute and then out of nowhere they are consumed by an overbearing force that either puts them on a manic high or a chronic low. It can happen anytime anywhere. The trigger is a chemical imbalance within them, not something affecting them from the outside.'

'How awful.'

'It is and prescriptive drugs are an effective way of inhibiting these episodes.'

'Do you think she was definitely off her medication?'

'I wouldn't start doubting DCI Reynolds if I were you. No doctor can guarantee bipolar drugs won't affect a foetus. So, women with bipolar have to decide between staying on their medication and running the risk, coming off it and suffering the consequences, or never having children at all.'

'So, I guess she was then.'

'Yes, and the fact DCI Reynolds told you makes me think he was warning you to go easy on her. Off medication it would be far more likely Primrose would take her own life not someone else's.'

'Crumbs, that's serious.'

'Yeah and confidential. That inspector really does trust you.' Toby stood up and closed the door behind him.

My reflection in the dressing-table mirror was full of guilt. It upset me that DCI Reynolds had had to compromise his discretion to set me straight and I now knew without evidence I really shouldn't have said a thing. I stared harder into the mirror and promised to God that I'd try to keep unfounded theories to myself in the future.

It was now time to get dressed and the thought of slipping into my ivory silk underwear, the last new set bought from Hillary's Honk commission, instantly put me in a better mood.

With a turquoise dress and drop earrings to match I left the room, happy at the thought of another outing with Toby.

23

'Oh, hi Susie,' said Lucy as I entered the kitchen.

'Sorry I wasn't there to let High Maintenance out into the field but Jim and me got back much later than I thought we would.'

'How was the lorry?'

'We had a right old time trying to get it up to speed on the country lanes. Great fun but it's a hell of a vibrator. No good for long hauls. Don't want our racers arriving with numb feet.'

I laughed at the thought.

'I just saw Toby by the car and he invited me to join you on a trip to a local museum.'

'We were hoping you'd come?' I said with a genuine effort to sound convincing.

'Na, not me Susie. There's a slim chance I'd go with you to a National Trust property on a Sunday, but not a museum, that's real boring.'

I was inclined to agree with her (particularly when it comes to a village museum). I've often wondered why the curators of the greatest and best museums feel the need to put absolutely every crumb, chip, flake and piece of an archaeological artefact into rows of glass cabinets rather than hold back a bit, give us a few magnificent things on display and save all the loose pieces in the archives for the boffins.

'We shouldn't be too long,' I said rattling my car keys out of my handbag, all ready to insist to Toby that I drive.

'No problem, I'm going to have a beer with the boys in the stable and Toby's told me dinner's in the oven so just give me a shout when you're back. He's amazin' ain't he?' Lucy smiled at me. 'All I have to do is lay the table.'

'Yeah, he's great,' and he's *mine* I said to myself. 'See you in a bit Lucy, thanks for everything. It's so nice staying with you.'

Aside from my jealousy over Toby, I genuinely meant what I'd just said. The ease and amusement of living with Lucy more than made up for how hard the horses had been to draw and I was surprisingly glad of her company over the last week.

This was not something I was expecting, considering I choose to live alone. A choice which gives me time and space to develop my creativity without interruption from others. I'm always trying to set my mother straight when she expresses her concern that my life must be 'so lonely poppet' and I assure her it's 'solitary', definitely not lonely. It isn't, and never has been, in my nature to need company. But don't get me wrong, I'm not a loser! I have great friends, I just don't have a need to be around them all the time.

If Mum really is worried I'm lonely then why didn't she give me a brother or a sister? The thought she might have wanted to and couldn't rattled me. As a family we've always been completely open about everything and I can't believe my parents would have hidden any troubles they'd had.

I let out a huff as I left the house. It's all

Toby's fault for pointing out I'm an only child. He's got me in a stew and this unsettling self-reflection was making me undermine my parents.

'I'm driving,' I said seeing him standing by his car. 'You're on holiday and deserve to have a pint or two if we find a pub.'

'That's kind but you've earnt a celebratory drink having finished your work.'

'Finished is an overstatement. Anyway, I'm very happy holding off until dinner.' I smiled at him. 'Come on, let's get going!'

★   ★   ★

The great height of Fontaburn Hall's flint wall took me by surprise, even though I was seeing it for the second time. I'd driven Toby the long way around to show it off as I don't think he'd believed me when I said 'you can't possibly see over it'. I slipped the car into snail pace as we passed the gates. Toby exclaimed, 'It looks beautifully kept inside there.'

'It really is a wonderful place, I wish you could see more of it. But as you now know,' I said with conceit, 'that's an impossibility thanks to Henry VIII.'

'It's nice it's so well kept. I can't bear it when people born with a silver spoon in their mouth don't respect their inheritance. It's all thanks to their ancestors they've got what they have.'

'Big houses and estates are quite a lot to take on though,' I said, unable to fathom the workload.

'But that's what comes with being born into a family who have things. This chap Archie, for example, is just one link in a custodial chain that's handed a unique legacy down from father to son for hundreds of years. It's his to take on, not his to give away.'

I liked Toby's reasoning, however, I countered, 'You've got to have the money to keep it going.'

'Which is my point exactly,' he enthused, 'working hard and taking on the responsibility of the task in hand. Every generation will start with money behind them, but they must manage their assets, put profits in the hands of savvy stockbrokers and cunning solicitors. Not have the pennies burn a hole in their pocket.'

I told him I like heirs who inherit debt and do everything they can to turn things around; he said my outlook was romantic. Which it was but that wasn't my point.

'What happens to a house like Fontaburn,' I asked, 'if Archie doesn't have an heir by the time his father dies and he moves out to take up the main family seat?'

'I don't know,' said Toby. 'I've never heard of that happening. Maybe a sibling holds it in lieu of an heir. Or it probably goes to the second son.'

'What about a daughter?'

'It could go to them these days, but ancient titled families have strong views on ancestral possessions going down the female line, particularly if a daughter marries and takes her husband's name.'

We agreed that there was likely much more

wrapped up in it than we understood and Toby left it in my hands to find out as he put it, 'on another posh outing'.

'Ah ha,' I said as the cricket ground appeared on our right, 'I'd wondered how close it was to the house.'

'Lovely pavilion, isn't it?'

'That'll be Archie. He talked to me about the upkeep of it for a bit but I'm afraid I wasn't really listening.'

'Cricket's not as boring as its reputation you know.'

'Oh, *I* know that. I actually really like cricket, I just wasn't very interested in the maintenance of the pavilion.'

'You like cricket?' Toby sounded surprised.

'Yes, I've got into it since moving to Sussex. Almost every village has a ground and the nearest one to me is very quaint.'

'So, you go?'

'Often, when the sun shines. It gets me away from the studio, which I have to force myself to do sometimes.'

'Force?'

'Yeah, it's important not to overwork a painting and it's so easy to do unless there's a good reason to leave the house.'

'And if there's not?'

'Then I have to make myself. I do it by believing my painting can improve on its own if I'm away from it. Silly really, but I tell you what, I jolly well hope my walnut still life has got better while I'm here.'

'That's so charming,' Toby smiled. 'I hope

you'll let me visit your studio one day.'

'Of course, I'd love that.'

'It's good you don't mind people seeing your work,' said Toby.

He went on to tell me an anecdote of an artist he knows who locks his door for fear of people snooping at what he's up to.

'I can understand that,' I said in reply. 'But my studio doesn't have a door as I thought it was a good way of getting over this issue. My art is me, it's the truth and all the more so if I let others in on the whole picture.'

'You've got a brave soul, Susie.'

'I don't know about that, and anyway letting people in can sometimes be very funny. Not that long ago I painted a barn across the field from where I live and two weeks ago I invited the woman who owns it to come and have a look. It's an enormous picture, about six feet by four. She stood in front of it, pointed at the bottom quarter and said, 'What are you going to put there?' 'Nothing! It's finished!' I replied.'

'And you don't mind?' Toby laughed.

'Not at all, it makes a great story and if I let comments like this get to me it would change the way I work. My first lesson to self was: don't let anyone's opinion change your style. My style is all I have that's true to me and I'm as brave as I have to be to share it with the rest of the world, it's what makes my work mine. If viewers like it great and if they don't I put it down to a difference in taste.'

What I really wanted to say to Toby was if you're willing to bare your soul and pour the honesty and truth of how you see and sense something into your work, then it will be as great a piece as you can possibly make it. But, I really didn't want to spring an emotionally indulgent conversation on him right now.

'I get it,' he said. 'I've always found Jack Vettriano's paintings lack what it is you've put your finger on. It's why Turner's late paintings are such works of genius.'

'Yes!' I said, overexcited by his knowledge and sensitivity.

I was pleased Toby had asked about my work — it boded well if we ever have a future together. It's important for me that whoever I end up with fully understands what it is to be an artist. I need a partner who encourages me to believe in myself when the chips are down. Someone who hugs me tight when I've failed and keeps their distance when I'm standing in front of a canvas, midway through a picture, with tears of frustration streaming down my face. I'm well aware that my artistic temperament is selfish but I also know nothing great comes without indulging in oneself, one's thoughts, one's desires and one's fears. This may mean I never find a partner for life but I'd one hundred per cent rather be married to my painting than married to someone who neither understands nor makes allowances for it.

24

I took my foot off the accelerator as Toby and I drove into Fontaburn village, which much like the Hall was incredibly well kept. In fact, the whole place was so immaculately empty it was as if the refuse collectors had cleared up all the people and taken away its soul too. The pavements were separated from the road by a mound of mown grass and hanging from every old-fashioned street lamp right the way down the high street were baskets of flowers, red as they always are.

Most of the buildings were redundant alms houses with a few remnants of Tudor architecture amongst them. Not that long ago this village would have been inhabited by the employees of Fontaburn Hall and their families, but its eerie atmosphere suggested most had moved on.

I parked right outside the museum.

'Where is everyone?' asked Toby.

'Strange, isn't it?'

'Hey, look at that.' Toby was pointing up at the museum's sign — a great big shield dangling above us. 'You can learn a lot about a family from their coat of arms, you know. Right away I can tell you the head of the family is a baron.'

'But Archie's father is a lord?'

'Yes, barons are generally always called lord except when described in a formal document.'

'I see, I think. And how do you know he's a baron?'

'That coronet of rank as they're known — heraldic language is so elegant — has six large silver balls, only four of them showing in two dimensions. This symbolises the rank of baron.'

'Where did you learn that?'

'I did an extra module in heraldry at university. I told you I was interested in ancient families.'

'You must be.' I looked up at the shield. 'So, the number of balls determines the rank?'

'Yes. A viscount has sixteen.'

'So, does an earl have thirty-two?'

'No,' Toby laughed. 'They have eight balls on spikes.'

'How confusing. What else can you tell from this coat of arms?'

'The shape is an inverted Tudor arch, which means the barony was ennobled in the sixteenth century. The colour blue symbolises truth and loyalty. The boar's head is a symbol of hospitality and I reckon the red rose in its mouth is for England.' Toby was on fire. I think I've just uncovered his specialist subject. 'The geraniums are a sign of true friendship and the pineapples of welcome. Scottish heralds on the other hand omit such fancies as ridiculous.'

'What's a pineapple doing on a sixteenth-century coat of arms?'

'Good spot. In medieval England it was a pine cone, which was later misinterpreted as a pineapple.'

'And the squirrels?'

'I don't know what they stand for.'

'Red head, ginger nut?'

'Very funny, but I don't think so. I bet there will be a blazon inside. That's a formal description of a coat of arms in Olde English.' Toby reached for the door. 'Let's go in.'

'Ah ha, visitors, are we?' said a busty woman, planted on the other side, with feet so small they reminded me of the joke that nothing grows in the shade.

'Hello,' we exclaimed, but our excitement was quickly dampened by our new companion.

'If you're coming in please bear in mind that we like to maintain a quiet reflective atmosphere in here so best keep any conversation to a minimum.'

'Talk about gloomy,' whispered Toby in my ear.

The museum was small, just one room with a chunky square desk in the centre where the curator had stationed herself. Three of the walls were cluttered with heavily protected photographs; newspaper clippings; correspondence; title deeds; and all sorts of things you'd expect in a museum of an ancient family's history. The fourth wall had a colourful mass of porcelain in glass casing, and then, circumnavigating the whole room, was a bossy 'keep back' rail with scales of thick plastic-coated information boards welded to it.

Toby had been right, Archie's family's fortune came from porcelain and, according to the text in front of me . . . *it was the sixth Lord Norland (Archie's great, great grandfather) who'd spotted* the potential for exploring trade links with the Far East in 1842 when China and Britain signed the Treaty of Nanking. Chinese coastal ports engaged in foreign trade and Lord Norland, together with his business partner Mr William de Bynninge, sailed for Shanghai. Here they set up a new company, choosing — in keeping with local tradition — a Chinese name, Piào Liàng, meaning 'elegant and bright'.

On the wall above this board were photographs recording four generations of Wellinghams and de Bynninges in business together. The most recent strapline read: *Wellingham Porcelain, trading as Piào Liàng. From left to right, The Honourable Archibald Barnabas Cooke Wellingham — Chief Executive Officer. Francis Archibald Lord Norland — Chairman.*

I turned to the curator. 'It's interesting,' I said as I approached her desk, 'that there's no mention of the current generation of de Bynninge in partnership with Mr Wellingham.'

'That would be right. Mr Wellingham has taken over as CEO and cut his ties with subsequent generations of de Bynninges.'

'Do you know why?' I asked as nicely as I possibly could — this woman was going to take some warming up.

'Well,' she said as her chest puffed up with pride and she squeezed out from behind the desk. 'If you take a look at that dated picture there,' her short arm was a perfectly adequate pointer in such a small room, 'you'll see that Mr de Bynninge and his wife, lovely looking isn't she, have two daughters and we can only assume

232

that without an heir he split his share in Wellingham Porcelain equally between his girls and resigned as a director.'

Charlotte's words, 'I count myself as Archie's oldest friend but if you widen the circle to professional relationships then I guess Primrose takes the title', rang in my ears. Was Primrose in this picture?

I turned to the curator. 'It seems odd that partnership ties have been cut just because there wasn't a de Bynninge son.'

'Well, madam, it's not a fitting role for an upper-class lady to become a director of a global porcelain empire.'

Toby, clearly more interested in the porcelain than the photographs, caught my eye as if to say, 'Now, now, Susie, don't even try to convince this woman otherwise.'

I often long for the day a female aristocrat becomes prime minister, or a judge, or a CEO of a global conglomerate. It would do wonders for the rest of us attempting to be taken seriously despite our gender. It is after all the upper crust who get the best start in life with private education and nepotism served up on a plate. Come on ladies, get your suits on!

'So, the de Bynninges,' I said, 'no longer have an active role in the running of the company?'

'That's correct. Although I happen to know Mr Wellingham often takes the elder Miss de Bynninge with him on factory visits.'

Ah ha! This woman was clearly a bit of a gossip.

'Factory visits?' I asked hoping she would tell me more.

'I'm led to believe Miss de Bynninge is now married — although her new name escapes me — and those of us who work here think it's a little inappropriate that she continues to travel with Mr Wellingham.'

'Doesn't her husband go too?'

'No, they go as a pair to a town nearby Shanghai.'

'What's the town called?'

'Wujiang.' Madam curator beamed as I was choked into silence . . . this was the exact place name Primrose had set Hailey straight on.

'To be fair,' she said, apologising at my reaction, 'Miss de Bynninge's not the only one to go on trips. Mr Wellingham has a charming friend he takes with him from time to time.'

'What's *his* name?'

'I'll never forget it.' She swelled with pride once more. 'It's Furr Egrant. Fancy being called that.'

'How funny!' I smiled at her. Little did she know what gold dust this conversation had been.

I went to join Toby by the porcelain and as I stretched out my hand to point at a beautiful teapot with a string of colourful butterflies dancing around its waist a sharp voice came hurtling across the room, '*No!* No touching. Those pieces are of great value and break very easily.'

I apologised, wondering how on earth this could possibly happen within a glass cabinet.

Toby drew me away. 'Have you seen the coat

of arms? It's here, painted on vellum.'

'Wow.' It was completely beautiful with colours so vivid it was hard to believe it had been done in 1539. Below it on a scroll was the blazon, written, as Toby had said, with such elegant language.

Arms — *Quarterly 1 and 4 Or a Geranium slipped leaves and flowering proper 2 and 3 Azure a Pineapple Argent Crest on a Helm with a torse Or and Azure A Boar's Head erased proper holding in the mouth a Rose Gules. Supporters On either side a Squirrel proper above each Squirrel and sprig of acacia.*

I swung around and asked the curator if I could take a photograph.

'Of course, madam. Most people who come here like to.'

'Hey, Susie,' beckoned Toby. 'Come and look at this.' He was pointing at an ancient family rhyme.

Cloak of dagger, friend of note
Stuck by the monarch's side and turned
 his coat.
Down with the Catholics, rid of the
 Romans
Wellingham rises from the life of a
 lowman.
Norlands of Norfolk, loyalty to the king
Time will tell if it's a punishable sin.

'These jingles are great fun. Quite a few ancient families have one although no one knows who wrote them or when they date from.'

'So, do you reckon Henry VIII ennobled the Wellinghams for their loyalty in converting from Catholic to Protestant?'

'I doubt it. Anyone who didn't want to get burnt alive renounced their Catholicism. It's far more likely King Henry, with his wandering eye, took a shine to Archie's great, great, great, great, great, great, great Granny and curried favour with her husband by giving him a title.'

'Do you really think husbands accepted titles on these terms?'

'Yes, definitely. It's proven. And if that's the case maybe the rose in the boar's mouth actually symbolises love and desire, you never know.'

I went back to the blazon. By its side was a table explaining the symbolism and, sure enough, the curly branches above the squirrels' heads were acacia leaves, which illustrate eternal and affectionate remembrance.

Toby's head gave a quick told-you-so nod. 'And,' he said, 'there you go, the squirrels express love of woods.'

'Makes sense, there were wonderful trees at Fontaburn Hall.'

'Hu-hmm,' came from the curator's desk. She was holding up a dangling keyring, 'These have the family crest on them if you'd like to purchase one.'

Out of politeness I moved towards her to take a look.

'Nice,' said Toby over my shoulder. The curator had gone to dust the porcelain cabinet.

'Archie had this crest embroidered on his evening slippers.'

'No surprise,' said Toby. 'Most toffs do. I bet he wore a signet ring too?'

'He didn't actually.'

'How unusual.'

Toby was right. Signet rings engraved with a family crest and worn on the little finger of a man's left hand have become common eighteenth birthday presents from aristocratic fathers to their sons. Maybe Archie's fingers had become plump with age.

Neither Toby nor I were in the market for a keyring so leaving it on the counter we both said 'thank you,' and left, out onto the empty street.

25

The thought of a soulless Fontaburn village pub put Toby and me back in my car with the cheerier thought of a drink on the bench outside Lucy's. As I mastered the narrow turning out of the village, saving my wing mirrors from the slightest scratch, Toby launched into the rather boring topic of the sixteenth-century Wellingham family within the context of British nobility.

I decided if I entertained him for a bit I'd get the best out of him when I introduced the juicier topic, as far as I'm concerned, of how the current generation's actions may have led to Hailey's death. So, when the opportunity arose I swung the conversation as far forward from the sixteenth century as I could and asked, 'Why are you so down on the de Bynninges?'

'Because, after four generations, William de Bynninge has cashed in and broken a history of business with the Wellinghams since 1842.'

'But he doesn't have a son so maybe he wanted the money to be split between his daughters?'

'Everyone knows Wellingham Porcelain is a successful business and therefore the de Bynninge daughters would have got plenty of income from their shares without having to sell and let down the family's legacy.'

I liked that Toby had a firm opinion on the matter and it wasn't that I was trying to provoke him when I asked, 'Why do you mind so much that Mr de Bynninge is cashing in?' I just didn't fully understand what he was getting at.

His voice took on a nostalgic tone, 'I suppose I have some sort of instinctive affection for the way things used to be in business, and, oddly, it does bother me that this Mr de Bynninge just broke off what was obviously a long-standing partnership.' Toby's body tensed and now I could hear the aggression in his voice, 'There used to be a real sense of responsibility in the way a proper family company worked. So different from faceless multinationals, where everything looks the same and everything's done on the basis of pure profit and the lowest common denominator. A family company is supposed to be different — they can care for their workers and suppliers better than the others. They have duties and there's a respect for history. Who knows, but it seems to me that de Bynninge is just throwing all that away. He's taking the money and running . . . '

I loved the fact Toby had such a social conscience, but I just couldn't stop myself butting in 'Listen,' I said, grabbing his arm and trying to get back to the here and now, 'I think Miss de Bynninge is Primrose Gerald.'

'Do you now?' Toby's voice was inflected with a touch of contempt.

'Yes, I do, because when I was at Fontaburn, Hailey implied she was going to Wujiang and Primrose firmly corrected her pronunciation. I also think Primrose was jealous that Archie invited Hailey on a trip.'

'But, according to the curator, Daniel also went on these trips.'

'But Daniel's a man so Primrose wouldn't mind that.'

'True, but, if Daniel fancies Archie, which I presume he does if he got into his bed, then he'd be just as jealous of Hailey.'

'Hey Toby, maybe inviting Hailey on a trip to Wujiang was the beginning of something bigger?'

'Nah, *you* would have picked up on it if it was that bad.'

'But, I think I did. Remember Archie told me at dinner that the topic of porcelain had caused a rift between some of them?'

Toby didn't say anything and as I was driving I couldn't look at him long enough to know if he was thinking about the effects of jealousy or not.

'I reckon Daniel could have killed Hailey with the poisonous bean we looked up.'

'But,' Toby wasn't buying it, 'a high oxalate concentration in Hailey's system is the only concrete evidence you have so far, and although it can come from eating plants, I'm absolutely sure you'd know by now if it was a plant that killed her.'

'Yeah, you're probably right.'

'I am right,' said Toby in that dogmatic way only a man can.

His insistence didn't ruffle me. In fact it made me very happy as it meant he was as invested in this mystery as I was and this inevitably brought us closer together.

'I tell you something,' he said lightening the atmosphere, 'Archie better get on and have a son, he's forty-one and not exactly hot stuff.'

'He's a nice guy though and probably wary of gold diggers.'

'Or, I reckon Daniel was on to something jumping into his bed, those red trousers in the photographs surely don't do it for the ladies.'

'Na, red trousers or not I don't think Archie's gay. Anyway, he's got plenty of time to have an heir, it's not like there's a clock ticking.'

'Do you want children, Susie?'

Crumbs, this was the most personal thing Toby had ever asked me. I was stuck for words. I wanted to say what he wanted to hear but in truth I'm not completely sure whether I do want children or not.

I took it for granted growing up that I'd get married and be a mother one day but now I'm in my thirties and still single, it crosses my mind that I might run out of time to have children and I'm never very sure how this makes me feel.

Out of step with my friends I guess, but then again, I channel a lot of energy into my work and I'd have to compromise this if I were to be a wife and a mother. There's also the possibility of not being able to conceive. If this were the case I'd tackle it with my belief that whatever challenges life throws at you, you must rise and overcome them. Having children is not the be all and end all for me. If I'm meant to have them I will but if not there will be something else in the mix I'm sure.

So, in short, I answered Toby, 'If I have children yes, I'd want them, but if I don't it wouldn't be the end of the world.'

'Very diplomatic of you.'

'I find life's much easier to comprehend if I believe it's outside of my control. I think if you start trying to order it, wishing for sunshine, putting words in peoples' mouths, planning to the nth degree, you end up disappointed if it doesn't pan out how you envisaged.' I'd got the bit between my teeth but I just had to finish, 'We're all so spoilt for choice now and when we don't get what we want we immediately blame it on something other than the rich pattern of existence.'

'That's all very well but sometimes life can be a real bugger. Look at Hailey. If she hadn't been staying with Archie for the weekend she might still be alive, that comes down to a simple yes or no to an invitation.'

'As sad and tragic as her death is I like to think it was outside of her control and that she died young for a reason unbeknown to us.'

'Jesus Susie, that's a tough line to take.'

'I don't mean it as harshly as it comes across, I just think for our own rationale it helps to believe there's a heavenly afterlife beyond all of this and some people deserve to get there quicker.'

'I doubt my mind will ever expand to that depth of comprehension but it's a nice way of looking at it.' Toby gave me a gentle admiring smile and switched on the car radio. Upon hearing the poem being recited on air, Toby's childish grin knocked twenty years off him. Afterwards, he explained that it was 'Sir Smasham Uppe by E.V. Rieu.'

'That's fantastic.' I loved it. 'What a great poem.'

'Isn't it? I learnt it as a boy, it was my first introduction to porcelain,' said Toby, relaxing back into the seat as we drove through Canny's gates.

26

'Wine downtime,' I announced as we got out of the car and Toby made a dash into the house to check on dinner.

The kitchen smelt as delicious as his arms looked when they tensed under the weight of the cast-iron pot he was lifting out of the oven.

'Yummee!' I exclaimed. Then, just as I turned to go upstairs, in need of a pee, Lucy's landline rang.

'Hello?'

'Susie dear?'

'Oh, hi Daniel.'

'I hope I'm not disturbing you?'

'No, not at all.' I looked at Toby. He was staring straight through me, his inscrutable face suggesting he might be a teeny-weeny bit jealous of Daniel's communication with me.

'I wanted to thank you for making me confess.' Daniel sounded full of glee. 'I'm no longer a key suspect.'

'That's great news, I'm so pleased for you.'

'Have you heard?' he said.

'Heard what?' I asked knowing it was indiscreet of me to be talking down Lucy's telephone like this, but she wasn't here so, for the time being, it was safe enough.

'The investigators found a blond hair on the lampshade in Hailey's room so that's narrowed it down to Archie or Primrose apparently.'

'Archie or Primrose?' I exclaimed. 'I'm very surprised they told you that.'

'Archie told me. He was called to the station on account of his hair colour and as I'm fortunately not blond I'm no longer a key suspect.'

'I see,' I said with the thought that Daniel was wasting my time. I had blonde hair and no one had called me in.

'I tell you Susie, it wasn't Archie.'

'You think it was Primrose?' I retaliated.

'I like to presume Hailey died of natural causes and that the hair is a false lead, although a most mysterious revelation.'

'Daniel,' I said, responsibility having got the better of me, 'I think I should give you my mobile number for future calls. This telephone belongs to the girl I'm lodging with.'

'I'm awfully sorry about that. Archie told me where you were staying so I looked up the number in the book. I never presumed you weren't in your own digs. Not to worry though, I'm leaving Norfolk, off on a trip to Sicily at the end of the week so you won't be hearing from me again.'

'Never?' I said sarcastically.

'Never say never! But farewell for now.'

He hung up, leaving no time for me to say goodbye or work out why on earth he'd stayed at Fontaburn so long. Blimey, I thought, perhaps Archie and Daniel really are more than just good friends.

'That's a hotline to you,' said Toby as I replaced the receiver.

'It was Daniel again.'

'What did he want?'

'He told me a blond hair had been found on Hailey's lampshade and therefore Archie and Primrose are now the only key suspects.'

'And you?' he said without missing a beat. 'On account of the hair colour?'

'It's absurd.' I pulled a chair out from the table and sat down. 'I reckon he just wanted to tell me *again* that Archie didn't do it.'

'I reckon this investigation is going to end up driving you nuts.'

'But why did Daniel ring *me*?'

'Oh, I don't know,' Toby rested his hand on my shoulder, 'I hate to see it having a negative effect on you. Please don't let Daniel get inside your head, he sounds like a pain.'

I looked up, as nice as Toby's words were they didn't stop my mind racing.

'Maybe Archie *was* in Hailey's room and if he was then it must have been Stanley who set off the alarm. But, why?'

'Come on, let's have a nice evening and stop this getting the better of you. It's not your responsibility to solve it.'

I stood up, Toby's hand withdrew, and I did my very best to reassure him. 'I'll stop tying myself in knots and put it out of my mind.'

It was insincere of me to say this as, deep down inside, I knew I *had* to keep all the clues in the forefront of my mind if I was going to solve Hailey's murder.

When I scampered upstairs saying 'I'm just nipping to the loo,' I had every intention of shutting myself in my bedroom and telephoning Sergeant Ayari.

'Thanks for calling, Susie,' came Sergeant Ayari's mellifluous tone. 'I'm still in the office and will be for a long time yet.'

'I thought I should tell you that I spoke to Daniel today.' I wanted my feigned honesty to strengthen her trust in me.

'That's very good of you to ring and tell me.'

'He told me the investigators found a blond hair on the lampshade in Hailey's room.'

'Mr Furr Egrant is absolutely right, but it hasn't ruled out any individuals thus far.'

'But I have blonde hair . . . ' Sergeant Ayari didn't know me nearly well enough to see through the panic in my voice. It had the desired effect, her discretion was compromised and she reassured me, 'The hair had Mr Wellingham's and Mrs Gerald's DNA on it.'

'How strange.'

'Not if Mrs Gerald ruffled Mr Wellingham's hair at any point over the course of the evening, or vice versa. However, the main focus of our investigation is on the concentration of oxalate in Miss Dune's system. Only once we get to the heart of this might supplementary information such as a stray hair come into play.' Sergeant Ayari's fine manner of outer professionalism and inner friendliness brought our conversation to a natural end.

I hung up and went to join my wine glass and Toby on the bench outside. He'd kicked off his shoes and his bare feet were tickling Red-Rum's tummy. It made me happy to see how at ease he was.

'Don't you just love an English summer?' he

247

said. 'It's the perfect temperature at this time of night.'

'Isn't it?' I smiled, glad he hadn't asked why I'd taken my time. 'Were you born in the West Country?'

'Yup, so I haven't moved far.'

'Well you have no need to move, it's a beautiful part of the world. I grew up in London but never wanted to settle there.'

'You say that, but sometimes I wonder if I'm missing out on a change of scene. I dream of quitting my job and moving abroad for a bit.'

'Oh,' I said with a shortness of breath. This wasn't good news for our potential relationship. 'Anywhere in particular?'

'Europe maybe or America, I've never been there.'

'Do you speak another language?'

'Nope so I guess America would be a good option.'

I smiled and my thoughts drifted to a conversation I'd had with Hailey about moving abroad. I still couldn't believe she'd quit her law training to come to London and find an English husband.

'American girls love English men,' said Toby smugly. 'I'd have a fine time in their country.'

'You'd have to love them too,' I joked.

'Only for a bit, I think I could do that.'

I gave him a reproachful look.

'You could come too,' he said.

'Is that an offer?'

'It'd be fun. We'd get a Winnebago, you'd bring your paints and I'd drive us across the continent. Think of the wonders we would see.'

'The Kentucky Derby.'

'Nashville,' added Toby.

'The Bonneville Salt Flats.'

'Grand Canyon.'

And so it went on, Toby and I travelling across America in our minds . . .

'Hoover Dam.'

'Death Valley.'

'Golden Gate Bridge!' we both exclaimed.

'How could you refuse?'

'I'm in,' I said wishing it were true.

'Oh God!' Toby jumped up and dashed into the kitchen, Red-Rum scampering after him. 'Bugger! Bugger! Bugger!'

He reappeared with a wine bottle in his hand and a grubby tea towel over his shoulder. 'I've overcooked the rice. It's a mushy mess with a burnt bottom.'

I consoled him, 'It's too hot for rice anyway,' and stood up offering to make a green salad instead. As I pushed past him, he didn't even try to move out of the way. It was as if he wanted our bodies to touch — and the sensation was electrifying. Maybe tonight would be our night . . .

27

'Lucy,' I called out into the yard. 'Dinner's ready.'

She came bounding across the ménage, her youthful figure bouncing in all directions.

'Thanks Susie, I'm looking forward to a good feast.'

Sure enough, and having guessed already from the tempting smell, Toby had made a pot of slow-cooked pork in a delicious marinade. We ate in the kitchen with the door open and the sound of birds rejoicing at the length of the days.

'How was the museum?' asked Lucy.

'You didn't miss much,' said Toby. 'Some lovely porcelain and a lot of dusky old photographs.'

'Susie's fair treating you,' said Lucy facetiously. 'There's way more interesting places than that around here.'

It annoyed me to be put down in front of Toby, but when he replied 'We'll just have to come back and visit you again,' I was thrilled he'd coupled us together as a pair.

'Are you off then?' asked Lucy. My heart sunk. I'd told Toby I was leaving on Thursday but hadn't actually asked him when he planned to go and I was still under the illusion that these happy days were going to go on and on.

'If it's okay, I thought I'd leave on Thursday like Susie.'

'No problem,' said Lucy looking as happy as I felt.

'You really don't mind if we stay till then? I've actually finished working with the horses but I'd love a free day to get my stuff together and have a breather before heading back to the grind-stone.'

I didn't want to take advantage of Lucy's hospitality but I knew if I could just stay another twenty-four hours I'd have a much better chance of getting to the bottom of Hailey's death. Other than Charlotte no one in the house party had known Hailey long enough to pre-plan her murder, and Charlotte's emotional response was either exceptional acting or as genuine as I believed it to be. The whole thing had a whiff of improvisation to it and I felt confident that if I could buy a little more time to identify the motive I'd uncover the truth.

'Please stay till Thursday,' smiled Lucy. 'I'm not ready to be on my own again. I'm going to miss your company.'

'If Aidan wants me to drop off the drawings in person I'll be back again relatively soon.'

Lucy had her mouth full but it didn't stop her from talking, 'I hope he does, it'd be nice to see you again Susie.'

'Well, as a thank-you for having me *and* Toby to stay, please can I cook dinner tomorrow night?'

'You two are spoiling me. Never eaten so well in my life. Kitchen's all yours if you mean it.'

'Great, I'll do us all a celebratory feast.'

Lucy asked if I'd mind making something with

251

the lump of beef she had in the freezer.

'Martin, the farmer across the way, gave it me and I've no idea what to do with it.'

'That was generous of him,' said Toby, and Lucy blushed for the first time ever.

When she explained, 'It was a nice try on his part, but he's got a wife,' I was pleased to hear she drew the line somewhere.

After dinner, I was first to bed and I was wearing the green willow. Once again Toby and Lucy had hit it off. She had that youthful ability to flirt outrageously no matter what the consequences and Toby (understandably) was enjoying every bit of it.

I'd tried my very best to laugh along and join in, but, in truth, the opportunity to go to bed without making it a 'thing' couldn't come quickly enough.

It was at last, when Toby offered us both another glass of whisky and Lucy jumped at the offer, that I apologised with 'I'm so sorry to be such a party pooper but I'm exhausted,' and said an early goodnight to them both.

I collapsed onto my bed with my telephone in my hands. I had three missed calls from Mum. A clear sign she was longing for a gossip rather than needing to speak to me urgently. If it was the latter she would have left a message, I knew that much. I didn't want to but I *had* to ring her. It was unfair not to report back on how my night at Fontaburn Hall had gone.

'Hi Mum.'

'Susie, darling.' She was already out of character. Usually I was poppet or sweetie, none of this Darling with a capital D. 'Hang on a sec, I'm just going to go downstairs, don't want to wake your father.'

'I can call in the morning,' I suggested but she'd hung up the receiver (wireless telephones are not something my parents are aware of).

'Susie? Susie? Are you still there?'

'Yes, Mum, sorry to call late, I've been very busy.'

'HOW was the weekend? I've been LONGING to hear? I do hope you wore the necklace I sent you? You are naughty not to have given me a buzz.'

Mum had that maternal knack of going straight from slumber to fully alert. No intermediate waking-up period. A trait instilled in women after their first-born.

'I enjoyed myself,' I said as I twiddled a stray thread from the duvet.

'Did you poppet? I'm so pleased. Were there lots of others staying? Any nice young men?'

'None my type but all very nice.' I listed the guests, each one prompting an interjection from Mum.

'How nice for you there was an American girl amongst them. They're so good at breaking up a stuffy atmosphere. I hear Archibald has a lot going for him.'

'He lives in a beautiful house.'

'Yes, I got Silvia,' (Silvia's my mother's young cleaner) 'to pull up a picture on the Google, absolutely beautiful house I agree but it's not the family seat, now that's quite something.'

'Yes, Mum. I see you've done your research.'

To give Mum her due she was as good at being teased as she was at admitting her own flaws.

'Susie,' she said. 'I do like to live vicariously through you. It's natural; you'll be just the same when you have children of your own.'

'Maybe,' I said, hoping not.

'When will we be seeing you next?'

This was my mother's subtle way of saying it had been some time since my last visit.

'I was thinking I could come up for the day and stay the night next Sunday?' I did want to see them but I also thought if I was there for the night it would be a good opportunity to ask her in person why I was an only child.

'This Sunday would be better.'

My parents rarely have plans and if they do they are hardly ever made over a week in advance. This Sunday, I knew, was better only because it was sooner.

'I have Mel staying this weekend.'

Mum liked Mel. Mel had married young, a banker with good looks and good connections, and Mum continued to hope her life would rub off on mine.

'Next Sunday it is,' she said sounding happy. 'We can eat in the garden; it's been wonderful weather here. I hope the drawings are going well? It's a big commission this one, isn't it?'

Mum had asked after my work! Maybe after fifteen years she's finally come around to the fact I would always be and only ever wanted to be an artist.

'Yes, I have six horses to draw, it's been tough

but I've finally got enough material.'

'Horses, that's a new one for you,' said Mum, making me sad she had no recollection that I'd talked her through the struggle of horses before.

'Clever girl. Sleep well.'

'Bye, I love you,' I said but she'd hung up, never one to linger after getting what she wanted.

I sunk back into my pillow, the thread of the duvet coming loose in my hand.

A thread! *The* thread. I shot up to sitting, my upper body stiff against the headboard. I'd picked a burgundy thread off Hailey's door. It was exactly the same colour as Charlie's V-neck jumper. The one Daniel had teased him about wearing. How had I not thought about it until now and why had I been so careless with it? I have absolutely no idea where it is . . . on the corridor; stuck to an investigator's shoe; squirrelled by a mouse and now lining its nest. It's highly likely it came from Charlie's jumper as his room was practically opposite Hailey's. Had he been bed-hopping too? Charlie, the one Daniel had described as having 'issues under the carpet'.

I read a book recently called *Rain*, an autobiographical novel of a young man on tour in Afghanistan. This novel had made me painfully aware of what my contemporaries on tour in Afghanistan had been through. It also got the point across of how difficult it is for these soldiers to integrate back into society. Poor Charlie was, according to Daniel, a similar case.

I heard the stairs creak and I could tell by the

lone heavy footsteps it was Toby.

I opened my door.

'Susie,' he said. 'I thought you'd already be asleep, you looked so tired this evening.'

'I'm okay. Just looking forward to going home I guess. It's been a long week.'

'Lucy's gone out somewhere, I'm going down in a moment to make a cup of tea. Do you want one?'

'Go on then, yes please.'

'I'll bring it up.'

I hovered about in my room, first sitting in the armchair, then deciding the dressing table seat would be better and Toby could have the armchair. Time passed and I moved to the bed, yes, the bed was soft and relaxed, that'd be best. Toby came in, handed me a cup and slumped into the armchair.

'Look at us,' he said. 'Tip-toeing around someone else's house. Good call of yours to stay another day, I saw right through that.' He smiled, his blue eyes twinkling with tiredness.

'Do you have any friends in the army Toby?' It was a random question put out of context but I lacked the energy to dress it up.

'Nope.'

'Charlie from the weekend fought in Afghanistan.'

'Did he talk about it?' Toby sounded confused.

'No, others mentioned it.'

'I'm not surprised he didn't, people who've been there can suffer all sorts of psychological side effects.'

'Do you think their experience would ever

lead them to random acts of violence on their return?'

'No, I don't. But, if it did there would have to be a trigger.'

'Like what?'

'Sounds or smells can spark memories but it's flashbacks during sleep that cause disturbed states.'

'How do you know?'

'Quite a few patients in the psychiatric unit in the hospital where I work are ex-servicemen and women.'

'Poor them.'

'Susie,' Toby sounded amused, 'what are you *really* getting at?'

'I'm wondering if a mentally unstable person could commit a crime without having any memory of having done so?'

'And . . . ?' Toby wasn't fooled by my straightforward expression and I knew now I had to be careful: he was getting to know me almost too well. There'd be no wool left to pull over his eyes if ever I needed to.

'Charlie's bedroom was almost opposite Hailey's and I found a thread from his jumper on her doorframe . . . '

'Definitely his jumper?' interrupted Toby.

'Yes, I'm sure. Daniel told me Charlie had issues and had been covering them up with gak.'

'Daniel's one big wooden spoon.'

I smiled at Toby. Maybe Daniel was a stirrer but I was far more interested in knowing if Charlie could have had an episode and done something to Hailey without knowing he had.

'I see where you're going with this.' Toby smiled. 'If you'd said heroin I'd have supported your theory, but cocaine more often makes people lovey-dovey or incredibly chatty, but rarely violent.'

'What about absinthe? Couldn't it have made Charlie hallucinate and induced a psychotic state?'

'That's so last century. No one now believes it corrupts minds. You must know the painting *L'Absinthe* by Degas?'

'Yes.' I knew the painting well, 'It's in the Musée d'Orsay,' which is somewhere I often visit on my Parisian lingerie sprees.

'Well, you'll agree then that the woman with the glass of absinthe in front of her and the indisputable blank expression doesn't look ready to commit murder, does she?'

'No!' I said, my voice full of glee that Toby had good art know-how. 'But, how, then, did Charlie's jumper get on Hailey's doorframe?'

'He probably went corridor creeping too.'

'But, if his jumper snagged he must have been leaving her room in a hurry.'

'Or he snagged it by mistake. But either way, Susie, you're forgetting the calcium oxalate in her urine.'

'We all know there's far too much oxalate in Hailey's system,' I said, rather disgruntled by Toby's narrow-mindedness, 'but maybe there was something else that killed her, or also killed her. Charlie could have suffocated Hailey.'

Toby seemed more interested in the writing on his mug of tea than me.

'Do you think I should tell DCI Reynolds about the thread?'

'Your decision, Susie.'

This was unhelpful.

'I'll sleep on it then.'

'Oh, okay.' Toby immediately stood up, 'I'm sorry, I'll leave you now. Goodnight Susie.'

Rubbish!

★ ★ ★

I got into bed with my computer. I wasn't ready to put psychotic fits to sleep yet. Google would have to guide me from here on in.

Psychotic disorder: a sudden onset of psychotic symptoms, which may include delusions, hallucinations, disorganised speech or behaviour, or catatonic behaviour. Lasting anything from tens of seconds to several minutes these fits are spontaneous and dangerous. Patients who become detached from reality during these episodes can go on to cause severe crimes which, when out of the fit, leave them with no recollection that they did.

Bingo! If Charlie fell asleep fully clothed (or at least with his top half on) and had a flashback to Afghanistan, it could have sparked a psychotic episode. Whilst in this state he might have set off on a mission to harm the first person he came across, as in next down the corridor: incapacitated-by-drink-Hailey. Charlie's military training would have given him the skills to carry out suffocation or worse, as swiftly and silently as possible. He could have snagged his jumper on her doorframe on the way in or out. And, according to this description, he may well have absolutely no idea he'd done so.

Even *I* knew this theory was far-fetched but if I shared it with DCI Reynolds first thing tomorrow his reaction might just tell me something I don't know. And, if Sergeant Ayari was having a late night, maybe there really would be fresh news for me in the morning.

28

I woke very early from the combination of excessive heat and a scrum of semi-conscious disturbed thoughts. A large part of me wanted to call DCI Reynolds and tell him about the burgundy thread. But, it was too early so I sent a text instead.

Hello, it's Susie Mahl, please can we speak when it's convenient, I have something I'd like to run past you. Thank you.

The new day was calling me outside and not wanting to disturb the others I skipped showering, put on my summer dress from Saturday, the one pretty outfit Toby hadn't seen yet, and tiptoed downstairs all set for an adventure.

Red-Rum was curled up in his basket in the kitchen and when he looked at me as if to say 'what are you doing up?' I thought I really should nip back upstairs and slip a note under Toby's door. It was only fair to tell him where I'd gone.

Hi Toby,
   Call me when you get this and we'll make a plan. I woke early so have gone shopping.
   Susie x

This was half-true. I needed to pick up a few ingredients for dinner but I didn't want to tell

261

him I was also going to Mass.

If I miss a Sunday service I like to try and make up for it in the week and I knew that, today, being in church would be a good place to clear my thoughts. With only twenty-four hours left in Norfolk the pressure was on to get my ducks in a row.

Moments after I was in the car my telephone rang.

'Hello Inspector.' I had him on the loud-speaker.

'Hello Susie.' He sounded surprisingly cheery for an early morning detective in the thick of a murder investigation. 'What do you have to tell me?'

'I forgot to mention I found a burgundy thread on Hailey's bedroom doorframe the morning of her death. It caught my eye and I plucked it off.'

'Is that all?'

'I think it's . . . '

DCI Reynolds interrupted me, 'I've got very good news Susie. You've beat me to it. I was waiting for a reasonable hour to call and tell you that late last night we were able to put a close to Miss Dune's case.'

This news punched me in the stomach.

'You've been a huge help to us all here and I'm very grateful for your willingness to co-operate.'

What I minded most of all was their solving the case without any vital input from me. It did nothing at all to help build my reputation as an amateur detective. A role I'd unashamedly been basking in recently.

When I asked what the outcome was DCI Reynolds replied in a wonderfully good temper, 'Quite simple in the end — although your telling us about the man in the striped jim-jams is what sped the whole thing up.' (I gave myself a very small pat on the back.) 'As soon as we'd diagnosed cause of death our tangential man in the striped pyjamas came clean.'

There was no time for me to interject, as DCI Reynolds was on a roll. 'One of the worst parts of these types of investigations, Susie, is suspecting innocent people who remain innocent all along. Thank goodness we didn't take up that glass of water with Mrs Ramsbottom. I would never have been able to forgive myself for causing her more upset.'

'I can only imagine,' I said, catching my brow furrowing in the visor mirror.

'We were wrong about murder, something I'm sorry about but couldn't have dismissed without the information we now have. Poor Miss Dune died of a very rare type of kidney stones that secreted an excessively abnormal amount of calcium oxalate.'

I couldn't believe it. I didn't believe it. Hailey only had stones in one kidney and Toby had assured me that wouldn't have killed her.

'Are you *sure*?'

'Absolutely certain.'

Toby *must* have missed something.

'Mr Wellingham,' said DCI Reynolds, 'was in Miss Dune's bed.'

I'd guessed as much.

'He was unable to wake Miss Dune and it was at this point he realised she was in fact dead.'

DCI Reynolds didn't go into any details, jumping straight to the point that, 'Mr Wellingham was afraid of being accused of killing Miss Dune. Full of panic he came to, in my opinion, the ludicrous conclusion that the quickest way to get help without being suspected was to set off the burglar alarm.'

'*What?*' I was shocked.

'Yes indeed, it is an unbelievable chain of events. Mr Wellingham crept past the Duke, fast asleep in the armchair as he said he was, into the billiard room and, hauling himself up onto the window ledge, he set off the alarm.'

'That's who I saw?'

'Yes, I think so, and in turn it was Mrs Mapperton who seemingly first found her friend dead. It's amazing,' said DCI Reynolds, 'what people think they have to do in order not to be unjustly accused. A lot of my time and resources have been wasted over the past week and I only wish a man as honourable as Mr Wellingham thought to tell the truth from the very beginning.'

I couldn't get my head around Archie's inhumane behaviour. What type of person wouldn't call an ambulance immediately if they thought someone was dead? And who would put themselves first, concerned they might be accused of killing the poor girl? It was staggeringly selfish and unbelievably cowardly. Did DCI Reynolds honestly believe it?

'He must have been absolutely certain she was

stone dead,' I said, it being the only vaguely reasonable explanation for Archie's actions.

'Yes, he assures us that she was and that much I believe.'

To me, Daniel's insistence that Archie didn't do it meant he'd been privy to the truth all along and I jolly well hope he would have spoken out if one of the rest of us had been accused of murder.

'Now, what did you want to put past me Susie?'

'I thought the thread I found on Hailey's doorframe came from Charlie's jumper.'

'Oh yes, you told me you'd found a thread. Rest assured Miss Dune died of kidney stones but just for your peace of mind, Charlie Letterhead confessed to calling in on Miss Dune in the early hours of the morning but on seeing Mr Wellingham already in her bed he rapidly retreated.'

'My goodness,' was all I had to say, although inside I felt mildly offended no one had attempted to jump into my bed.

'We've all been let down, Susie. I feel the same disappointment as you but at least we've got to the bottom of it. Thank you for your input, I'm so glad to have met you in person.'

'I just wish I'd been more help.'

'You were a great help. Don't underestimate yourself, you have a keen eye for detail. I'll never forget your description of Miss Dune's bedroom, quite the best memory I've ever come across.'

'Thank you.'

'Thank *you*, Susie. All the best and bye for now.'

'Bye.'

I immediately felt like pulling a handbrake turn and rushing back to tell Toby the news, but with St Cuthbert's Culhead in view I craved the peace and quiet of a church.

29

Eight thirty wasn't unusual for a weekday Mass, but there were many more people in the congregation of this largish country church than I'd expected. Fair enough, most were of the age of people looking for things to fill their few remaining days on earth, and then there were the usual goodie-two-shoes, short men and in-your-face women who'd only be missing if a meals-on-wheels volunteer had called in sick.

I filed in and sat near the back. It was nice to catch the breeze coming through the open door. There was no music but thankfully the priest's tuneful voice carried the rest of ours along.

He greeted us with open arms, 'The grace of our Lord Jesus Christ, and the love of God, and the communion of the Holy Spirit be with you all.'

'And with your spirit,' we solemnly said.

'Brothers and sisters, let us acknowledge our sins, and so prepare ourselves to celebrate the sacred mysteries.' His eyes dipped to the altar with a brief pause for silence and my attention was caught by a blond mass of shaggy hair a couple of pews in front of me. The figure beneath it appeared youthful in comparison to the majority of the congregation.

The priest's head rose and loud and clear we recited together, 'I confess to almighty God and to you, my brothers and sisters, that I have greatly sinned, in my thoughts and in my words, in what I have done and in what I have failed to do.' Striking our breasts, we said, 'Through my fault, through my fault, through my most grievous fault.'

BANG! The church door shut in a gust of wind and my shoulders shot up with fright, although my eyes remained focused on the youngish man in front of me. His head swivelled . . . it was Archie! He was staring back towards the door. I was completely stunned — I'd automatically assumed that his family were Protestant.

I just about managed to join in on the tail end of The Absolution with an 'Amen'. But that was all. I heard none of the Penitential Act. With Archie in view, my head was flooding with fresh memories of all the theories I'd had about the weekend.

The priest's voice took on an almost silent tone when not singing. He muffled the gospel into his dog collar with his head so heavily bowed I doubt he'd notice if we all got up and left. I stared vacantly at Archie's back. So far I don't think he'd noticed me.

Blond hair, that's what they found on Hailey's lampshade. The very same skew-whiff lampshade I'd noticed. All of which made sense if Archie was in her bed but the DNA matched Archie and Primrose and what if it was Primrose . . . There would be no logical explanation for that.

The Lord's Prayer rolled off my tongue, and the words, 'Safe from all distress,' in the priest's embolism struck me: was Hailey's murderer still on the loose?

'Peace be with you,' was upon us. I smiled sweetly at the old man behind me who had the only hand close enough to shake. He looked as uncomfortable as I always feel at this moment in a modern service.

Back on our knees, I began to worry that the forensic pathologists had come to the wrong conclusion. And if I am the only person who doubts the diagnosis then I am the only one (and maybe Toby once I've filled him in) who will be pursuing this.

In unconventional form the priest brought communion up the aisle, stopping at the end of the pews to serve those of us filing out. As a result there was no chance of Archie's path crossing mine.

I prayed on my knees for my family and friends then asked with all my heart for clarity and forgiveness.

'Go forth, the Mass is ended,' said the priest.

I waited in my pew so as I could try to catch Archie's eye when he came past. He looked up and a flicker of surprise grasped his expression as he registered my presence.

'Susie Mahl!' he said with gusto on the porch steps, excusing himself from courteous old women wanting to say hello. As he greeted me with the posho's kiss on both cheeks I admired this uncharacteristic confidence I was seeing in him — he was playing his role of squire with aplomb.

'Come,' he said leading me up the path of the

graveyard, the narrowness of it pushing us close together. 'I'm so glad to have bumped into you,' Archie smiled. 'I want to apologise for all that kerfuffle over the weekend. What you must think of my rabble of reprobates.'

'Not at all,' I said. 'It was so kind of you to include me,' and then catching my breath, not wanting to waste this golden opportunity, I added, 'Poor, poor Hailey. What a way to go.'

Archie paused. 'You *have* heard, haven't you?' his voice was chastened. 'DCI Reynolds assured me he'd be in touch with you all.'

'Yes, it's just so sad she died.'

'She was such fun wasn't she?'

'Yes,' I said. 'Had you known each other long?'

'No, not at all, Charlotte brought her to the party; none of the rest of us had ever met her before.'

'Oh gosh, how awful.'

'Yes, poor Lotty, although she's much better now she knows there's nothing any of us could have done.'

Archie stopped to let me through the gate in front of him.

'Are you rushing off?' he asked.

'I don't have to.'

'Well, if you've time why not come back to the Hall for coffee. I'd rather like to discuss you drawing Yin and Yang?'

'Oh, how great! Yes, please. I'll follow you in my car.'

'Marvellous.'

Soon after we were on our way Radio 4 cut out to my telephone ringing over the loudspeaker.

'Hello?'

'Hi Susie.' It was Toby. 'Thanks for the note. I've been out for the count. Stayed up far too late reading my book.'

'That's okay. You'll never guess what, I've just bumped into Archie.'

'In the supermarket?'

'No. I'll explain later but do you mind if I have a quick cup of coffee? I won't be long.'

'With him? Are you *sure* you want to go alone?'

'Oh, yeah, I'm sorry, I never said did I? They've closed Hailey's case.'

'What? Who?'

'DCI Reynolds. I spoke to him this morning. He says Hailey died from a very rare type of kidney stones that produced an excessive amount of calcium oxalate.'

'Enough to kill her?'

'Apparently, but I don't believe it.'

'It'll be true if they said so.'

'But, Toby, you didn't think so.'

'I'm not a nephrologist but I can't honestly believe it from the findings I saw, which makes me think there must have been other tests or another report.'

'What happens if there wasn't?'

'There must have been.'

'Maybe the medics wanted a quick conclusion?'

'Impossible, the compliance department would have pulled them up.'

Archie's Land Rover indicated left.

'Toby I'm going to have to go, I'm sorry, we're

about to arrive at the Hall.'

'Just quickly,' he said, 'I was thinking we could go to the beach at some point today, are you keen?'

'I'd love that; I'll be back as soon as I can.'

I hung up, thrilled at the thought of swimming in the sea. Only last night was I regretting the fact I hadn't made time for it.

30

Archie turned over a brick under the belladonna plant and unlocked his front door. I was half expecting a déjà vu of Daniel standing on the doorstep but he was no longer here. Yin and Yang rushed out, their nails clipping the paving stones as they made for the lawn.

'It's such a beautiful day,' said Archie. 'Let's sit in the garden, there's a table over there, I'll bring the coffee out.'

'Okay.'

I was a little put out he didn't want me in the house but I can be oversensitive at times so maybe there was nothing in it. Both his dogs were sniffing and snuffling around me, yet another visitor in a long week of investigative intrusion. And as their excessive curiosity kept them close by, I sat down at the round cast-iron table, and did a very quick sketch of each.

'Can I have a look?' said Archie laying down a tray.

'It's only a preliminary drawing.' I turned the page for him to see. 'I've never noticed it before but a lurcher's posture almost echoes a racehorse's.'

I was hoping Archie was going to continue the point, me having done my very best to introduce racehorses into the conversation but instead he said, 'I'm sorry we never got to discuss your art properly on Saturday evening.'

He began pouring a detestable-looking murky brown liquid into two porcelain cups. Poor Archie really must be at a loss without his staff — coffee obviously no longer has instructions on the packet.

'Milk?' he asked holding up a small elegant jug with, yes, the Norland family crest on it.

'No, thank you.'

'So, Susie, let us say I'd possibly like you to draw Yin and Yang, how would you go about it?'

Archie's non-committal approach is one I'm quite used to amongst aristocratic clients. Old families often suggest they're short on spare cash, keeping their cards close to their chest. I knew Archie would bite in the end, they always do once I let on how lucky *I* am to be drawing *their* pet.

I talked him through my terms of business. 'I'd come here and spend a happy three hours minimum with your beautiful dogs, taking photographs, sketching and hanging out, getting a feeling for their characters and how they move. I would then get back in touch with you when I've finished the drawings.'

'I see, that's how it works is it, or do you sometimes draw on the spot?'

'I do lots of sketches on the spot but I always finish the final picture at home. It helps not to have the owner-looking over my shoulder.'

'I can completely understand that.' Archie's deliberately enchanting smile was on full display. 'Now, you mentioned draw-*ings*. Does that mean you'd do two separate pictures? I'd much prefer them to be together in one.'

'No, I could definitely draw them together. It would make a really nice picture, Yin being so black and Yang so light.'

'Okay, great. Now, how are we going to portray them?'

Anyone creative knows the one thing you can't do is 'tell' an artist how you want the picture to be. If it was this easy we'd all be churning out perfect portraits. But, no, we have to wait for the spark — a flick of a tail, a pause of a paw — this then dictates the characterful pose.

'To be completely straightforward,' I said, 'I can't draw truthfully unless I'm left to decide the pose and composition, on the agreement you only pay if you're happy with the final picture. Absolutely no hard feelings if not.'

'That sounds a good deal to me. Can we agree on it?'

Oh heck! I couldn't realistically afford to turn down two dog portraits but I really didn't want to tie myself into a commission with Archie just yet. First, I wanted to be convinced Hailey wasn't murdered, and right now, although alone in it, I wasn't.

I flicked through my sketchbook as if it doubled up as a diary, giving myself time to figure out how to show willing without committing.

'I'd really love to draw spritely Yin and adorable Yang but I have a lot on my plate at the minute. Would it be at all possible for me to visit you when I return with Mr McCann's horses, probably in about ten weeks or so?'

'Of course,' came his welcome reply. 'Whatever works for you. I'm in no rush.'

Archie took a final sip of coffee and then, as if it had just popped into his head, which undoubtedly it hadn't — him being a successful businessman in his own right — he said, 'I suppose I should ask how much you charge?'

'I have a flat fee per pet, not per drawing. Here,' I got a card out of my wallet, 'it's all on this, travel is charged on top.'

'What a marvellous painting that is,' he said looking at the front of it and I decided maybe Archie did have taste after all.

'Thank you,' I smiled. 'It's a parasol in Tuscany.'

'Oh yes, of course, blue are the hills that are far away.' He looked up and the intensity in his eyes flushed me with awkwardness. 'This painting has a calm nature I've rarely seen in contemporary art.'

Not one bit of me wanted to discuss the personal nature of my work with Archie. I *had* to divert the conversation but all the topics that came springing into mind were far too bold: Catholicism; his setting off the burglar alarm; how long Daniel had stayed; had he ever heard of these rare kidney stones; his family museum . . . Yes, his family museum: this was the crux of the knot in my tongue, I knew too much about Archie to ask anything at all.

I've only ever been in this position once before, when I won a competition that led to a day's drawing in the Royal Collection. In the afternoon, there was a drinks reception and I found myself in a room with the next in line to the throne. Not wanting to miss the opportunity of speaking to him I hovered on the outskirts of the sycophantic crowd, waiting for my moment of introduction. When I eventually got to the front I was absolutely lost for words. I knew so much about this man, whether truth or speculation, and he didn't know me from Adam. With a glass of champagne in my hand I envied what was in his and found myself asking, 'Where did you get your cup of tea from?'

How embarrassing is that!

The attentive waitress rushed off at his request and as we waited for her return the Prince spoke to me about my career with genuine interest, taking the time to engage and be supportive, something I'll never forget.

Now, as I forced down one final sip of filthy coffee I drew attention to the family crest on the saucer.

'Yes, that boar would frighten off the riff-raff,' said Archie. 'I've always wished my family would do away with the rose so as his head would have more space but it's bad luck to tamper with one's crest so we're stuck with this curly confusion.'

'Is the rose a symbol of England?'

'Ah ha! My father would tell you that but in fact there's more to it.' Archie gave an insinuating chuckle, gosh he was in a good mood, and I put it down to relief from the kidney stones verdict. He went on, 'According to the oral history that's come down through my ancestors Henry VIII took a shine to my great, great, great, great,' I smiled as Archie spelt it out, 'great, great, great, great, grandmamma and allusions to this are weaved into our family's crest.' With excitement he pushed the tray to one side. 'If you look here,' he pointed at the centrepiece of the table, 'it's seen better days but this is the Norland coat of arms.'

'Oh yes, look at that,' I exclaimed, as if seeing it for the first time.

'The red rose can be a symbol of love and desire and the acacia leaves stand for eternal and affectionate remembrance.' He pointed at the different elements, explaining them with a fluency that obviously comes with the title.

'No one actually knows,' he said, lifting his head, smiling at me, 'if my grandmamma in question was a mistress to the King. But, I like to think she was, although my father won't hear any mention of it.'

With a sudden burst of daring confidence, I asked him when his family reverted back to Catholicism.

'With me,' he answered proudly. 'Although I didn't instigate it. When my dear mama gave birth, she longed for her little boy, me, to be christened a Catholic. She got her way with my father by saying it would be our family's way of revenging the infidelity in the past.'

'And your father agreed?'

'Let's just say my father likes to please my mother so he didn't stand in her way.'

Wow, Archie's mother had it easy.

'Probably like you,' he said, 'I was making up today for having missed Mass on Sunday.'

'Yes,' I smiled at him, us having found an isolated patch of common ground.

'More coffee?' he held up the cafetière.

'No, thank you. One cup's enough for me. By the way, I bumped into Primrose and Stanley at Ingle races on Monday.'

'How amusing. I used to watch my horse race there.'

'Did you co-own it with Victoria Ramsbottom's husband?'

'I did indeed. It makes me sad to think about it. Poor Vicky is really suffering. I didn't realise quite how much until she rang yesterday to apologise for leaving early on Saturday night.'

'Did something upset her?'

'She found a photograph of her husband and awash with emotion she borrowed it to copy. Didn't want to have to explain in front of you all so she rushed off home. It's no wonder the pudding was forgotten.'

'How incredibly sad,' I said, longing to believe this really was why she left early.

'Isn't it?' said Archie. 'Having been friendly with her husband I feel protective of Vicky, alone and in need of income, which is why I employed her to cook at the weekend. I'm hoping the Geralds might jump on the bandwagon and give her future work.'

'Stanley and Primrose have recently moved near here, haven't they?'

'Yes, I'm so lucky one of my oldest friends came to live so close. I'm very fond of Primrose. Our families have known each other a long time.'

Archie's words made me wonder if he'd have liked to marry her. And if so, why didn't he? Surely Primrose — my friend Snoberina

279

— would have wanted to marry the Honourable Archibald Barnabas Cooke Wellingham rather than Stanley Gerald, the second son of a family who have a first name as a surname.

'What was her maiden name?'

'de Bynninge,' he said and with a terrible combination of self-congratulation and surprise I let the word 'Seriously?!' shoot out of my mouth.

'Yes. Why?' Archie challenged. 'Do you know them?'

Having dropped myself in it I saw no reason to stop, 'No, but, the de Bynninges are in business with your family, aren't they?'

'They have been for years but not any more.' Archie promptly stood up and, giving me no choice in the matter, he instructed, 'Come and see a statue I've recently bought? It's down here, in the rose garden.'

He'd left the table and was off. No great speed at that. Archie's legs were struggling with the aftermath of Saturday's spurt of exercise.

'What do you think?' he asked as I ducked under the arched arbour into a circular courtyard with an enormous, and I mean enormous, bronze hare in pride of place.

How I hadn't seen this animal protruding above the hedgerows on my tour with Daniel I do not know, but now, here it was in full view, heads above everything else. It had legs akimbo, one arm on a hip and the other rigidly protruding with phallic connotations.

This was the most skin-creepingly unattractive, anthropomorphic leporid sculpture I'd ever seen. And having learnt the hard way in life that a difference of opinion with most people is taken as a personal criticism, I knew, when Archie asked, 'What do you think?', it was in fact a rhetorical question. All I had to do was agree. But, I find it impossible not to say what I'm thinking or at least not do injustice to what I'm thinking.

So, no matter how bad it was I decided to crack a joke in reply, 'Where's he off to?'

Archie laughed. 'I like that! He's headed for the hills.'

And as we turned back the way we'd come I avoided pointing out that Norfolk has no hills.

'Do you own a greenhouse?' I asked.

'Not here, Susie. You sound just like Daniel. He's always nagging at me to get one. He thinks it's more likely I'd get permission to grow the seeds he wants to bring back from China.'

'Why is Daniel so keen on plants?'

'He's bonkers about Chinese medicine and consequently a right botany bore.' Archie's feet attempted to speed up. 'I'm afraid Susie, I must be getting on but it's been lovely to see you.'

'Thank you for asking me to draw your dogs. It's very kind of you.'

'Don't mention it, I'm pleased you'd like to.'

Archie pulled open with a squeak the small decorative gate into the yard and told me how glad he was that we'd bumped into each other. 'I'm particularly pleased,' he said, 'I've had the opportunity to apologise for the very sad death at the weekend and all the investigation fuss you've been wrapped up in. I'm so sorry.'

We've been wrapped up in because of *you*, is

what I thought. Archie the man in the stripy pyjamas who'd wasted everyone's time by not having the decency to admit straightaway that Hailey was dead. I wasn't willing to accept his apology and grasped the moment to ask, 'Why didn't you call an ambulance as soon as you realised Hailey was dead?'

Crisp and clear Archie replied, 'I set off the alarm to get help as soon as possible without any of my visitors being held accountable.'

And there it was, the first glimpse I'd had of Archibald the Chief Executive Officer, the authoritative tone in his voice, seeing me on my way. And as I sailed down his drive, I wondered to myself why the thought that one of us would've been held accountable had ever crossed his mind.

31

Toby looked up from the bench outside Lucy's as he heard my car arrive.

'Where on earth did you bump into Archibald Wellingham?' he said snapping his book shut and jumping up.

'I went to Mass,' I said, no longer holding back now I was here to witness his reaction.

'You're as bad as my mother. She's forever going to Mass. You'd think she had a stream of sins.'

Phew, Toby hadn't winced at the mention of religion and even better, he didn't crack a bad joke about Catholics. I don't have strong views on what others believe or whether they believe at all but I would find it difficult to be with someone who belittled my faith. It's something I'm private about, but it is important to me.

'What on earth was a Wellingham doing in a Catholic church?'

'Great isn't it? First Catholic heir since the sixteenth century. Archie's mother is a Catholic.'

'That's so funny and absolutely typical of you to have bumped into him in such highly unlikely circumstances.'

'Isn't it? Hey, what's that book you're reading?'

'Do you know it? It's excellent.'

Toby handed it to me but I'd never seen or heard of it before.

'It's translated from French. All about a nanny who isn't as innocent and perfect as she seems. I'm very nearly finished so I'll lend it to you before you go.'

'My friend Sam wouldn't like that.'

'What?'

'You lending me a book. He feels sorry for authors. It's one less sale of very few sales nowadays.'

'What about libraries then?'

'I think he'd say they're just as bad for not buying in bulk any more.'

'Your friend Sam sounds a bit of a naysayer,' said Toby in a rather irritating tone.

'No, he's not, I'm painting him in a bad light, he's great and knows more than anyone I've ever met.'

Toby's eyebrows rose as his chest puffed out and he grew at least an inch.

'Other than you, of course! Is Lucy here?'

'No, you're the first person I've seen all morning. Are you on for the sea?'

'Absolutely, I love swimming in the sea but do you mind if I sort out a few things for dinner first?'

'Not at all.'

I put the kettle on and got tonight's lump of beef out of the fridge. It had thawed and left a pool of watery blood in its dish. Toby started prodding it.

'Oh *blast*,' I moaned. 'With all that's happened this morning I completely forgot to go shopping.'

'Never mind, we're bound to pass a shop on

our way to the beach.'

Toby watched carefully as I cut the encasing fat from the bulk of the meat and put it in a casserole dish.

'Aren't you going to brown it first?' he sounded confused.

'Nope, I don't believe in browning, I think it dries meat out.'

'I've never heard that.'

'If you stick to recipes you won't have. I like to go my own way and I only ever take other people's advice when they've made something really tasty.'

'You must have been impossible to teach.'

'Probably, but I always put in extra time to work things out for myself.'

'That's a long way to go about learning.'

'Yes, but it gives me a thorough understanding of how things work, which then allows me to do what I love doing: trying to find a better and more efficient way.' I smiled at Toby as if to say even if I fail it doesn't stop me.

Toby sat down at the kitchen table and began flicking through the local parish magazine. It annoyed me he hadn't asked about Hailey's closed case *or* coffee with Archie. I was longing to tell him, but I wanted him to volunteer an interest.

By the time I'd cut up an onion, chopped garlic, searched the kitchen for any dregs of red wine, placed it all in the pot, covered it with water from the kettle and put it on the hob to boil, he *still* hadn't said a thing.

I couldn't wait any longer. 'Toby?'

'Yes?' he looked up motionless as if the only thing he wanted to hear was 'it's time to go,' and other than that reading the magazine would get him through.

'Could Hailey really have died of kidney stones?'

'Yes,' he said, his head remaining steady as a cucumber.

'Honestly? Even though you said she didn't when I showed you the autopsy?'

'There must have been another autopsy if the police have closed the case — and I really think you should leave it all behind you. Curiosity killed the cat you know and I think if you keep digging around, you'll blacken your reputation.'

My face fell and he immediately got up, crossed the kitchen, tapped me on the shoulder and suggested we should be 'on our way'.

I didn't get it. How could he accept this conclusion just like that and forget the case altogether? I wished we could at least talk about it retrospectively and learn from our mistakes.

'Honestly,' I said, 'you think she did die of kidney stones?'

'Honestly, yes.'

Eeek he sounded cross and I really didn't want to spoil (I can hardly bear to think about it) our last day together, which is why I said, 'I'm sorry,' and left it at that.

Much to my delight, he pinched my arm and scampered upstairs leaving me waiting for the pot to boil. I stared into it, turning the ingredients with a wooden spoon, watching the water begin to burble. Little bubbles slowly popped up, *pop pop pop*, as if they were mimicking people in my mind, trying to push someone's name to the surface.

Tatiana's name quickly sunk to the bottom for the very fact it would have been easy for her to slip a poisoned mushroom into Hailey's first course and she didn't. Tatiana *could* have murdered Hailey another way but there are too many irons in the fire to introduce more. Charlotte, heavy Charlotte, was also not rising to the surface. She's Hailey's friend and the last person I'd suspect. Then there's Victoria Ramsbottom's questionable innocence simmering away, but it's going to be very difficult to prove her guilt without trampling over her vulnerable state. I longed for her to be innocent and so wanted her sudden exit to be a result of snitching the photograph frame, not placing a poisoned glass of water by Hailey's bed. George, large and slumbering, wanted to get Hailey drunk but certainly, I'm sure, didn't want to kill her. And then there's Daniel who's been hot on communication, as if enjoying the trickery of the situation. His insistence that Archie didn't do it makes me think perhaps he has an inkling of who did. Combine Primrose's family's broken business ties with the Wellinghams, and her and Daniel's reason to be jealous of Hailey, and we have two possible suspects bubbling on the surface, jostling with Archie and Stanley in their stripy pyjamas, and Charlie with his burgundy jumper.

'Right,' said Toby, giving me a fright. 'I've been looking at the map and reckon we drive directly

287

east to the beach. It's not far.'

'How wonderful,' I said scooting past him to get my stuff.

He insisted on driving, which was actually quite a relief. I was feeling the effects of having woken early and once we were in the car the breeze passing through our open windows was the only thing that stopped me from nodding off. And as I mindlessly focused on the distant horizon its uninterrupted solitariness intensified the loneliness inside me. I'm now the only one pursuing the cause of Hailey's mysterious death and with my bikini on under my dress I was looking forward to the sea taking this unsettled weight off my mind.

'Those are special,' I said alluding to Toby's very red sunglasses.

'You like them do you?' he replied, cocking his head but keeping his eyes on the road.

'They have a style of their own.'

'They're my sister's, I nabbed them off her years ago and surprisingly she's never asked for them back.'

'That is surprising,' I said with a laugh.

'Sunglasses are for posers anyway and as I don't use them for anything other than driving it makes no difference to me what they're like.'

Toby's lack of vanity gave him a good dose of old-fashioned masculinity, something I like in my men, and if it were not for the fact he was always cleanly shaven, his unruly hair would have suggested he *never* looked in a mirror.

We'd reached the coast in no time but, being Norfolk, we had a lengthy walk from the car park through sand dunes and salt marshes before reaching the sea. And by the time we did, we were both hot and eager to whip off our clothes and get straight in to the water.

There were enough other people around to lighten the atmosphere, a family of four building sandcastles and a scattering of lugworm hunters. Toby stripped down to his shorts and announced a race. But he beat me to the surf by miles. I was left behind struggling to get my dress over my head without my bikini riding up in all the wrong places.

Breaking his front crawl, he turned and waved, smiling and waiting for me to catch up. And as I waded in towards deeper water, I felt thankful that the sea was perfectly calm. I'm a real wimp when it comes to big waves and I didn't want to drop my guard this early on.

'Okay?' he asked as I swam towards him, struggling to smile without getting a mouthful of salty water.

'Isn't it bliss?' I called out between breast strokes.

'Are you up for a bit of a swim?'

'Of course.'

We set off side by side, gliding through the water, parallel to the coast, nattering almost all of the way.

'You must swim in Sussex, don't you?'

'All the time. There's a long pebbly beach between two craggy spits just twenty minutes from my house. It's great there as the coastline slopes straight in to the water so it's deep enough to swim very close to the edge.'

'Afraid a shark will come and eat you?' he joked.

'Always!'

When we turned to swim back our small pile of belongings was a tiny pea in the distance and by the time we reached them I was beginning to get cold. Toby was keen to stay in a bit longer so I left him to it and went to get dry.

I lay flat on my back, wrapped up in a towel, enjoying the heavy du' doom of a heartbeat that needs to settle. I looked up and released my thoughts into the vast blue void of Norfolk sky, letting them float free and disperse. Sending them away for a bit until I was ready to think Hailey's death through one final time.

I felt Toby's presence even before he reached me and I wondered if Hailey had known her killer.

'Susie? Are you in there?' he said shaking his head above me, spraying what water was left in his curls. 'It looks like you're away with the fairies.'

'You should try lying down and staring straight up at the sky, it's so wonderful to see only one colour.'

Toby placed his bag between us, rolled out his towel and joined me in my view.

'From an artist's point of view how many shades of the sky do you reckon there are?'

'Several hundred thousand.'

'Nah, no way! It's blue, grey, off white and that's about it.'

'Red in the sunset.'

'And yellow at sunrise,' added Toby. 'But that's

nowhere near several hundred thousand.'

'Well, last year, every day at ten o'clock in the morning I painted a four-by-four-centimetre square of the sky. Three hundred and sixty-six squares later, leap year up, and no two were the same.'

'What a great idea! I'd love to see the picture? Where is it now?'

I turned my head to face him. 'It's in the Tate Modern.'

'Really?' he pushed himself up on his elbow.

'It was way beyond my wildest dreams to have a picture hanging in their collection but somehow it found its way there.'

'You're so modest Susie. I can't believe that. Congratulations!'

Toby sat up, fumbled in his bag and gently threw a cling-filmed sandwich onto my bare tummy.

'Oh, wow. Thank you so much, I'm famished.'

'Swimming always makes me hungry too. I hope you like avocado and bacon? I toasted the bread a bit to stop it going soggy.'

We sat, staring out to sea, chatting about nothing in particular. I was finding it hard to tell if Toby is one of those wanderers who enjoys dipping in and out of other people's lives or whether his sand-crusted toes wriggling as he spoke suggested he did actually have stronger feelings for me. I wished I had Lucy's natural ease with the opposite sex as that way I'd find it far easier to make the first move on Toby. But I'm just not the sort and my inhibitions were holding me back.

'Toby,' I said leaning over his bag longing for him to notice and come towards me before I had to finish my sentence.

'Yes?' he got up to roll away his towel.

'Nothing.' I brushed away the thought and began packing up.

He held out his hand for me to hold and as we walked barefoot in the warm sand he kissed me softly on the cheek and drew away.

I had absolutely no idea how to play this. No man I've fancied has ever kissed me on the cheek without going further. And now the moment was gone, he'd trotted in front and picked something up. 'Do you know what this is?'

'A razor clam?'

'Spot on.' He handed me the dark-grey shoehorn-shaped shell. 'Have you ever caught one?'

'No.'

'We should try sometime. We'd have to get to the beach very early and follow the tide out looking for holes in the wet sand. Then, as soon as you see one you pour lots of table salt into it and dig with a trowel as fast as you can. The hope is that you'll catch them as they come to the surface.'

'Really? That works?'

'I've never actually succeeded but I've tried lots.'

I smiled, longing to say 'Great! When shall we go?' but instead I dropped the grey shell to the ground and clenched my fist in frustration at the most maddening internal dialogue I had going on.

Toby was the one who'd kissed me but it was such a quick peck, I didn't know if he was testing the water and wanting me to make the next move or had just done it for fun, on the spur of the moment, without any pre-thought or afterthought.

We were now out of step, him making for the edge of the marsh and me dawdling wondering if I'd missed the opportunity to tell him I really like him. As I looked ahead I longed to pull my fingers through his salty hair, hold onto his hand and run up and down the dunes as fast as we could.

'Look.' I pointed in to the marsh. 'That's samphire. We should get some for dinner.'

'Great idea.'

I was up to my ankles in the squelch trying to pull it up.

'Here, take this.' Toby handed me a penknife and with my bottom in the air I gathered a good bunch.

'It looks like legless stick insects doesn't it?'

Toby laughed. 'Here, stuff it in my bag.'

'Are you sure?'

'Yeah.'

It was only half past three when we got back to the car — plenty of time to eat a Mr Whippy sitting on the bumper of the open boot.

Toby went into a humorous monologue about the 'types' you get in these upmarket villages, 'DFLs' (down from Londoners) as he said they were known. And as I laughed I wished he'd pause and give me a proper kiss but, when he announced, 'let's head', I knew unless I could man-up and take charge, it wasn't going to happen.

On our way back, we stopped at a farm shop. I left Toby milling about outside reading the newspapers on a stand next to the dog-water bowls while I went in and grabbed the things I needed. The vegetable display alone looked like a work of art, all sorts of colourful round things piled high, making one reluctant to pluck at them for fear of a landslide. A bar of dark chocolate with sea-salt crystals caught my eye at the till and even before the cashier's encouragement it was in my basket with the thought that if we stayed up late tonight it would go down well.

Ry Cooder played in the car all the way home but unfortunately it was set loud enough to excuse the no talking. If I had it my way we'd be discussing our families. I wanted to know more about Toby's sister who lives in Spain, what his upbringing was like and how much he saw of his parents. Little details like this interest me. It's part of what makes us who we are. But, because Toby rarely asks a direct question, I thought it best to hold back.

The silence sent me off, theorising about his impersonal side. Maybe he has something to hide? Or maybe he grew up in a family who didn't discuss things and simply doesn't have the skills to know how?

It upset me to think Toby might be bearing the emotional strain of having buried episodes from his life deep within and I wished he knew he was safe with me. What he was yet to realise is that nothing in his life would put me off — as long as I heard it from him first.

32

My hands were full of shopping and when I edged open the kitchen door with my foot I found Lucy sitting at the table eating crackers, nonchalantly allowing Red-Rum to lick up the crumbs. As soon as she saw me she grabbed the packet and offered me one.

'No thanks, but I could do with some water.'

'I'll get it.' Lucy jumped up towards the sink and Red-Rum leapt the distance to the counter. 'Where's Toby?'

'I'm not sure, I thought he was behind me. We've just come back from the most wonderful swim in the sea.'

'It'd be good for me to do that sometime but I can never be bothered to walk around all those watery parts.'

I laughed as I peered out the door to look for Toby. 'Smile Susie,' he called out and quick as a flash, his camera snapped at me.

'Oh dammit!' I drew my head back inside as I heard him shout, 'You look great with your tousled hair.'

'Sexy, that's why he likes it,' said Lucy as she handed me a glass.

I put it on the table whilst I fished the samphire out of Toby's bag and dropped it into the sink.

Lucy leant over me, 'Gads, what is that? Is it *alive*?'

'No,' I laughed. 'It's samphire for dinner tonight. It's a delicious crunchy green vegetable we picked down on the marshes.'

She stuck her hand in the sink and pulled out a strand.

'Don't eat it now,' I yelped. 'It tastes filthy raw, but will be delicious once I've cooked it, just you wait.'

Lucy dangled it in front of Red-Rum's inquisitive nose. It set him off clawing at her wrist and as she gently cuffed him round the head he sprung to the floor and scampered out the door.

'What time's dinner?'

'We could eat at eight if that suits you?'

She laughed as Toby came through the door.

'Why are you giggling?'

'We're going to eat at eight!' exclaimed Lucy.

Toby smiled. 'Either of you know if there's a garage near here? I need to buy some oil for my car.'

Lucy jumped at the chance to answer, 'The closest one is left out the drive, first right, join the dual carriageway and you'll see it on the left. There's a bridge soon after that will get you back on to the other side of the road.'

'Perfect, I'm going to head down there now. Anyone need anything?'

'No thanks,' we both said at the same time.

Lucy offered to help me in the kitchen but other than find the electric beaters there was nothing more for her to do. So off she went to 'get on with the final rounds of horsey stuff for the day' and I set to making cherry fool.

The yoghurt and cream stiffened and, as I swirled the deep dark red coulis through the white mixture, I couldn't shift my mind off the thought of blood. If only Hailey's murder had been messy it would have made it so much easier to trace the truth. I put the fool in the fridge and went upstairs to have a wash.

★ ★ ★

I lay in the bath with the window open, listening to the birds having an early evening chirrup. Even on the hottest of days I like a bath. And as I let the warm water consume my salty skin I went over my cup of coffee with Archie. It was at the mention of Primrose's maiden name when the atmosphere had changed and I *wish* I knew why.

My salty hair was one matted lump and as I covered it in conditioner and pulled my fingers through it several strands came loose in my hands. Strands of blonde hair just like the one they'd found on Hailey's lampshade. The one with Archie and Primrose's DNA on it.

The bath took in a great big gulp as I sat up and gripped my fingers round the roll-top edge. Could there be any possibility whatsoever that Primrose and Archie shared the same DNA?

I thought harder, my grip tightened and a huge smile swept across my clean face. Maybe, just maybe, they were half-siblings. And if so 'their childhood kiss and cuddle' will have forced Archie's father to tell his eldest son the truth: the pretty girl he's kissing is in fact his half-sister.

If this was true it made perfect sense why Archie would have rejected such a beautiful family friend. And if poor Primrose was and is ignorant to the scandal then she'd understandably be jealous of any girl with her claws into Archie.

I was still finding it incomprehensible that Archie would've set off the alarm for fear of one of his visitors being held accountable for Hailey's death. Did he suspect foul play all along? If so, he clearly thought someone under his roof was capable of murder. This combined with the heady thought of illegitimacy was making it very hard for me to keep my rationale. More than ever I wanted Toby to bounce my idea off. But, there's no use bemoaning him, he'd deserted the cause.

I had the maddening truism, 'theories are no good without evidence to back them up' ringing in my ears and if *everyone* else is convinced Hailey died of 'a very rare type of kidney stones', then my only saviour is finding something concrete that proves them all wrong.

★   ★   ★

I sat wrapped up in a towel, staring into the dressing-table mirror. I'd tempered my bouncy sea hair into a plait and put on my favourite underwear (of that which I brought with me) in the hopes it would do what it could to cheer me up.

If I was at home right now, and a large part of me wished I was, I'd walk straight out the front door and up to the trig point high on the Downs. The view from there stretches for miles over patchwork fields scattered with farm animals, the valleys give way to glimpses of the sea, and chalky headlands are there for me to drop my troubled thoughts over. This expanse nourishes my soul, it reminds me of the simple things in life and never fails to banish the creative turmoil in my head, sending me bouncing back home with a vigour to keep going.

Instead, here I was, staring out of Lucy's spare-room window, Norfolk's invisible horizon intensifying the loneliness of my thoughts.

Who would have believed my mother's social surfing would result in a weekend where someone died? Mum's bound to hear rumours on the grapevine, not much goes down it and slips her by. But, I don't want to be the one who tells her first. It's not that she's a malicious gossip but Mum doesn't always think of the consequences before opening her mouth, particularly within her bridge circle and they're meeting tonight.

33

'Nice dress Lucy,' I said as I stepped outside to find her and Toby giggling on the bench. She smiled modestly and complimented me on mine.

'I don't often wear a frock,' she said in her honest way. 'But as it's your last night I thought I'd make an effort.'

'I think you both look lovely,' said Toby. 'Susie, a glass of wine?'

'Yes please.'

'We've been holding out for you to come downstairs,' he grinned. 'Lucy do you want some now?'

'Nah, I'll stick to the beer tonight.'

Toby poured the drinks as Lucy set the table and I got dinner on the go.

There was a buzz in the kitchen that cheered up my mood. Toby insisted on helping and I was glad to have him standing so close. He piled the samphire on a platter and as soon as I'd clarified the butter and added lemon he took charge of pouring it on top.

I shredded the slow-cooked beef while the wraps warmed up in the top oven. Toby's tummy gave a great rumble of anticipation and Lucy laughed as I tapped him on the shoulder to say. 'That's a good sign.'

We sat in a trio with Toby at the head, and as soon as Lucy picked up on the process of layering shredded beef and spicy tomato chutney into a tortilla she joined in with great enthusiasm for a dish she couldn't get her head around how on earth I knew how to make.

'Shall I put some on your plate?' I asked holding up a serving spoon full of samphire.

'Always good to try something new,' said Lucy with a sceptical look on her face.

'You'll love it,' said Toby shovelling a forkful into his mouth.

'What do you think?' I smiled as Lucy put a strand in her mouth.

'It's okay,' she said licking the salt off her lips. 'But not as good as a tomato, which is the only vegetable I really eat.'

Toby finished the rest of Lucy's samphire and I got up to clear the table. Half a bottle of white wine and one glass of red down and I had that happy slightly sloshed feeling, glad to be rid of completely coherent thought.

'Jesus,' said Lucy rushing to the door. 'Why does this frigging cat have to bring me his conquests?' She wrestled the bloody mouse out of Red-Rum's jaws and stepped outside to chuck it away, him scampering after her wanting to play.

'That was delicious,' said Toby as I caught him filling up my glass, his eyes then following me to the fridge. It's been some time since my last snog and I'd forgotten the warm glow one gets when mixing alcohol and attraction.

I put a fool on the table, which got a 'I love this stuff,' exclamation from Lucy as she sat back down with Red-Rum curled in her arms.

'Did you make these as well Susie?' she asked

as Toby offered her an almond biscuit.

'Afraid not, they came from a packet.'

'Oh great, I don't have to be polite then. Mind if I don't eat it?'

'I'll have it,' said Toby plucking the biscuit from her hand.

'Where are you headed tomorrow?' Lucy asked him as I savoured my mouthful of pudding.

'I'll be on my way home to the West Country.'

'That's a long way to go in one day.'

'I'm planning to spend the night in Reading, which will break it up a bit.'

'With friends?' asked Lucy lowering Red-Rum off her knee.

'Visiting my son.'

Good god, I almost choked. The fool was somewhere between my windpipe and nostrils attempting to come out as I struggled to get it down. Toby has a *son*. I *can't* believe it.

'That's nice,' said Lucy innocently. 'How old is he?'

Toby's eyes purposely (I'm sure) didn't engage with mine although mine weren't exactly attempting to engage with his. I felt completely miserable that he had a past he'd hidden — did he think I was too conventional to understand? I could feel the shock in my face tingling through my body and was for once very glad Lucy was impervious to the atmosphere.

'He'll be eleven tomorrow.'

'Right little grown up,' said Lucy. 'What are you giving him?'

'A remote-control helicopter.'

Typical, I thought, a spoiling present from an

absent father. I took a huge gulp of red wine and, clearly grasping for an opportunity to engage, Toby rapidly filled my glass up again.

'Oooh, isn't he a lucky little chappy,' said Lucy.

I could hardly bear to sit through the entirety of the conversation and by the time Toby got up to clear the bowls I was well on my way to Drunkdom.

Lucy announced there was ' . . . a party at Rob's place. He's spent every evening this week preparing. You should come,' and Toby turned from the sink, looked straight at my delirious eyes and said, 'I'm going to duck out, don't want to overdo it.'

'Susie?' asked Lucy.

'That's so kind but I won't this time.'

'Alright then, I'll see you both in the morning. Well probably the afternoon.' She gave us a cheeky look.

'I'll be leaving early,' I said getting up to say my goodbyes. 'Thank you very, very much Lucy, you've been such a great help to me and I've loved staying with you.' I steadied myself with the table and then in a state of insobriety, I enveloped her in a hug.

When Toby got up and did the same, I couldn't care less.

'You're both welcome here whenever you want,' said Lucy and fled, taking a six-pack of lager rather than a coat.

Toby and I didn't flinch as the ding of her bicycle bell sounded through the open door and jarred against the awkward silence between us.

34

I started to manically clear the table, unable to contain my upset as I clattered things into the sink. My shoulders were tense and I couldn't think of a single civil thing I wanted to say. Toby had sat back down and I heard the glug of wine as he refilled his glass.

'I've wanted to tell you about my son, Susie. He's called Tom, his mother named him after her father.'

'Why didn't you?' I snapped while wiping the soap suds off my hands.

'I don't know. I didn't want you to judge me before you knew me.'

'I thought I did know you but obviously not.' I tried hard not to sound cross but it was difficult. I *was* cross — having a son is a major part of knowing someone.

'You do know me. I love my son, I really do, but he's tarnished with the whoopsie brush and always will be.'

I was in no mood to be amused. I turned to the table and picked up my glass. There wasn't nearly enough washing up to keep me busy for long.

'Are you married?' I asked sitting back down.

'Heavens no. Tom's mother and I never actually went out. We were good friends from university and made the mistake of sleeping together. Only once, but she got pregnant and neither of us agreed with abortion.'

'Why didn't you marry her?'

'We were young, very young. I was a medical student and she was training to be a lawyer. I would have got married for Tom's sake but Liz and I both wanted to give each other the chance of true love. Liz is a great woman and I knew all along she'd never want me for her husband.'

I wasn't interested in knowing why not. If there's more that Toby's hidden from me I'm in no state to cope with hearing it right now. But, unfortunately, my silence prompted him to continue.

'Liz is a career girl, a modern woman who wanted a househusband. I wasn't willing to give up my job for her and neither of us was any good at compromise. It's worked out for the best, it really has. She's married a nice guy and Darren makes a great stepdad for Tom.' Toby's voice was calm and kind but it made no difference to how hurt I felt.

My head was beginning to throb. I would have understood if he'd told me about Tom earlier but springing it on me, this far into our friendship, shattered all the trust I thought we had. How dare he have concealed the truth at the same time as leading me on.

I ached with disappointment, having fallen for a gilded version of Dr Toby Cropper and allowing my imagination to run forward into a future together.

I looked up, Toby's face was drooping like an old labrador's. He was playing the helpless card. That way men have of shifting the blame as if they've done nothing wrong. Why is it they find it so difficult to reflect on their mistakes? All I needed was for him to say sorry . . .

'You can ask me anything Susie and I'll tell you. It's not as complicated as you might think.'

It was *his* complication I was concerned about but I was exhausted by the thought of bearing a grudge. I'm not one for playing games and would always rather get to the bottom of things than tear through emotions and harm each other along the way.

'I wish you'd told me earlier,' I said with a slim hope he'd apologise and I could stop longing to put the words in his mouth.

But Toby said nothing. His eyes were fixated on a splinter in the table that his fingers began picking at.

'I thought we had something good going on,' I said.

'We do.' He looked up at last. 'You've become a great friend.'

'Friend?!' I let slip by mistake.

Toby looked at me intently, 'You mean to say it meant more?'

'I thought, I hoped, it did.' I blushed. Drink had got the better of my tongue and unashamed honesty was taking over. How I wished I could play it cool, not give him the pleasure of knowing how much I liked him. But I'd blown my cover and it was hopeless to attempt to back-track now.

'You've hardly given me any signs in the whole time I've been here.' He was now riled. 'How was I supposed to know you wanted something to be going on between us?'

I was taken aback by this accusation. Was he completely clueless?

Toby pushed his wine glass to one side and fervently continued, 'The only thing that has got a grip of your attention is Hailey's death. Even with the case closed you can't resist trying to dig it all up again.'

'That's unfair.'

'No, it's not. Every time I've tried to take you away from it or insisted you drop it you bring your little theories back into the centre of everything.'

'Go on then, give me an example.' His anger had quashed my heartache and I was all fired up to bat it back.

'When isn't there an example? Drawing the horses, it's the only thing we talked about, going to the races you obsessed over that nice couple, visiting the museum filled you with theories and then today when you came back from coffee with Archie I tried not to bring it up but you just couldn't resist.'

I stared into my glass. He was right, it was obvious now, but I was not in the mood to back down. The very thing that brought us together in the first place, investigating murder, was now tearing us apart. I'd been under the impression, until today, that we'd been equally invested in solving Hailey's death, just as we were with Lord Greengrass's. But, no, Toby had fooled me and he was now using my obsession with it against me.

'Someone may have been *murdered* Toby and

I was there. I can't just drop it. To me that would be wrong and anyway it's ridiculous to suggest it's been my way of avoiding paying you attention.'

He took a slow sip from his glass, his eyes making no attempt to engage with me as I got up and left the room. I wasn't going to have a petty argument and particularly not with drink inside me.

Red-Rum was on my pillow again and this time I made no attempt to move him. We curled up together, him purring in my ear, giving me the comfort I so desperately needed. I shut my eyes, too furious to cry and my teeth clenched at the realisation I'd thrown away my self-composure and now lost whatever it was Toby and I had.

My body was awash with alcohol. The room was spinning and my thoughts were in crazy disarray. I could feel my heavy head sinking into the pillow as I tried to overcome the dark cloud seeping through me. It was like a poison in my being.

A large part of me longed for Toby to knock on my door and when Red-Rum decided he wanted out I made sure Toby would hear and therefore know I was awake. But he never came and as I snuggled in between the bed sheets, wrapping myself in a cosy cocoon, my mind wavered and I drifted into thoughts of Hailey's system collapsing under an excessively abnormal amount of calcium oxalate. This in its own way was a poison of sorts. Resulting in kidney stones, the reason given for her death but maybe, just maybe, it came from something else. This conundrum destroyed the last tiny ounce of energy left in me and so drowsily I slipped into sleep.

35

I woke all of a sudden, with a furry mouth and no clue what the time was. I'd been out for the count, as good as dead, and the only sign several hours had passed was the daylight through the window.

I'd forgotten to draw my curtains, something I haven't often done since giving in to my father's will. When I was little he'd never let me wake to natural light, sneaking into my room when I'd fallen asleep and shutting out the night, as if he knew better.

I sat up in bed. *Oh curses!* Toby had an illegitimate son. My chest expanded as I furiously inhaled and with the exhalation of resentful breath my shoulders slumped.

It's like Antonia Codrington had warned me, 'If you go for an older man who's still single, Susie, you have to be aware they might have a past.'

Hearing about Tom, by the sounds of things a happy child whose parents get on, shouldn't have made me as angry as it did. The fact was it had taken me by surprise and I'd overreacted. I could love someone else's child, I knew I could. I just wish Toby had been open about it from the beginning.

I gazed out the window and thought about it from little Tom's point of view. Although it goes against my religion, maybe Toby and Liz had been fairer on him by giving each other the chance of finding true love. I have a friend who got his girlfriend pregnant at university and did what I thought at the time was the right thing to do, he married her. But they're now unhappy, they've fallen out of love and it's not nice to see.

I stretched for my telephone. *My goodness!* It's only five o'clock. I looked down at the duvet knowing there's no way I could go back to sleep. I may have softened to Toby's domestic situation but as immature as it seems, even to me, I now more than ever wanted to solve Hailey's death and prove him wrong.

My eyes were crusty and as I cleared their corners with my fingers a startlingly bright ray of sunshine came sparkling through the window, reflecting off the white sheets, blinding my sight.

Every blink I took set off another blotch of black dancing around the room. I couldn't cope. I shut my eyes, allowing the cells in my retina to recover in darkness and pulled my knees up to my chest in despair of the day to come.

My head began to throb and I blamed the duvet for being white. If it was a colour it would have absorbed some of the light rays but no, it's not, and every single wavelength of light in the visible spectrum had bounced off it into my eyes.

I hugged my knees tighter and opened my eyes. The sun had disappeared behind a cloud and a great shadow cast over my room. It was dark and sinister, and riddled me with fear of 'the end'. What will become of us when this life is over? Hailey's eyes had shut the world out, leaving her in darkness never to wake again.

I needed to get up and out, go for a breather and inject life into my limbs before taking on the long journey home. My body was stiff, having lain comatose in sleep, and as I stood up slowly I knew exercise was all there was for it. I crossed the room in that way one does with a body that's yet to loosen up. Rather similar to Archie's yesterday I remembered.

Crickey! Cricket. Why hadn't I thought about it before . . . lunch in the pavilion. No one had mentioned it, not even DCI Reynolds and Sergeant Ayari. Did this mean it hadn't been searched?

I had to rush, *right now*. Get to the ground before the early morning dog walkers were out.

As quickly as possible, I got into my clothes and pulled on my trainers. No time spare to do up the laces. Not one bit of me was feeling jaded any more.

I grabbed the yellow Marigolds from the sink, stuffed a plastic bag into my pocket and bolted from the kitchen out of the door.

36

Leaving a trail of footprints on the dewy grass, with no time to circumnavigate the boundary, I scampered straight across the square heading for the charming blue-and-white pavilion Archie had tried to tell me about. Any conscientious groundsman would be furious, but acting on thoughts like this was far from my mind.

If Hailey died from something she ingested at lunch, then traces of poison were what I was looking for. Some substance that would take time to work its way through her system and kill her in the early hours of Sunday morning.

What a sight I must have looked in yellow rubber gloves hoisting myself over the veranda, the gates of which were chained shut. Blast. The door was locked, the windows too, and both shielded by internal blinds.

I swung my leg back, all set to kick my way in, when inbuilt good manners brought it to a grinding halt. *Susie!* I thought, don't let yourself get out of control.

Round the back of the pavilion, out of sight from the village, I found two quite small free-standing wheelie bins. Out came my leg again, and my arms, carefully toppling one over. *Dumph!* it went on the dry ground, the lid flipped open and nothing came out.

It was empty. A big deep dark cavern of emptiness. Not even an unbranded plastic bag stuck to the bottom. I left it for dead as I wobbled the other bin from side to side. And as it groaned under its own weight, I creaked back the lid and immediately shut it tight again. The stench was so bad I was almost sick on the spot and as I gagged I prayed that if I opened it again I'd discover something vital inside.

Holding my breath, I flung back the lid and took out the top bag to lighten the load. I gave a great shove, the bin crashed to the ground, and as the sound of bottles and black bags tumbled out I wafted the air to disperse the dreadful smell before putting my head inside.

I untied one of the sacks and sunk my yellow hand into its revolting contents. Out came more sandwich crusts than any hungry seagull could eat; tangerine peel; cocktail sticks with glacé cherries left to rot; half-eaten scones and a mountain of tea bags. I gave my hand one last ruffle before the stink became too much to bear and I had to leave this one for now and try the other.

I wiped my hands on the grass, looking away for fear of gagging again. And as I untied the knot of bag number two my heart stepped up a beat at the sound of the glass clanking inside. With no thought for mess, I tipped its entire contents onto the ground.

The pile of empty bottles at my feet smelt like a Soho gutter the morning after a frivolous parade. With one final shake a few vegetable crisp packets fluttered out onto the ingredients of Primrose's punch. There was an empty bottle of gin lying next to the thick glass of some rare peach liqueur and by its side rolled a fancy bottle of blue curacao.

An empty packet of Fortnum & Mason's finest filter coffee stuck to my glove as I scrabbled through Fever Tree tonic cans to reach the plastic bottle at the bottom of the stash. I grasped it and the crystal blue liquid sloshed and frothed up the neck as if there were some chemical inside.

'Antifreeze,' it said on the label, 'tailored for the Tiguan.' What on earth was this doing in a cricket pavilion bin? It's the height of summer for heaven's sake.

Then, the name of the car hit home . . . a Tiguan — it's exactly what the Geralds had. I knew it was. George had teased Stanley at dinner for having a 'spivs' car in the country and Primrose had retaliated, 'Oh George, that theory went out with the war, it's nonsense gents only have a green 4×4 in the country any more. We love our black Tiguan, don't we darling? Smartest car we've ever had.'

Now, I'm no chemist but I knew this blue liquid could be my answer to it all.

A high-pitch whistle came from the other side of the pavilion. I glanced around the corner, charging across the cricket square some distance away was a stocky miniature English bull terrier, mobility restricted by what used to prompt my grandfather to say, 'that dog should be wearing underpants'.

I stripped off one glove, flapped the plastic bag out of my pocket and slipped the bottle inside. The voice calling 'Governor, Gov, here boy,

Govvy,' was getting closer but I knew if I was unbelievably quick I'd have just enough time to stuff the majority of the rubbish back into the bins.

The voice was coming from the right of the pavilion, so swiftly and carefully I crept down the left. With gender on my side — no one would suspect a blonde girl in a dress to have been digging about in a pile of rubbish — I strolled unhampered around the cricket-pitch boundary and, as I unlocked my car, I felt the wind in my hair.

If antifreeze could kill, I knew who would know.

37

I returned the Marigolds to the sink and made two cups of tea. I urgently needed Toby's co-operation. He'd give me a reliable answer far quicker than I could search for one on Google and therefore I owed it to him not to be cruel.

'Knock, knock,' I said standing outside his bedroom door feeling proud of myself for rising above the underlying issue, thinking perhaps there was a reason he didn't tell me about Tom.

There was a grunt that I took to mean 'come in'.

'I thought you'd like some tea,' I said putting a mug down on his bedside table.

'Susie?' he'd rolled over to face me. 'What is it?'

I made no excuses for my entry and sat down in the mini armchair at the other end of the room. Toby's colour was high and his face expressionless, no doubt he was wishing I'd go away.

'I had to come and tell you.'

'You've had a dream?' he butted in and we both laughed.

He was so good at breaking an atmosphere. I liked him for that.

'I've just been to Fontaburn cricket ground and found a bottle of antifreeze in the wheelie bin behind the pavilion.'

Toby kept looking at me and it was hard to tell

what he was thinking or if he was awake enough to think at all. His chest began to appear above the duvet as he sat up.

'One: what were you doing rooting around in bins, and two: why have you woken me up to tell me that you've found a bottle of antifreeze?'

'Please don't be cross. I know you've been trying to get me to stop my investigation and it's not that I wanted to go against you it's just I couldn't resist trying to . . . '

Toby finished my sentence, 'Prove everyone else wrong.'

I was hurt by his comment. I shut up and very nearly left the room.

'Susie, I'm sorry, it's just, after our discussion last night and all, I'm surprised you've woken me so early to bring up the same old subject of Hailey's death.'

'*Shh, shhh*, we don't want to wake Lucy.'

Toby quietened his voice but it didn't take away the sting in his tongue. 'I really did think you'd managed to drop it once and for all.'

'It's lucky I haven't, honestly, please let me explain. Can you just help me out one last time, *please*? I need to know if someone can die from drinking antifreeze?'

He pulled the duvet up and pushed the entirety of his upper body back into the headboard.

'Yes.'

'Yes, you *can*?' my body was tingling.

'Car antifreeze is generally ninety-five per cent ethylene glycol. This is a toxic alcohol, which when drunk is broken down by the body into glycolic acid and oxalic acid.' The monotone explanation rolled off his tongue, him giving me the answer with no wish to do so.

'Oxalic acid!' I exclaimed so loudly I'm sure Lucy must have woken. I clasped my hand over my mouth.

'Don't worry,' said Toby. His tone was still dull. 'I don't think Lucy came home last night. I lay awake a long time and didn't hear a thing.'

It consoled me to hear he'd struggled to sleep.

'*If* Hailey drank it, how would it have killed her?'

'The toxin would have poisoned her kidneys.'

'How?' I asked. Accuracy was all I wanted right now.

'Calcium oxalate would have accumulated in her kidneys, damaged them and led to anuric acute kidney failure.'

'If they did, is there any way the medics could have missed it?'

'The signs of ethylene glycol poisoning are not specific and share very, very similar signs and symptoms to the likes of kidney stones. Anuria is non-passage of urine and can occur from an obstruction such as kidney stones.'

Like that of any brainbox, Toby's ego couldn't resist giving a thorough, if a little tedious, answer to a question he knew all about. There were no 'sort ofs' or 'thingamajigs', he gave me every detail I could have possibly wanted.

On and on he went ... 'Because calcium oxalate is the same by-product produced from kidney stones and as Hailey had kidney stones it might've masked ethylene glycol poisoning.'

'No wonder they made the wrong diagnosis.'

'What *you* think is the wrong diagnosis,' said Toby, but it didn't perturb me. I ploughed on regardless, gleaning the information I needed, now knowing he'd answer any medical questions I wanted.

'Is it easy to test for antifreeze poisoning?'

'No. It costs a fortune to measure blood ethylene glycol concentration so many hospitals don't have the ability to perform it.'

Then came Toby's rocket. 'If the investigators were in any doubt over the cause of death they wouldn't have closed the case. They have concluded Hailey *wasn't* murdered and so should you.'

I sipped my tea making sure not to show the slightest reaction to his proclamation. This got under his skin and I could tell it did when he tried to persuade me there was no way Hailey would have drank such a vivid blue liquid, even if it tasted sweet.

'Toby,' I raised my head. 'That's exactly my point. Primrose's cocktails *were* blue. I'm absolutely sure Hailey's drink was spiked at the cricket.'

'You're wanting it to make sense.'

'But let's say she *did* drink antifreeze, what symptoms would she have shown?'

Toby knew I'd been upset by him last night, which was now perfect. He was on the back foot and as he's neither nasty nor unkind I knew he was going to play into my hands.

'You may as well know,' he said defeated, 'that someone poisoned by ethylene glycol shows very similar symptoms to someone who's drunk too much.'

Toby pulled his fingers through his dishevelled hair. He wasn't looking at me, he didn't share in any of my excitement. His high colour had subsided to pale cheeks and it took a lot of pleading to get him to re-entertain the idea that Hailey was poisoned.

'What are the exact signs she would have shown early on?'

'Dizzy, lacking co-ordination, slurred speech, confusion and thirst,' he said with a half-smile.

'That's exactly what we wrote down.'

'*You* wrote down.'

I rushed to my room to get my sketchbook.

'Here it is.' I handed it to him open on the list of symptoms: *Slurred speech; Energetic; Dizzy; Thirsty; No urination.*

'You have a point,' he said finally. 'But the signs are very close to alcohol poisoning and with ethylene glycol they don't always kick in immediately. A person can look well for several hours before showing signs of poisoning.'

'But the combination of these symptoms, the excessive levels of oxalate in the autopsy report *and* the bottle of antifreeze surely gives us . . . ' I corrected myself, '*Me*, enough reason to go to the police.'

'Your call, Susie, but I'm staying out of it. It wouldn't do me any good challenging the conclusions of other medical professionals.'

'How long would it take to kill her if she drank it?'

'You don't give up easily do you?' he said.

'I *need* to know. I have to be sure.'

'At the very least twelve hours and at the most around thirty-six hours.'

'Hailey died in that window.'

'Yes, she did.'

'How would she have died?' I asked.

'What do you mean?'

'Would her heart have stopped? Would she have choked on sick?'

'Oh, I see.' Toby was slowly becoming more forgiving. 'If someone drank it they'd probably slip into a coma and die soon after.'

The talk of death silenced me. Poor Hailey was dead. This put things into perspective and I grasped the opportunity to smile at Toby, regardless of how I'd felt last night.

He looked back at me with pity. 'Susie, I think you'd be taking too big a risk by going to the police. You'd have to tell them you'd doubted the forensic pathologists' conclusion and gone out on your own to prove them wrong. DCI Reynolds obviously trusts his men and who are you to tell him they're wrong?' Toby took in a deep breath. 'I don't want you to make a fool of yourself, all you have is a bottle of antifreeze found by rooting around in a bin.'

An emotional lump formed in my throat and to keep the tears at bay I continued the fight. 'The antifreeze is branded for a Tiguan. The *very* car Primrose and Stanley had.'

'You don't know if the Geralds' car was even at the cricket or if the antifreeze had been chucked away by a cleaner for the simple fact that no one has any use for antifreeze in a cricket pavilion.'

'Too true,' I said with a smile. 'Thanks for not refusing to discuss it.'

Toby let out a pffft. 'Your *poor* parents, you must have given them an exhausting upbringing if you've always needed such thorough explanations.'

The word upbringing brought Toby's son Tom in to the forefront of my mind. Arguing last night had created a reserve between us and I didn't want the memory of it to fester under the carpet.

'I'm sorry I was so outspoken last night.'

'No worries.'

He cut me off. Nothing more was said and the tea I'd brought him remained untouched. I left the room feeling sad. Sad that Toby wasn't backing me and sad that we'd damaged whatever it was that felt so good between us.

I dragged my feet downstairs and sat at the table drinking black coffee, which only darkened my thoughts. I didn't even bother to open the front door, despite Red-Rum clawing at it. The air in the kitchen was stale and I didn't care. My whole being felt empty and I'd lost the drive to carry through my theory on Hailey's death. The only place in the world I longed to be right now was home but not one bit of me felt strong enough to take on the journey.

There was a loud thud on the other side of the door. 'Oh, hi Susie,' said Lucy as she came crashing in. 'Hell of a party.'

'I can tell,' I said with an unavoidable grin. Lucy's dress was crumpled, her legs were grazed and her glittery make-up smudged around her bloodshot eyes.

'There's some coffee in the pot,' I said, glad of her presence forcing me to lift my mood. 'I can heat it up if you want some.'

'I'd vomit if that hit my stomach. I have to go to bed, sorry Susie.'

'Don't apologise, it's your house. I'm leaving soon so thank you very much. You've been a wonderful landlady and thank you for having Toby too.'

Lucy's pale face hung off her worn-out body. She looked like she might faint any minute so I decided against slowing her up by giving her another hug.

'Bye Susie,' she just about got out before her eyelids began to droop.

I gave Red-Rum a cuddle goodbye and went upstairs to pack my stuff. It wasn't till I was in the driving seat all ready to go that I glanced across at the antifreeze bottle in the plastic bag and decided that for once in my life I was going to heed someone else's advice. I wouldn't go to the police; I wasn't prepared to take the risk.

It's not that I minded the thought of being wrong; it had more to do with losing Toby's respect and spoiling any chance of a future together (if that was even a vaguely realistic thought).

I let out a breath and took a deep one in, encouraging myself to grow up and go and say goodbye.

Toby was up and dressed and packing his bag.

'Time for me to go,' he said.

'Me too, I was just coming to say goodbye.'

'Off to the police, are you?'

This stab made me so furious that in the fiery heat of anger I changed my mind then and there, 'Yup.'

Toby advanced towards me and kissed me coldly on both cheeks. 'Thanks for a happy few days in Norfolk, safe journey home.'

'And you.'

I turned and left, there was nothing more to say.

Goodbye Pluton Farm Stables! Norham Police Station here we come . . .

38

'Madam? May I help you?' called out the receptionist as I breezed past her on my way to the lift.

'Sorry,' I turned back, 'would it be possible to visit Detective Chief Inspector Reynolds?'

Mandy, as her badge told me, picked up her telephone, dialled an extension and took an inordinate amount of time to get back to me with the news that, 'Detective Chief Inspector Reynolds has a day off.'

'He's not here?'

'No. I'm afraid he's not,' she said far too kindly considering my disgruntled question. 'Is it urgent? I can pass you on to his number two if you'd like?'

'No, it's okay. Thank you though.' Sergeant Ayari wouldn't do. This time I had to go to the top.

I rushed back to my car but as I sat in the car park, staring at the whitewashed wall that had previously absorbed my thoughts of Mrs Dune, I couldn't decide if I was on a wild goose chase or not. I longed for the wall to tell me the answer but it wasn't giving anything back. The decision to pursue this was entirely down to me.

Brinng . . . brinng . . . I'd called DCI Reynolds on his mobile, *brinng . . . bring . . .* having decided if he didn't answer I'd take it as a sign and give up. *Bring . . . bring . . . bring . . . bring . . .* Where was he? *Brinng . . . brinng . . . brinng . . .* Come on Reynolds, *Brinng . . . brinng . . . brinng . . .*

'Hello?'

Phew. 'Inspector, it's Susie Mahl.'

'Susie, to what do I owe the pleasure?'

'I'm on my way home to Sussex but I wondered if we could have a chat before I leave?'

'Of course, go ahead.'

'Is there any chance we could do it in person?'

'I'm not at the station today I'm afraid.'

'Can we meet elsewhere?'

'If you tell me what it's about we can go from there.'

I begged, '*Please* can I just come and see you? It won't take long. I'd rather not say it over the phone.'

I knew DCI Reynolds's good manners and kind nature would make it impossible for him to brush me off.

'*I'm, I'm,*' he stuttered over his answer, let out a sigh and said, 'I'm at home and you're welcome to drop by, although we'll be heading out for the day in an hour or so.'

He gave me his address. The name of the village rang a bell. Oh yes! I'd just come through it on my way to the station . . . ten minutes and I'd be on his doorstep.

★ ★ ★

DCI Reynolds's tidy home was nestled in the middle of a row of identical houses. They were part of a new development on the edge of a very pretty village. Modest living but sympathetic architecture and not a single step in sight.

The bonnet of the car parked next to number thirty-nine was up and DCI Reynolds very nearly caught his forehead on its rim as he rose to my arrival.

'Susie, that was quick. You've caught me at it, filling the washers. Won't be long. Hang on a sec.'

His head together with the watering can disappeared back under the bonnet.

Only at this moment did I realise he was balding. DCI Reynolds was tall with plenty of hair and I would have never believed, before now, he had an empty patch on top. If my partner was balding I'd encourage him to shave it. I've always had a soft spot for men with a number one.

The filling up of the washers was taking longer than I predicted and my thoughts took off on a hairy tangent. I was remembering once overhearing a wife commenting on their gamekeeper, 'I do wish he wouldn't shave his hair darling, do you think you might have a word?' This request prompted a discussion, 'Yes, I will my dear, it'd be simply dreadful if our Tommy did the same. So frightfully common.'

Their conversation went on, 'His new school friend Stuart is awfully hairy. A result of cross-class breeding I'm sure,' and on . . . 'Yes,' said her husband, 'thank heavens you and I are only hairy on top.' 'My darling if you'd married a German you'd have had to make allowances for underarm growth.'

This exchange of contrary idioms enlightened

me on aristocrats' obsessesion with hair and left me confused as to how a natural phenomenon could become such a stigma.

You only need visit Hoxton to see for yourself the celebration of hair in this day and age. However, with country folk out on a limb, squirrelled away in their gentrified pile, getting with the times takes a bit longer and I should think it will be several years yet until we come across a trimmed moustache hanging off a stiff upper lip.

'Now do come in Susie,' said DCI Reynolds at last. 'If you wouldn't mind getting the door, my hands are dirty.'

I opened it to a well-turned-out woman who was standing on the other side, holding a damp cloth in her hands.

'Thank you, pet. This is Susie Mahl.'

'Hello,' I said bending down to take off my sandals having already seen her slippers.

'Come through to the lounge Susie. Would you like a drink?'

'No, thank you.'

'Now, if you wouldn't mind sitting on the settee, I've done something to my back so forgive me for taking the armchair.'

'I'm sorry I called you on your day off and I don't want to waste your time but there's something I really want to tell you.'

'Go on then.'

'I have a friend who's a doctor.' Oh damn, I knew I shouldn't be bringing Toby in to this but I'd begun now. 'And when he said he'd never heard of kidney stones excreting enough calcium oxalate to kill someone I was surprised.'

DCI Reynolds didn't know that I knew Hailey had one healthy kidney but that didn't matter for now.

'Yes, I was surprised too.' He smiled and his charming face made me realise it was going to be very difficult to get this man to think sceptically.

'I'll be honest,' I said. 'All along I've thought Hailey was murdered. I can't explain why, I just did.'

'Female intuition, eh?' DCI Reynolds was being funny but I didn't let it put me down, I had his attention and he was sympathetic to me wanting to talk.

'Without going over everything I'll launch straight in with where I'm at.'

'You do that Susie.'

'I woke very early this morning and remembered no one had ever mentioned carrying out a search at the cricket pitch in connection with the death.'

'We really should have covered all bases,' DCI Reynolds's eyes rolled and I was surprised he'd dismissed the point with such ease. Furthermore, I think he thought our chat was over when he said, 'It is kind of you to have come out of your way to tell me this Susie.'

Maybe police budgetary constraints meant they couldn't do everything but DCI Reynolds was in for a shock if he thought this was all I had to say.

'The thing is,' I looked straight at him, 'I went to the cricket pavilion this morning and in the bins, I found a bottle of antifreeze. I think the cocktail Hailey drank before lunch must have been spiked with antifreeze.'

There it was, it was out.

'Delia, Delia,' he called out as he got up and went towards the open door.

Delia was a pretty woman in an even prettier paisley frock. Much younger than her husband but still very much in love.

'Come in, I'd like you to hear this.' She sat on the arm of a chair and, as DCI Reynolds made his way slowly back to his, he began . . . 'Of an evening Delia and I enjoy sitting down and watching a good whodunit. Don't we D?' He smiled at his wife who smiled at me.

'Yes,' she replied.

'Only last night Susie, we were gripped by, what was it this time?' he looked to his wife.

'*A Brush with Death*,' said Delia.

'Yes, yes, particularly good series that. I'd highly recommend it Susie. Last night the murderer killed his victim by lacing the blueberry cooles.' He turned to Delia. 'That's what it was called wasn't it D?'

She turned to me. 'He means coulis.'

'Lacing the coulis with antifreeze and it's just your luck Susie that we didn't believe it possible so Delia here got straight on her iPad to check the facts and blow me down you can die from the smallest amount of common everyday antifreeze.'

'In this bag,' I got up to show DCI Reynolds, 'is the bottle I found.'

'You haven't touched it, have you?' He sounded alarmed.

'No, I had gloves on.'

'Of course, you did.' He turned to his wife, 'Susie makes a fine amateur detective.'

'Yes,' said Delia with excitement.

I sat down. 'The bottle says it's made specifically for Tiguans. The Geralds have a Tiguan.'

'What's a Tiguan?'

'It's a car,' I said rushing into my full explanation, 'Primrose Gerald made cocktails for everyone using blue curacao. The colour of this spirit could have easily disguised the antifreeze slipped into Hailey's drink. I'm sure it must be the case as the timings tie up.'

DCI Reynolds's elbows were clamped to the armrests of his chair, his torso braced, 'Only Hailey's as none of the others were poisoned. Go on Susie,' he coaxed.

'It was several hours after cricket that Hailey's system packed up from what we all now know was an excess of calcium oxalate. Calcium oxalate is a by-product of ingested ethylene glycol, and antifreeze is often ninety-five per cent ethylene glycol.'

'Gosh, what knowledge you have.'

Delia looked a little baffled.

'If Hailey died from drinking antifreeze, it makes sense, doesn't it?'

'Well, there are several factors within this we have to prove right before any type of conclusion can be drawn, but no doubt about it that bottle in the bag you have there is reason for me to think we mustn't be too hasty in writing off the case.'

I was bubbling over with excitement.

Reassuringly, DCI Reynolds told me his wife was involved behind the scenes in all his cases. 'If I wasn't able to let my grumbles out to someone Susie I'd go mad. Delia's my confidante. Now, just this once, do you have a theory of why you think Mrs Gerald murdered Miss Dune?'

I swallowed the lump in my throat, which had reappeared on account of accusing someone I'd hardly even met. A vulnerable person at that.

'Well, there are several threads, none of which I have concrete evidence for but all of which point to Primrose and I'd like to share.'

'Understood,' said DCI Reynolds.

'When I arrived at Fontaburn on Saturday afternoon I picked up on Primrose's jealousy of Hailey having been invited on a trip by Archie to Wujiang, a place in China he's visited several times before with Primrose. It's where Archie's family have a porcelain factory. I know this having visited the family museum in Fontaburn village on Tuesday. Archie alluded to it when he confirmed at dinner that the topic of porcelain caused a rift between some of them on Friday night.'

'You're saying Mrs Gerald was jealous of Miss Dune?'

'Yes, I think Primrose's motivation for murder was jealousy. Archie is very fond of Primrose, he told me so, and I know from others at the weekend that they were romantically involved when they were younger. Considering this, it seemed strange to me their relationship hadn't lasted, and to cut a long story short I've done a bit of background research into the two families and I think, although I probably shouldn't be saying it, that Archie and Primrose share a father.'

'You say they're half siblings?' interjected DCI Reynolds.

'Yes, I think Archie's father would have had to tell him this when he saw them getting a little too close.'

'That poor man,' said DCI Reynolds, although it was unclear if he meant the father or the son.

'I reckon Archie ended the relationship and never gave Primrose the real reason why. And if Primrose wanted Archie for herself she would be forever jealous of any woman who looked like she might be about to woo him.'

'My, Susie, this is quite a back story and one I wouldn't want spread.'

'If it was Mrs Gerald,' said Delia, 'And you can find a trace on the bottle, no one need know anything else.'

I agreed with them that it would be best not to make Lord Norland's infidelity public if we could help it.

'So much for a day off.' DCI Reynolds pushed himself up by the arms of his chair. 'I'm sorry D but we'll have to go to the garden centre at the weekend.'

'That's okay, it's of minor importance right now.'

'Susie, I don't know what to say. You could have just proved us all wrong. It may fall on my head that the case was concluded but I'd never let this get in the way of the truth. Murder is a very serious thing and when there's any doubt in an investigation, no matter how late in the day, it's always important we hear it out.'

The three of us were now standing in the porch.

'You must go,' said Delia, who had come alive with the recent news. 'Right now!'

'Yes,' said DCI Reynolds. 'And if it was up to me Susie, I'd take you with me but I'm afraid it's not and I'd be breaking rules of confidentiality if I did.'

'She could remain in the waiting room,' said Delia coming down on my side.

'That's a point. Do if you'd like to.'

DCI Reynolds pecked his wife on the cheek and off we set, in convoy, to the police station.

39

'If you're happy sitting at reception Susie, I'll come straight back down when there's news.'

Mandy recognised me but said nothing as DCI Reynolds explained, 'This young lady is going to wait here for a while. She's with me so don't worry.'

He went to the lift with the plastic bag in his hand and I sat down in one of the bucket chairs just inside the entrance door. I took John Updike's collection of short stories out of my bag and let it take my mind off the wait.

Time dragged and I spent most of it hoping I'd been right. It's not that I wanted to punish Primrose but if she was in the wrong I thought it was important to separate good from evil. There was no anger inside me, just remorse that poor Primrose had, if she's guilty, truly suffered from her mother's mistake.

If Mrs de Bynninge's good looks hadn't caught Archie's father's eye none of this would have ever come about. My revelation, if right, would ruin the Geralds' future and I just hoped Stanley had it in him to forgive his wife. She'd need him more than ever in the years to come.

'Madam,' said Mandy, her forefinger beckoning me to her desk.

'Yes?'

'DCI Reynolds would like you to go to his

office. The lifts are behind me, over there, it's the fourth floor.'

'Thank you,' I said, relieved to hear it was at last time. I still wanted to get home at some point today.

'Have a seat,' said DCI Reynolds closing the glass door of his office.

I couldn't take my eyes off him.

'I can confirm,' he said sitting down at his desk, 'that we've found DNA evidence linking the antifreeze directly to Mrs Gerald.' There was reserve in his voice and this made me worried I'd created the most abominable mess. I sat tight as he continued. 'This does not mean for sure that Mrs Gerald is guilty of murder. We mustn't go jumping the gun, pardon the pun. We still need to find evidence that Miss Dune did indeed die of antifreeze poisoning and, unfortunately, we do not have the method to determine this here. I'm led to believe it is a very sophisticated test.'

I gave a half smile.

'Don't panic Susie, as we speak Sergeant Ayari is accompanying Miss Dune's body, which is being transported to a London hospital where they have the means to measure ethylene glycol levels in her blood.'

'How long will that take?'

'We'll have an answer by . . . ' DCI Reynolds squinted at his watch and totted up the time. 'Four thirty I'd say.'

'This afternoon?'

'Yes, this afternoon.'

'Okay,' I said wondering how I was going to contain myself until then. I was desperate to know the outcome and wished I could share my anxiety with someone. 'Are you able to call and tell me the result when you hear?'

'Of course I will,' said DCI Reynolds with a smile. 'Actually Susie,' his face fell and I couldn't think what was coming, 'You said you were on your way back to Sussex, didn't you?'

'Yes.'

'Just to be on the safe side why don't you ring me? I don't want you answering my call while you're driving.' He was amused by his own authority.

'Of course. Four thirty on the dot.'

DCI Reynolds was in a good mood, I could tell by the speed in which he shot up out of his chair. His poor back!

'How did the forensics find evidence of Primrose's DNA?'

'Spot of luck,' he said standing by the door. 'One of Mrs Gerald's fingernails must have chipped off when she was mixing her cocktails. The forensics found it in the solution.'

DCI Reynolds accompanied me to the lift.

'You've been a pleasure to work with Susie, many thanks for your co-operation.'

'I just hope I haven't wasted your time, particularly as it's your day off.'

'Between you and me you've saved me yet *another* trip to the garden centre.'

DCI Reynolds grinned as the doors of the lift shut and I descended, wishing Toby and I hadn't had our spat.

40

The journey to Sussex was long and hot and the congestion over the Queen Elizabeth II bridge left me in no doubt that it *is* the busiest estuarial crossing in the United Kingdom.

I had both front windows wound down instead of turning on the air conditioning, and by the time I'd crossed the final county border my bum was well and truly stuck to the second-hand leather seat.

Home had a feeling of desertion to it. The ants were at it again, nibbling away at the front door-frame, and the sitting-room floorboards creaked under the load I was carrying. At first whiff, I thought the whole place had taken on a new odour in my absence, but no, it was only stale hot air freed as soon as I opened the windows.

From the car into the studio I lugged my materials, sketchpads, tins of pencils, rubbers and charcoal. I took my canvas chair and easel through the house too, carrying it all at once to avoid making too many trips.

My house is small but long and has a strange knack of egging me on to take as much as possible in one go. There are no internal doors, no steps, no corners to turn, it's an eighteenth-century cottage joined to a small modern extension that's flooded with light. The perfect arrangement for me to work in one half and get cosy in the other.

I flicked on the kettle and scattered the pile from the letterbox on the kitchen table. There was an envelope that I knew contained the results of a recent competition I'd entered. And seeing it gave me that horrible feeling inside of not wanting to open it for fear of it containing the wrong answer. That was exactly how I felt about the arrival of four thirty, knowing there was a fifty-fifty chance of being right in what DCI Reynolds was going to say.

★ ★ ★

I felt winded by the prospect of picking up the telephone but I pressed the call button and held it to my ear.

'DCI Reynolds speaking.'

'Hello, it's Susie.'

'Susie, are you home?'

'Yes.' I took in a deep breath to try and regulate my breathing. There was no way I was going to get many words out if not.

'Well, here I am sitting at my desk with a very different outcome in front of me. A diagnosis that Miss Dune died from ethylene glycol-based antifreeze has been confirmed. The tests they ran in London found high levels of oxalate in her kidneys, which indeed my forensic pathologists found here. I do not blame my team for drawing the wrong conclusion, they did what they could from the limited means they had. They found both glycolic acid and calcium oxalate in Miss Dune's system.' DCI Reynolds paused. 'Please forgive me Susie if I read from the report in front of me, that way I'll be sure to get it right.'

Full of relief that I hadn't created a problem I leapt around the kitchen, able to be quiet but momentarily unable to keep still. Hailey Dune was poisoned by ethylene glycol-based anti-freeze. My dogged determination had paid off. I'd had theories, I'd needed evidence and I'd done it.

DCI Reynolds was conscientiously covering all points. I sat down and tuned in to what he was saying. After all my convictions, when I came back down to earth this was what my conscience would need to know.

'The kidney toxicity of ethylene glycol occurs twenty-four to seventy-two hours post-ingestion and is caused by a direct cytotoxic effect of glycolic acid. The glycolic acid in antifreeze when ingested is metabolised to glyoxylic acid and finally to oxalic acid. Oxalic acid binds with calcium to form calcium oxalate, which accumulate in the kidneys causing damage leading to anuric acute kidney failure. Death by antifreeze has been reliably diagnosed by the measurement of Miss Dune's blood ethylene glycol concentration.'

There was silence down the line.

'Thank you,' I said.

'No, thank you Susie. The truth would never have been known if it wasn't for your tenacity.'

'It was just a feeling I had.'

'Well, it's not something I often encourage but if I were you I'd be inclined to trust your instincts in life.'

'Maybe,' I said with an ambiguous giggle.

'Once again if you could keep this under your hat for now it would be a great help to me. Mrs Gerald is being escorted here now.'

'Does Archie know?' I asked, rather hoping he did.

'Yes. I encouraged Mr Wellingham to stay away from the station but he came here regardless and caused quite a scene in my office. This has led to a leak and now I have Sergeant Ayari doing my dirty work, pleading with the *Norfolk Post* not to release print until after Mrs Gerald's hearing.'

'Oh no. Poor you. Of course, I won't breathe a word to anyone.' I meant it, Toby included . . . at least for the time being.

'Thank you, we'll keep in touch.'

I hung up the telephone and let out a long breath. My work was done, the tables had turned and Primrose was going to be arrested.

I laced up my boots and set off up the Downs. All I wanted now was to see *that* view.

41

The wispy clouds spiralled towards the horizon and the hills appeared soft and gentle in the low sunlight. Skylarks twittered invisibly above my head, the sheep huddled under the shade of the gorse and I was pleased to find no one else treading the South Downs Way.

I walked much further than I had energy for. The momentum of my feet was dictated by the words spiralling around my head as I composed a letter to Toby. I felt exhilarated by the prospect of putting down on paper all the things I had wanted to say and only once I was home did I struggle to recall what I'd got straight in my head.

I sat down at the kitchen table with my favourite fountain pen and a blank piece of paper.

Kemps Cottage
Norland Lane
Thursday 23 August

Dear Toby,
If I could get this letter to you as soon as I signed off, I would. I can't let one more day pass with misunderstanding between us. I don't know where to begin. I sat down with a bowl of crisps that's now empty, night is closing in, the ink pot is drying up

and this letter is the hardest to write.

You and I haven't known each other long but I've so enjoyed becoming friends and I mind desperately that we left on uncertain terms.

It was unfair of me to react so self-centredly when you mentioned Tom and I am truly sorry I let unprocessed inner feelings come out when they did.

You were right when you said I need an explanation for everything. This must be very tiresome but it's who I am. It's not that I don't trust other people, particularly you, it's just I've never been able to learn by being told. I like to know the ins and outs of everything before coming to a conclusion.

When I was very young I asked my mother whether she would ever lie to me. She said, 'Of course not, poppet.' I then asked if Father Christmas really existed and I'll never forget the look on her face. I had her on the gallows. She swore me to secrecy and told me the truth. From that moment on I think I became obsessed with the truth and I am sorry you got the brunt of it recently.

For what it's worth and as this letter will take some time in getting to you I wanted to let you know that DCI Reynolds reopened Hailey's case when I went to him with the bottle of antifreeze. Medics at a hospital in London identified high blood ethylene glycol concentration and Primrose's DNA was found on a fingernail in the bottle. I don't want any of this to come between us and as it stands Primrose is yet to be convicted. I am under strict orders to keep quiet and I trust having told you, you will too.

I was so thrilled you came to stay with luscious Lucy, as I now like to call her, and I could not enjoy mucking about with you more. You're one of the few people one leaves thinking time has been too short so, I hope we will be in touch again soon.

I trust your journey back to Dorset went okay and that Tom liked his helicopter. I bet he did!

Being back at work must be a bit of a shock to the system but hopefully not too much piled up when you were away.

Love from Susie x

42

My weekend with Mel had been and gone. She left me on Sunday afternoon full of expectation that Toby would get in touch. She said, 'He *has* to congratulate you on convicting Primrose.' I'd told Mel all about the murder case. It was just too good a story to keep to myself and when I'd spilled the beans she insisted, 'We must celebrate with a drink or two.' We sat out on the patio, late into the night, indulging in reminiscing about our university days, and laughed so hard I'm still surprised my stomach didn't ache.

But, it was standing on the doorstep just before she left, when Mel ordered strict instructions: not to count the hours waiting for Toby to get in touch. She went on to say something only a really good friend can, 'Susie, it's in your character to want things to happen immediately and when they're out of your control you mustn't criticise people for doing it at their own pace.' Mel liked the sound of Toby, 'he's a doctor to boot', and I could tell in her departing eyes she really wanted this one to work out.

Obviously, I've found it completely impossible to heed her advice and it's now been one hundred and sixty-eight hours since she left and not a squeak from Toby. Each new day I long for a card in the post and the hours in between I go over and over what I would say if he calls.

347

Countless times I've almost dialled his number but stopped myself at the last minute in the hopes he'll get in touch first.

Tomorrow will be a week since I sent my letter and each day that goes by I am finding it a tiny bit easier to cope with no news. In fact, I'm almost reconciled to thinking the worst: our friendship might well be over.

I cancelled my weekend visit to my parents. I couldn't face the thought of exposing my troubled heart and seeing my mother share in my disappointment. When I rang to tell her, 'I can no longer come,' she completely understood that I was 'too taken up with drawing'. It's a creative place I've been in before and Mum knew from experience it wasn't worth her putting her foot down and insisting I visit.

What I'd told her was half-true as, for once, the emotional turmoil of my personal life hasn't affected my art. In fact, the fury inside me has me drawing in a new manner. Full of frustrated energy, an emphatic approach has brought out a talent for portraying the colossal aura of an enormous, fit horse. Boy Meets Man is almost complete. One monumental beast bursting out of an A1 sheet.

I really feel some supreme being had a hand to play in it and, combined with the adrenalin of sleepless nights, who knows how long this will last, but right now I'm full of confidence to move straight on to another. Great Knockers's blank sheet of paper is at the ready and with Mel's help I've chosen a particularly good frisky pose. It shows her immense character and, if I can capture the movement softly, Great Knockers's equal elegance should shine through.

The unfortunate outcome of not going to my parents is, it's put the question of 'Why am I an only child?' on the backburner. I can't possibly ask it right now. I'm in the doldrums already. No place for the blissful foundations of my childhood to be pulled from beneath me. That is, if my parents really have concealed something from me.

First things first, I needed to cure my aching heart, and as any girl knows, the only way to address this successfully is to find a new handsome project to focus on. Sussex hasn't in the past thrown up the goods but I'm going to pull myself together and organise a good fun night out.

Postscript

Almost a year to the day later I received a letter and a newspaper clipping through the post from DCI Reynolds:

Norfolk County Police
Special Investigation Unit
Friday 16 August

Dear Miss Mahl,
I felt a good old-fashioned form of correspondence was necessary for the news I have to deliver. I hope in years to come you will revisit this remarkable outcome and pat yourself on the back. Us policemen and women do not like to leave loose ends untied and without your intuition, intelligence and exceptional attention to detail, Miss Dune's case may never have reached the correct conclusion. I write on behalf of my whole team and those forensic pathologists directly involved in the case to express our grateful thanks and eternal respect for you and your skill as an amateur detective. The police force would be a lot better off with many more of your calibre within it.
Mrs Primrose Gerald confessed to the manslaughter of Miss Hailey Dune at Norfolk Magistrates Court yesterday morning. The murder charge has been allowed to

lie and Mrs Gerald has been sentenced to eight years' imprisonment.

If you are ever passing do let me know. You will always be welcome in these parts and I hope we meet again one day. I could do with an accomplice, however I know you are pursuing your career as a painter and I wish you every success in your endeavour to do so.

With grateful thanks and warmest wishes,
Roland
Detective Chief Inspector Reynolds

The Norfolk Post, Thursday 15 August:

MANSLAUGHTER, Fontaburn Hall, the inside story

Breaking news from Norfolk Crown Court . . .

Primrose Arabella Gertrude Gerald, 38, of Mongumery Castle, Jiltwhistle, has pleaded guilty at Norfolk Magistrates Court to the manslaughter of Miss Hailey Dune, who was at a house party at Fontaburn Hall, home of the Honourable Archibald Cooke Wellingham, next in line to the Lord Norland title. Mrs Gerald was sentenced to eight years in prison.

The court heard that Mrs Gerald poisoned Miss Dune, spiking her drink with antifreeze, which in turn caused Miss Dune's internal organs to fail in the early hours of Sunday 19 August. Mrs Gerald claimed she had found screen wash in her husband's car and on the spur of the moment spiked Miss Dune's cocktail. She had only recently met Miss Dune, and although Mrs Gerald could not say why she had done it, her intention had been to cause Miss Dune discomfort and not to kill her.

Mrs Gerald's doctor gave evidence that she suffers from a mental disorder and she could be prone to extreme behaviour. She had also recently moved to the area and had found the move stressful.

Judge Bright gave a recommendation that Mrs Gerald serve at least five years in prison.

Acknowledgements

Brian Catling, Professor of Fine Art at The Ruskin School of Drawing and Fine Art. Rosemary Morton-Jack for introducing me to Jane Dowling.

Thomas Woodcock the Herald of Heraldry. Marissa Ramsey for guiding me through a murder trial. Lucy Keane, my link to Garry Moore racing who let me in to their yard at the busiest time possible. My betting buddies, Tudor, Jarvid, Beatrice. Claire Hopkinson who knows everything there is to know about a horse. Beloved Sam for his unwavering support. Jenny Parrott my truly wonderful editor. Super-efficient 'I'll get on to it' Harriet Wade. Everyone at Oneworld, the family team behind Susie Mahl. It's to you all I owe an ENORMOUS thank you.

We do hope that you have enjoyed reading this large print book.

Did you know that all of our titles are available for purchase?

We publish a wide range of high quality large print books including:
Romances, Mysteries, Classics
General Fiction
Non Fiction and Westerns

Special interest titles available in large print are:
The Little Oxford Dictionary
Music Book
Song Book
Hymn Book
Service Book

Also available from us courtesy of Oxford University Press:
Young Readers' Dictionary
(large print edition)
Young Readers' Thesaurus
(large print edition)

For further information or a free brochure, please contact us at:
Ulverscroft Large Print Books Ltd.,
The Green, Bradgate Road, Anstey,
Leicester, LE7 7FU, England.
Tel: **(00 44) 0116 236 4325**
Fax: **(00 44) 0116 234 0205**

A BRUSH WITH DEATH

Ali Carter

One cheeky wink and Lord Greengrass was flat out on the ground, deliriously gasping for life, his eyes flickering with a sparkle of hope that the shadow on the wall had come to help . . . In the village of Spire, murder is afoot. Rich landowner Alexander, 9th Earl of Greengrass, is caught with his trousers down in the village graveyard before meeting a gruesome end. Luckily, Susie Mahl happens to be on hand. With her artist's eye for detail and her curious nature, she is soon on the scent of the murderer . . .

CONVICTION

Denise Mina

It's just a normal morning for Anna McDonald — until she opens the front door to her best friend, Estelle. Anna turns to see her own husband at the top of the stairs, suitcase in hand. They're leaving together, taking Anna's two daughters with them. Left alone in the big dark house, Anna can't think; she can't take it in. So she distracts herself with a story: a true crime podcast. There's a sunken yacht in the Atlantic, multiple murders, and a hint of power and corruption. But Anna realises she knew one of the victims in another life. This is a murder case she can't ignore. As she throws herself into an investigation, Anna's past and present lives are about to collide, sending everything she has worked so hard to achieve into freefall . . .